All That Matters

D1409647

ENDORSEMENTS

All That Matters kept me awake at night even when I thought I was too tired to read. This heart-wrenching mystery, with its complex characters and psychological twists, compelled me to keep going until I had the answers I craved.
—**Clarice G. James**, author of *Party of One*, *Doubleheader*, *Manhattan Grace*, and *The Girl He Knew*.

All That Matters is an emotionally charged page-turner with engaging characters and plot twists that will keep the reader guessing until the very end.
—**Thomas Kies**, author of the Geneva Chase Mystery Series

Found a dime today. Like a bright, shiny star, it appeared suddenly before my feet, in a spot where a moment before was but bare earth. I thought of this small coin's symbolic significance, so central to the tale in *All That Matters*. I picked it up, and clutched it close, as one may hold onto even a glimmer of hope, in the wake of overwhelming loss and despair.
—**Scotty Brown**, Free-Lance Writer and Graphic Artist

Andy Davidson masterfully ties the charm of the Carolina beaches; beauty of the Pennsylvania farm country; and Italy's historical ambiance in the suspense thriller, *All That Matters*. Think of Swayze and Moore in the 1990 blockbuster *Ghost* as mysterious discoveries of liberty dimes, impossibly dated 1996, the same year as a murdered girl, provide clues to finding her. Woven through this page turner, deep family secrets come alive through a brief encounter with a death row mass murderer.

—**Thomas P. Gill**, author of *The Bridge, Return to Emerald Isle, Randy's Way, and Tuesdays are for Turtles.*

Andy Davidson knows how to take you on a journey. This one is a journey. Threading mystery and tragedy, grief and redemption together with his trademark wry humor and breathtakingly human characters, this story will hold you until the last page and then some.

—**Kaley Rhea**, author of *Off-Script & Over-Caffeinated: A Novel*

"Cooking and life, it's all about the wait." Mee-Maw's words were true for her granddaughter Carol and stuck with me after I finished reading this story. Davidson weaves a complex tale of hope and second chances for a mother whose daughter has been missing a year and whose husband is now estranged from her. All Carol wants is her daughter back, and despite people telling her she needs to move on, she refuses to quit her search. Davidson kept me guessing to the end. On a deeper level, this story explores the psychological complexities of grief and bitterness while the main characters learn to love and live again.

—**Kristen Hogrefe Parnell**, author and blogger at KristenHogrefeParnell.com

All That Matters

Andy M Davidson

ELK LAKE PUBLISHING INC
PUBLISHING THE POSITIVE
Plymouth, Massachusetts

Copyright Notice

Cover and Interior Design: Derinda Babcock
Editor(s): Sue Fairchild, Cristel Phelps, Deb Haggerty
Author Represented By: Credo Communications, LLC

PUBLISHED BY: Elk Lake Publishing, Inc., 35 Dogwood Drive, Plymouth, MA 02360, 2021

Library Cataloging Data

Names: Davidson, Andy M (Andy M Davidson)

Everything That Matters / Andy M Davidson

318 p. 23cm × 15cm (9in × 6 in.)

ISBN-13: 978-1-64949-214-2 (paperback) | 978-1-64949-215-9 (trade paperback) | 978-1-64949-216-6 (e-book)

Key Words: Adoption, kidnaping, North Carolina coast, Pennsylvania, Italy, Relationships, Family

Library of Congress Control Number: 2021937424 Fiction

DEDICATION

To those who have lost life ...
and never lost hope.

And the people of Perry County
who graciously adopted this child as your own.

ACKNOWLEDGMENTS

It's a weird thing, this dime phenomenon. It sounds mystical and metaphysical. Yet, many peoples of all faiths believe they have experienced a reaching-out by those they have lost. Despite all explanation, it keeps happening in this post-modern age.

As a psychologist, I used to explain it away as denial, a defense mechanism that needed to be overcome so the patient could move on with their life. Now, I know it is not that simple. No, even in people of faith, death is still a mystery, and life is not so simple. When a child is lost, parents only want one thing—it's all that matters. We want their life back. What we need more than anything is family.

A year after our son died, we went to buy a Christmas tree for the Hanna's Hope fundraiser at the Market at Cedar Point in North Carolina. I knew Mary and Jeff lost their daughter Hanna in a motor vehicle accident, and I wanted Lori to meet her. Mary saw the pain in another mother's eyes. This beautiful mother took off her special dime necklace and gave it to the woman she'd just met—my wife. Mary explained dimes were a way of reminding us our children are not lost, they are not missing, they have been found by God. Mary gave us more than I expected.

And the magic began. That spring I came up from the beach and washed the sand from my feet in our outdoor shower when I saw it—a dime lying in the corner. I left it lay. The next day, I looked, and the dime was gone, but on the third day, it was back. Since then I have found dimes in the weirdest of places and other parents have told me their dime stories. Note to self: be careful what you say to a writer, it may just end up in a book.

This a story for everyone who wants to experience the unexplainable. A story not just about a dime but about family—about life. And a story for anyone who still hopes beyond all reason. You may think you see yourself in this story and that's okay, but please remember, every character comes from an overactive mind whose hands still write. Yet, in some way, all are milky reflections of me and you.

First, I want to acknowledge the tireless Sue A. Fairchild, part editor/part magician, who took my second-born and grew her into the story everyone will want to read. Once my first manuscript was completed, like many writers, I thought it perfect. Sue unmuddied the waters and allowed sunlight to filter through my clouded words. She brought clarity to my voice and wings to my vision.

Next, to my indomitable publisher, Deb Haggerty, to whom I owe my writing career. In a world of business, it is nice to know there is still a place for family—it's Elk Lake Publishing, and ELP is the place writers call home. I sent ELP my first ten pages, and Deb kindly told me it was nice to see me trying new things. Her response was as polite a rejection as only a mother could give. I went back to the keyboard and after a year of serial editor abuse, I came up with ten good pages of copy. I sent them back to Elk Lake Publishing to ask about my options. Deb wrote back, "This is good writing, we might be interested." Wow, my second book, my first novel, made it back to Deb's refrigerator door. It was more than I expected.

I must acknowledge my Lori, who shared her hometown with me over forty years ago. Until I drove through the town square for the first time, I didn't know such places still existed. I immediately fell in love with her little town, and I fell in love with my future helpmate, stealing kisses while stacking hay on a moving wagon in the irregular fields of Wheatfield Township. A true metaphor for our life if ever there was one. Lori has read these pages with trepidation that she may see herself. Please know I could never fictionalize my living, breathing angel. Simply, no one would believe you are so.

And lastly to Jeff and Mary Miller, I must acknowledge your kindness, you, who through a simple act, showed us how to survive a complicated life.

Be joyful in hope, patient in affliction, faithful in prayer. (Romans 12:12)

CHAPTER 1

The beachball hit her square in the face.

"What was that?"

Carol looked up to see a little girl in a one-piece. The two stared at each other for a long moment, both stunned for more reasons than an errant ball or a dislodged slumber.

You could be my little girl's friend. You could play catch, dig castles, and catch sidewinders. You two could hold hands and walk off the beach for a peanut butter and jelly. You could live and so could Becca.

Waves crashed and pushed the tide under her chair, melting Carol's feet into the sand. Birds squawked, a mom yelled for her kids, and a dog splashed nearby. The little girl in the lime suit with the tiny faux bow ran away after her ball, now dancing along the surf.

Just go.

Carol gathered her chair, grabbed her lotion, and pulled her cell phone from its sandwich bag. Looking at the screen, she noticed Sis had called.

I should go and get ready, put on my drab dress, sunglasses, and smile just a little. I should believe them, accept it. I should move on.

Carol slogged across the last dune to the weathered, green-tinted steps and then put on her flip-flops to avoid another splinter. Shadows drifted past the dunes, but her sunglasses still clung to her face. Her phone vibrated, the light visible through her mesh tote.

Nuts.

"Carol, it's Maxx. I know it's been too long, but I wanted to call before the funeral."

Why did you answer? Come on, Carol, think.

Carol's fog rarely lifted but she had learned to fake interest when she needed to be someone else or to move along with the remains of her life.

"It *has* been too long. You're supposed to be here for me—for us."

"I know ... you're right, Carol, but I'm back. I had to figure some stuff out, but I'm back."

Oh, now you're back.

"I can't talk now, Maxx. We'll talk later. Bye."

Despite her husband's disappearance for several months and the reprimand she'd just given him, she wasn't ready for his return. Her chair shifted from her back and her towel fell to her feet.

I'm so tired.

Her pressured heartbeat and labored breath pounded in her ears as she pushed through the last of the sand that overlapped her walkway.

This was easier with my kindergartener and her toys. Please God, I want them back.

Her flip-flop caught a raised nail and folded over itself, causing her to stumble.

"Ugh! Nothing's right."

"You're going to be late," Sis yelled from the upper deck. "I ironed your blouse."

"Great," she muttered.

Carol dropped her beach bag and chair in unison. Her phone followed before she pushed through the mildew-stained curtain and lowered her head under the outdoor shower. The shower curtain separated her from the real world while old razors and pieces of forgotten soaps reminded her there was one. She stood with one foot on top of the other on weathered pressure-treated boards in a feeble attempt to keep warm. As cold water coursed down from overhead, she stretched her arms to either side, and clutched the lattice work—a sacrificial posture as if nailed to her own cross.

After a deep breath, she pleaded, "God, just take me."

The cold water caused her muscles to tense, and she jerked her head back for a moment, clarity coming for the first time since she'd been told part of her daughter's remains had been recovered. While life went on at a dizzying pace around her, she remained sequestered in a cocoon at the edge of the beach—empty, paralyzed.

Keep moving. Funeral today.

Carol sighed.

The day darkened as the water turned from warm to hot and steam rose from the broken lattice barrier. She shook the water from her head but couldn't shake the memory of her daughter.

Why did he call now?

Carol knew Maxx had left his job and taken off to the wilderness after months of no news about Becca.

Just stay gone.

She heard a crash upstairs in the house and pictured Sis banging around the kitchen. Her two-storied beach home on stilts had become Carol's fortress, but her sister's arrival was a necessary intrusion. Carol put her head back under the cascade, letting the heat beat against the back of her neck, trickle down her back, and patter across her toes. She squeezed her eyes tight, but tears poured from them, mixing with the water from the shower.

After a few moments, she opened her eyes. Becca stood in the corner of the shower.

"Oh my gosh, oh no."

Mommy, lookey at my dime.

Carol blinked, letting the water run around her eyes and off her chin. She could see Becca's pink suit, almost feel her matted hair, and saw her little toes curled on the pressure-treated floor. Carol clutched at her heart, pierced by the vivid reminder of her little girl who she could no longer hold.

"God, please make this real. Let me hold her," she pleaded. "God, please."

Becca pointed to the floor. Through the waterdrops something glowed in the corner of the shower stall.

Sunlight through the floor?

Steam rose around the light. Water flew as Carol shook her head.

Mist? Jeez, you're losing it, Carol.

Carol blinked more and then pinched the upper part of her nose with her forefingers and rubbed both eyes. The sharp light remained, but Becca had disappeared in the mist. Her moment of near contact left a false satisfaction that quickly evaporated—like waking up after dreaming of someone who'd died. The dream had ended, but her nightmare continued as she lived a life without her little girl. If she could, Carol would have evaporated with her.

She cocked her head to the side to loosen the water in her right ear and wash the sand from her left. She could see the outline of a circle on the floor of the shower and bent to get a closer look. A dime lay on one of the floorboards.

What is a dime doing here?

She went to one knee. As she picked it up, she noticed the date.

1996 ... Becca's birth year.

The dime grew hot between her fingers as she felt the copper ridges with her other hand. The steam heated around her, and she dropped the hot coin.

The dime seemed suspended in air before floating its own path back to the floorboards below. Then, the coin caught an edge and spiraled into a gap between the boards. Steam drifted up into the stall as Carol dropped to both knees and pulled at the boards with her water-wrinkled fingers.

"Becca!"

Carol tore at the curtain, then stepped into the sunlight, and dove onto the sandy ground to get a look underneath the shower. A glimmer of light caught her eye. The dime.

She turned her head to one side, burying her water-logged ear in the sand as she stretched for the dime. The sand dug under her nails causing a sharp pain. Her body was now half underneath the floor of the shower stall and her fingers just missing the edge of the dime. Her shoulder ached from pressing against the shower floor joist.

The dime means something. It must.

On the ground, Carol smelled the mist, and caught a whiff of fragrance—jasmine, Becca's favorite. It was Carol's grandmother's favorite flower and perfume too. With Becca gone, the smell of jasmine usually caused Carol to crumple, but today felt different.

She desperately clawed at the dime, pushing the balls of her feet further into the sand. Finally, her fingers reached the dime, but then her hand disappeared into the vapor. She could see the date—1996—but then the mist enveloped her arm.

Carol grabbed the dime, and a jolt of burning heat spiked through her palm. She yelled and her head jerked backward, hitting a rusty iron drainpipe. Her face hit the sand.

CHAPTER 2

Upstairs, Sis rummaged through the cabinets. A saucepan fell out onto the granite counter before hitting the floor.

"Carol, I don't know how you do this. I don't think you even own a proper colander." She gave up looking for paper towels and added them to her list on the fridge. After rummaging through the freezer, she found a frosted-over green box at the bottom. *Is this one of those low-calorie meals?* She shrugged. At least it was food.

Sis wiped away the frost and read the instructions before placing the box inside the microwave and pushing a few buttons. The Smart Sense meal began to rotate inside. The wait seemed interminable. She pulled open the door before the third beep and nearly burnt her fingers on the carton. She rummaged through another drawer for a fork and then curled up on the Sunbrella couch on the porch.

She heard the faint sound of a cry or maybe a song—she didn't know which. Undeterred, Sis turned on the TV and focused on her meal.

Sis had been frequenting Carol's beach town since Becca's disappearance. She stood by Carol when she met with the police, when she talked to the press, and even one time when she went on TV to plead for Becca's return. Through it all, she'd remained stoic for her grieving sister. She'd cooked up chicken corn soup in a big pot she'd brought with her and made whoopie pies and shoefly pie in the fall and ham and green beans in the spring. She'd even made pork and sauerkraut at New Years, much to Carol's dismay when it smelled up the whole house for days. She brought a bit—sometimes too much—of home wherever she went.

Coming to take care of Carol and living out of her suitcase had taken a small toll on Sis. Every day, she faked a smile as she encouraged Carol to get back on her feet—and not just to go to the beach. But her advice went unheeded and her frustration grew.

Just yesterday they'd had yet another fight.

"Maybe you could get a job. What if you did some work, I mean instead of exercising so much? Have you thought about dating?"

"Sis! That's enough," Carol yelled.

While Sis had the patience of Job when taking care of livestock, her sister was another story.

Sis clicked through endless TV channels now but found nothing to spark her interest. She turned off the TV and heard a muffled yell from below. Startled, she recognized her sister's cry. Sis dropped her meal on the screened porch floor and hurried down the steps and around the landing. It mattered little she was dressed in only a slip and no shoes. Carol needed her.

The water from the shower still ran and spilled out to the bottom of the weathered steps stained green from mold. The slick surface, the quick turn, and the aged wood resulted in a quick and ungraceful slip. Sis saw her own feet rising to near eye level before she landed between the shower stall and a little girl's rusty bike.

"Aww." She clutched her hip and felt some blood where she'd caught the edge of the bicycle. "That's gonna leave a mark."

Briefly dazed, she felt her head through her mass of freshly washed curls. No blood and no bump. She looked around for her square-framed glasses and saw them lying in a puddle near the shower stall. She grabbed at them and pushed them on so she could assess the damage.

"Carol," she called.

Her sister was lying prostrate on the ground, partially beneath the shower. Carol reached toward an ugly cut oozing blood on the back of her head, but Sis grabbed her hand.

"Sis, it was Becca. I saw Becca."

"What?"

"And an old dime, but 1996 ... her birth year. She could be alive."

"Calm down, Carol. You have a nasty bump back there." Sis felt her own hip bleeding more through her slip but remained focused on her sister—like she often did for the countless farm animals back home.

Sis turned to see someone running up to her.

"Oh my, would you look at you two?" Daphne exclaimed in between breaths. "How did you—"

"Not now, Daphne," Sis cut off the neighbor. "Let us take care of you, Carol."

Her sister shut her eyes. "Becca could be alive."

CHAPTER 3

Carol awoke with a start on the couch and looked around her home. Absent were the big-box store pictures of children playing in the sand or seagulls standing in line on the beach as the sun melts on the horizon. She'd thought them too cliché. Mirrors accented the walls instead. She'd heard they made a room look bigger and reflected more light. She squinted now as the sunlight hit one just right.

"Where's Sis? Is she all right?"

"Your sister is shopping, Caroline. She got a little banged up when she fell, but she'll be okay."

Carol turned toward the voice. "Daphne?"

"Yup, next-door Daphne."

"Sis fell?"

"Yeah, don't you remember, silly rabbit? She slipped on the steps when she heard you yelling and found you half under the shower stall. Do you remember anything?"

"Dimes. The Lady Liberty Dime, but the date said 1996 which doesn't make any sense at all. People call it the Mercury Dime because of the winged headdress. But that's a symbol for liberty. Wings, like Peggy used to have."

Daphne sat across from the couch on an oversized chair while she thumbed through last month's *People*. She smiled. "You just keep talking, Caroline. Piggy's got wings, and dimes are falling from the sky, you say?"

"No, Peggy is Becca's stuffed Pegasus, not Piggy. Never mind, and don't call me Caroline. Where's Sis?"

"Sis is at the store. I'm here, Caroline. Sis is okay. Everything is fine. The house is fine. You're fine ... well, sort of. Sis called off the burial service—it's all taken care of."

"Burial ..." A tear made its way to the pillow. Carol envisioned Becca playing in a field of flowers. Butterflies landed, and dimes dropped from the petals as black birds flew by. "Jasmine." She smiled.

"Here, take this." Daphne handed her two pain meds and a ginger ale.

"Is this diet? I don't drink diet."

Daphne stood over her. "You always drink diet. Just drink it."

"How did you get here?" Carol squinted into the light. "I always lock the door."

"Sis asked me to check on you."

"Sis talked to you? Does she have your number?"

"Don't worry about it. Sis wanted to get you some Jell-O and more pain meds or something."

Carol took the medication offered and the diet ginger ale.

"Well, maybe Sis left the door unlocked." Daphne shrugged. "Everything was pretty hectic. Do you remember anything? I mean, what were you doing under your shower? I came over when I heard you scream."

"I was getting a dime."

"Just a dime?"

"It wasn't just a dime—it was Becca's dime."

"Rebecca? She's dead; her funeral was supposed to be today."

Daphne was often abrupt but this time her words unsettled Carol more than usual. "Not to me—I have her dime."

"You have her dime?" Daphne had returned to her chair and was riffling through the rack for another magazine.

"Well, I had her dime, but I lost it in the mist."

"Caroline, your daughter passed on."

"You don't know that. And don't call me Caroline. Maxx called me that and I hate it."

"Where is Maxx?" Daphne stopped looking for another magazine and faced her.

"He left. Haven't heard from him in months. Well, he called earlier. He was supposed to be at the funeral, but I can't count on him. He was backpacking, trying to get his head straight."

"Does he think Becca is still alive?"

"To Maxx, Becca never died."

Carol sat up and turned away. She didn't care if Daphne saw her crying, but she needed a tissue and some water.

"Well, what can we do about that now?"

Carol knew when she was being patronized. "Nothing. Just jasmine."

"Huh?"

"Never mind."

"I see." Carol could hear her flipping magazine pages again. "Should be easy, just find a sandy dime underneath an outside shower, and find a little girl who's been missing for almost a year and whose DNA turned up three states away in Pennsylvania. I guess I should stay with you. You need help, Sugar."

Daphne had been little more than a nosy neighbor in the two years they'd known each other. Carol called her high maintenance. She'd felt relieved when Daphne left for California shortly after Becca went missing. She no longer had the energy to coddle Daphne's mercurial temperament. Now that she'd returned, she'd taken to popping in and helping herself to the wine.

"No. I need some time alone. Besides, Sis will be back soon."

"Suit yourself." Daphne tucked the magazine under her arm and left without another word.

Carol slowly rose from the couch. Her head pounded as she shuffled to the kitchen. A note on the fridge said, "Went stor'n." Sis's way of saying she was grocery shopping. The note was signed, "Food First."

Carol sat at the window and kept checking her phone—first for a text, then for an email, and then for a call from Maxx or Sis. She could go on like this for hours, days if she needed—she'd had lots of practice.

Carol feared going through the ugliness of loss, so she played her game of Becca in a bubble. She imagined Becca floating above, waiting to be found even though Carol felt like the one who was lost.

The sun dipped in the sky when she finally rose from her seat by the window. She glanced at Becca's dusty room and, for the first time in months, walked inside.

She sank into the comforting rocking chair as she stared at the pink and blue animal wallpaper. Everything in the room was as it was before Becca went missing. Her stuffed Pegasus, "Peggy," slouched on the toy wooden rocker next to Carol. The much-loved horse's head folded down at the neck and its crumpled legs flopped over the armrest. Carol lightly touched the stitches on either side of its back.

She picked up Becca's pillow to fluff it, then pressed it to her face. The fragrance of her fabric softener lingered. "Jasmine." *How can that be?* Time had slowed down after Becca disappeared. *Has it been a year?*

Carol opened her eyes and glanced down to where the pillow once lay. There lay another shiny dime. *Another dime? What is this?* She picked it up and saw 1996 stamped on one side.

Seeing a second dime unsettled her, but, in a curious way, Carol liked it. Her imagination sparked and memories of her past and her desire for a future all combined and caused a chill to cross her skin. Her eyes widened and her pulse quickened again. She felt alive once more.

The dime grew brighter and hotter in her hand. Her fingers still hurt from the first dime. Again, she dropped the coin, but this time she saw the woman's head roll around and end up behind the Romanesque chifforobe where Becca used to play dress up. Unable to move the heavy oak furniture, Carol got down on all fours on the dusty floor and peered beneath the antique. Lots of dust, but no dime. Gone like Becca. Gone.

Carol sat back on her heels and combed through her hair with her fingers to think. *Make sense of this, Carol. Make sense.* But her senses failed her. Her sight, her smell, her hearing, even her touch seemed to betray her. *What's happening to me?* She had no answers. She returned to the pillow feeling overwhelmed.

Her mind spun. *Dimes? Becca? Jasmine? What does it all mean?* For months, Carol imagined Becca's whereabouts. Images of Becca would stop Carol in mid-sentence, in the middle of a walk, or simply in the middle of life. This seemed different. This felt both real and surreal and went beyond Carol's logical, deductive reasoning. She wanted her daughter back but couldn't be disappointed again. It would kill her. Yet, she had to know—had to find out if Becca was still alive. There could be no doubt. Carol smelled Becca's fragrance once more as she lay the pillow down, smoothed out its wrinkles, and caressed its edge before turning out the light and leaving the room.

Carol hurried into her office where she picked up her laptop, typed in "dime," and got too many hits. She narrowed her search to "Lady Liberty dime," and discovered the coin had only been minted from 1916 to 1945.

But Becca's dime said 1996. She kept researching, caught up in the mystery—her time and hurt forgotten. *1996, Becca's birth year.*

She read out loud, "The Lady Liberty dime is also known as the Mercury dime because of the winged headdress the woman is wearing. This headdress is known as a Phrygian cap, which is worn by the Roman god Mercury."

Interesting. Roman.

Carol had been an Archeology major in college and was fascinated by all things Roman. She'd even gone on two digs on the outskirts of Rome and Pompeii before and after the summer of her senior year. Friends thought her erudite when she'd adorned Becca's room with Roman mythology. She'd found the old chifforobe with Roman figures in a consignment shop.

Carol seemed to recall a belief about dimes showing up after someone's death.

But Becca is not dead. She isn't. They only said she was dead. They brought me a pile of ashes and a bracelet and said it was Becca. But it just couldn't be.

The police had told her to pick out a spot to bury the remains, but the DNA seemed less than conclusive.

She remembered the day the officers walked up her wooden steps and knocked. The male officer had looked away, but the younger female officer's pained expression told most of the story. Carol had led them inside her house. He'd insisted she sit down. Instinctively, the female officer had reached out to touch Carol's shoulder.

Carol flinched. "What, what?"

He studied the rug beneath his feet. "Ma'am, we ... they ... they found some remains. It's not much, but a number of hairs were enough to link them to your daughter's DNA."

"Okay. What are you saying?"

"We also found this." The female officer opened a manila envelope and let a plastic bag slide onto the coffee table.

"That's Becca's bracelet." Carol's eyes widened. "Where is she, where is she?" she screamed.

After a long pause, much too long for Carol, the officer told her about Harold Baker, a convicted serial killer who was linked to multiple murders. Becca's DNA turned up at a site he used to burn his victim's evidence. The burn pit held evidence from several of his victims.

"Baker was in jail at the time of Becca's abduction, but we think it was the work of a copycat. Maybe someone who admired Baker. Someone who wanted his admiration. It's sick and a lot to take in, I know."

"I can't imagine what you're feeling," the female officer inserted.

Carol looked at her and then him. *How could you know anything?*

"Here's a picture of what looks like a little tank top. Do you recognize it."

Carol looked briefly at the picture before shutting her eyes.

The officers waited. "Ma'am?"

With her eyes still shut, she nodded.

"Ma'am, we ... they ... I mean the chief investigators believe Becca is dead. They found human ashes and bits of bone in the pit. Likely they were dumped there after cremation. Baker didn't deny knowing about Becca, but he's never confessed to any of his crimes and just plays word games."

"Were they Becca's ashes?"

"We believe so."

"You believe so?"

"Well, ashes don't carry DNA but because her DNA and other victims' DNA were found in various articles, they feel certain Becca's remains were located in that pit."

The word *pit* sickened her. Carol's lip had quivered. She had tried to talk, but nothing came out. She was surrounded but alone. Weakness invaded her bones, no longer held together by anything living as if she was lying in the bottom of that pit. She had begun to rock back and forth. Carol had died that day.

"Some of the ashes were delivered to our department. We would like to deliver them to a mortuary with your permission."

A fog settled on Carol, and words no longer held meaning. Voices grew distant.

"Is there someone you can call?" she remembered them saying.

"Sis." It was the last thing she said before they rose, said something about being sorry for her loss, and headed out the door and down the steps.

The officer seemed so unsteady, Carol thought. He'd simply repeated what he'd been told, but his words seemed less than convincing. Now all she had was a bag of green ashes she wasn't sure held her daughter and the rantings of some psychopath on death row. It seemed too convenient. *And why the green color?* No one knew. The police wanted to close the case, and the press wanted a story, but Carol wanted her daughter.

Forcing her mind back to the present, she typed "dimes and death" and swallowed hard. She tried to skip over anything suggesting death but now she couldn't avoid the topic. She winced at descriptions of grieving parents as the room turned dark.

When the screen dimmed, she plugged in the power cord and continued to read about a man who'd found dimes in the most unusual places after his father-in-law died. Then about a woman who'd found a dime in her dead son's shoe. Psychologists called the phenomenon cognitive synchronicity. Jung had theorized that people often have similar occurrences because they share a collective unconscious. Today, theorists believe it is simply a matter of mathematical probability. To the grieving, dimes did not seem to be a coincidence but a connection to the departed. Dimes meant something.

"Shrinks," she mused. "If they only knew their science is rooted in Roman mythology." She read on.

Seeing the number ten (or finding dimes) is often a message of validation that you are receiving guidance and insight from your angels and from the realms of spirit. Release any fear or uncertainty and know that you are loved and supported. Things are working out for you for the highest and greatest good. Call on your angels to help align your thoughts with what you want to experience in your life.

She wanted to believe but it was too much, too fantastical, and all too spiritual. *Angels. Right.* Yet she felt an overwhelming sense of love and peace for the remainder of the day.

The house darkened and cooled toward evening. She knew the beach would be deserted and always thought it sad the tourists left at the best time, just so they could eat and drink and forget their harried lives.

People come and go. I wonder what they know. Carol relished the sunset. *One day closer to Becca.*

Like so many evenings before, she walked out to the back porch to catch a glimpse of the last bit of orange, purple, and scarlet. When she looked down over the railing, she saw nothing out of place.

She looked at her steps. They were clean, and the area around the shower, smooth and undisturbed. When she looked at the shower stall, everything seemed to be in its place. The two canvas beach chairs were hung, and the towels had been draped over the railing. "I can't believe Sis cleaned up." She smiled and gazed at the sunset.

A few minutes later, she heard the low rumble of a car and saw Sis pulling up the drive. She got herself down the steps to help with the bags.

"What's this?" she said as she peeked into several bags. "I can't eat a thing you've bought." Carol's foray into all-natural foods was well known.

"We'll see about that," Sis remarked.

"I feel nauseous anyway. I couldn't eat right now."

"Hey, you're close to forty, you need a little puddin' on those bones." Sis lifted several bags from the trunk and turned toward the house. "Call it insurance. It'll be there when you need it."

When the food was put away, Sis insisted on cooking up a frozen lasagna. Carol didn't fight the meal. At least Sis paired it with a nice salad. They drank water instead of wine because Sis worried about Carol's head.

Sis did most of the talking during their meal.

"I was just talking to the bagger at your Piggly Wiggly, and he says he's going back to college next week. I should take him some pie next time I go. Do you know Mrs. Shaeffer on the corner? No? Well, she knows you and says you left your beach towels outside in the rain last week. I can't believe your minister has been married three times. He'd never get a church in Duncannon. Nice enough and all, just a little squirrely."

Carol picked at her salad.

"Really?" Sis exclaimed. "You didn't know any of this?"

"Really."

After their meal, they sat together but on opposite ends of the sectional couch. Carol petted her cat as Sis flipped through the TV channels. She stopped on an episode of divorce court.

"I thought this show was over," Sis remarked.

"Sis, change the channel."

"Oh ... right. I understand." She turned off the TV.

"Understand?"

"You know ... Maxx."

Carol laughed. "What's Maxx got to do with anything?"

"Well, you tell me. I mean, if you want to. You really haven't said much since I've been here. I get it, but Carol, it's me."

Silence had never bothered Carol in the past. Her work required it, and her current life demanded it. But now, the quiet squeezed every bit of energy from her life.

"Since Becca went missing, things have never been the same," Carol started. "How could they be? We'd talk a little, but it was mostly, 'Get this,' or 'Why didn't you take your shoes off,' or 'That shirt is dirty.' He didn't say anything of substance. He'd catch me staring at pictures. One time, he caught me staring at him. 'What are you looking at?' he asked. 'Nothing,' I lied. 'How could you?' is what I really thought."

"How could he what?"

"I hate myself for blaming him. I mean I don't really but there were those moments ... I couldn't help myself. I couldn't shake it. It was like I was so worried about blaming him, afraid I was becoming bitter that it swallowed me. I felt lost. Who am I kidding? I am lost. Nothing is real, nothing matters, just Becca, not Maxx, not me, not anyone."

"Not me?"

Carol felt her body go slack. She knew her face showed no expression. She turned to Sis with unseeing eyes.

Sis's eyes darted about the room. She picked up her glass of water and wiped the condensation. "Don't I matter?"

Carol ignored her comment. "We were strangers, Maxx and I. Ships in the night, right until there was nothing left. I blame him for leaving, but well, I wish I could go too, but I can't. She could show up some day, right here. Tomorrow maybe. And I have to be here. I can't leave. We had the storybook marriage. People used to envy us. Now I feel their pity and hate them for it. There, I said it. I hate them." Carol's chin raised defiantly toward her older sister.

"Oh, Carol."

"Oh, don't look at me like that. It's the truth."

"Do you hate me?"

"No, Sis. I could never hate you, never. You have always been here for me. Always."

"Then let it go."

Carol sat back against the sofa cushion and furrowed her brows. "What do you mean?"

"You heard me—let it go. Everything. Get out of here, take a vacation, take a cruise, meet a guy. Sound crazy? So is sitting here doing nothing. Get away. Get out of Dodge."

"Meet a guy? You're crazy. That's not at all like you, Sis. You didn't get a guy when Sid died. I mean Maxx and I didn't even sleep in the same room at the end. No, we didn't argue. I mean, we tried but just didn't have the will. He'd go downstairs. I'd go into my room. Besides, what's the point? The only point was—is—getting Becca back. Nothing else matters. Nothing." Carol slapped the arm of the sofa. "At first, we held on to each other—day and night. He'd go with me into town. I'd go with him to his stuff. It was just us. Sure, the church said they were there for us. Sure, we got casseroles from the neighbors, but after a week or two, it was just us."

"But you grew up in the church."

"We all did. We had to. But after college, I was too busy with my work, and archeologists aren't much on faith. So, when Joey died, that pretty much did it for me. But after we adopted Becca, Maxx thought we should take her to Sunday school."

Sis blurted, "What about us, your family?"

"I can never go home. Mother still blames me. She'll never forgive me for Joey. There's nothing there for me and never really was." Carol's eyes darted from Sis to the back of the room then back to Sis. Her guilt of her brother's untimely death mixed with her missing child churned her stomach. Her breathing shallowed.

"Our hometown was just fine for me." Sis's tone turned cold. "I married Sid, and we had everything we needed. We had family. I guess you were too good for that."

Carol fussed with the fringe on the couch afghan.

"I guess you were made for bigger things."

"Nonsense, my life took me away from home. But Maxx and I hated it. We didn't hate each other—we hated *it*—our life. The life we were handed after Becca disappeared. We just stood still. Sharks can't survive standing still and neither could we. We tried to keep everything the same. I guess we wanted it that way because, in our eyes, Becca will always be six. We can't change our phone number, we can't move, we can't even change our voice mail in case someone tries to find us. We're stuck. You know what that does to a relationship? Doing nothing kills."

Carol looked right at Sis, and Sis didn't flinch.

"Carol, the police could always track you down."

"I know, but it's how a parent worries. Besides, I don't trust the police anymore. I ... I don't trust anyone."

Now Sis looked down. "Does Maxx have someone else?"

"No." The remark seemed out of place and unsettled Carol. The comment hurt but she wouldn't show it, not to Sis. She got up and saw her darkened eyes in the mirror-tiled wall. Seeing her image only caused more pain, but she didn't want to face her sister.

"I'm just ask—"

"No. I would know. Maxx wouldn't do that to me. He said he left for the both of us."

"Carol, I heard you yelling, 'Mommy's coming' earlier. Then when I was outside, I heard you say, '1996.'"

"Becca's birth year. There's more." Carol spilled out how she'd found another dime stamped with 1996 in Becca's room, but how the design was from the thirties and how the dime gave off a mist and how she smelled jasmine. She turned to Sis. "Look, see the little burn mark on my finger?"

When she looked up, Sis was looking at her—not her finger. She sat still and quiet. Sis was never quiet and never still.

"What?"

"Carol, we all know you've been under a lot of stress." Sis paused and wrung her hands. "Please don't take this the wrong way."

Carol stood up and squared her body toward her sister. "Look, I know what stress is. My daughter is missing. M-I-S-S-I-N-G. I put up flyers, and I waited. I put up more flyers. Waited some more. Do you know what it's like to find your daughter's flyers torn, lying on the street, with people walking on them?

"Someone drew pointy ears and a pitchfork on one. Another one had wings and a halo. We walked in a line poking at weeds in the woods when there was a rumor someone saw a little girl down by the sound. Do you know what that is? Is that stress? No, that's real. Every time I poked, I felt Becca wince. What I'm telling you is this is real, and if you don't believe me, then you can leave too."

Sis reached out to touch Carol on the shoulder, but she moved ever so slightly. "Oh, honey, it's not your fault."

Her words, meant to comfort, rang hollow to Carol. Anytime someone said that phrase, she only felt more guilt.

Sis's head bowed. "I'm not going anywhere."

Carol felt perplexed by her sister. One minute, she seemed supportive of her feelings and, the next, dismissive of her actions. But Sis was her last connection to her past. Her brother, Joey, and her father were gone. Joey's wife and children had moved away years ago. Carol couldn't face her mother, but she longed for Mee-Maw, her surviving grandmother, the silent matriarch.

"I'm missing something. I just know it. All I need is to work through this." Carol stared at the mirrored wall. "It's a research problem. I just need to find the right question, then I can solve the problem."

Carol, the archeologist-turned-mother, pulled out her kindergartner's erasable markers from beneath the coffee table. She found a sticky notepad in one of the end tables.

Sis sat up straighter as she worked. "What are you doing?"

"Something. I'm doing something. Finally."

At first, she wrote notes and stuck them to the tiles, and then she drew lines, arrows, and circles connecting them in an algorithm. Different color notes and different color markers all had significance. Her notes converged into something like a physics problem on her makeshift blackboard.

Carol's default was to step back, get the big picture, and organize. "Everything has a place—everything," she would often say. She looked the picture of perfection. So perfect, in fact, that one misplaced dime had sent her into a tailspin. Carol cringed as she thought of the time she had made Becca stand in the corner for drawing on the wall. Why couldn't she just have taken a deep breath and moved on?

"It looks like you're diagraming the space shuttle's reentry pattern," Sis remarked.

But Carol continued to draw lines and connect circles. The harder she worked, the more critical Sis became.

"I just don't want to see you hurt, honey."

"You're right," Carol said. "This is all wrong."

She wiped it all down—taking the sticky notes with each swipe—and started again. *Keep it simple, that's what my proctor would say. Occom's Razor—the simplest explanation is the best.* On the left side of the mirror, she wrote, "Becca," in the middle, "Dime," and to the right "Significant Others." Somehow, they were connected. Somewhere, there was meaning. Somehow, she would find it.

"What's 'Significant Others' mean?" Sis asked.

"Well, Maxx and me, for sure. The people in Becca's life. Maybe there're others we need to focus on as well."

She wrote down significant dates while Sis surfed the internet for pictures of dimes and began asking questions.

"Who's Mercury ... why wings ... what's a Phrygian cap?"

Carol stopped to give Sis a crash course on all things Roman.

Then Sis began reading about numismatics. "The edge of a dime has 118 ridges. Did you know how much silver, copper, and even gold went into each dime and where they were minted?"

Carol ignored her question and began a timeline starting with Becca's birthdate: June 1, 1996. Then the day she went missing, and the day her ashes were reported found, just a few months prior to today. She wrote down words that had meaning: Peggy, her stuffed horse; jasmine, her favorite flower; and words that she ended in "ey," like "lookey." She wrote down anything significant in Becca's young life.

Sometime around 3:00 a.m. they looked at the blank column under "Significant Others." The two sisters looked at each other, took a collective breath, and Carol started more scribbling.

"Focusing on Maxx isn't getting us anywhere," Carol said.

Suddenly, Sis came alive and started writing in the subcategory. Friends, neighbors, male and female, old girlfriends, old enemies, work people, customers, suppliers, anyone they could think of. She wrote down what Maxx liked to do, what he hated, and what motivated him. She wrote habits and peculiarities.

Carol watched Sis nearly fall from a chair when she reached to circle a word.

They took a break.

Carol felt disheartened. "It's a mess. It isn't working, not this time. I'm missing something."

Looking at their work, Sis asked, "What's it all mean? It just looks like some weird science experiment—I don't think this is the way to go, but I'm no scientist."

Carol feared Sis was right. "I don't know but we're going to find out. You are right about one thing—it is science. We just need to use deductive reasoning to rule out the confounding variables. When only one variable remains, we can produce a grounded hypothesis. Then we'll establish an experimental design, an N of one, perhaps, and try to disprove the null hypothesis."

Sis frowned and looked up between her bangs.

"What I mean is—we'll know where Becca is," Carol said. But a small amount of doubt crept into her words.

"I just don't get it. What are you trying to do?"

"I guess I'm organizing, getting the facts where I can see them. I'm a neat freak, you know that. So, I'm organizing my mind, of sorts. I keep thinking I'm missing something. I'd hoped seeing it up here would shake it free."

"Well, did it?"

Carol shook her head. "Not yet."

After a pause, Sis said, "Carol, I love you, but if you are a scientist and all, then you can't rule out the possibility, the real possibility that Becca is—"

"Not now, Sis."

The word "dead" could stop her in her tracks—paralyze her like a nightmare. That word could keep her frozen while the monster drew ever closer.

The sisters fell asleep with cell phones resting on their stomachs, markers still in their hands, paper plates on the counter, and a grape juice box still in the sink.

CHAPTER 4

Carol woke to see Daphne reading the sisters' handiwork. The cat stirred in the corner and the coffeepot kicked on for the morning ritual.

"These two have been busy," murmured Daphne. "What are they up to?"

"Daphne?"

"Oh!" Carol's neighbor startled and put her hand to her chest. "You didn't answer my knock, and the door was open."

"I'm sure I locked it last night after we finished our lasagna." The box lay in the corner. Carol watched as the cat licked the cheese stuck to the cardboard. "What are you doing?"

"Just thought I'd check on you to see if you're okay."

"Just great." Carol's head throbbed from the lack of sleep and water.

"So, what's all this?" Daphne waved her hand at the papers strewn about the living room.

"Well, it may sound crazy, but I found a dime, maybe two, and they're connected to Becca somehow. Seems that dimes are often signals from the grave. I don't believe in ghosts, but I believe in Becca."

"So, if it's from the grave, then Becca *is* dead."

Carol shook her head. "That's something I'm not ready to consider. Not yet—maybe not ever."

"Carol ... please, I feel like whatever you're doing here is just gonna hurt you all over again. We've been through this already."

"I know, but I gotta believe."

"Believe what? It's been a year, Caroline."

"Well, yesterday, I watched a dime roll under Becca's Roman chifforobe. I did a bit of research, and it seems the dime may be a Lady Liberty dime. I think the woman on the dime is trying to tell me something. She's the Liberty Goddess—most people think it's Mercury, but she's a Roman goddess."

"Rome, you say?"

Sis stirred on the other end of the couch. In the kitchen, the coffee maker gurgled the end of its cycle.

"Sis, sorry if we woke you."

"Oh, Daphne, no, I must have smelled the coffee."

Carol noted an edge to her voice. She and Daphne were often at odds. Years before, Sis became head cashier at the hardware store after her husband Sid died from an early heart attack, but Daphne took off for the West Coast after her first divorce.

"Anyway, Carol, I say move on from this tragedy," Daphne said as she moved to fill some coffee cups. "Just move on. That's what I did. And that's what you need to do too."

"Are you talking about Becca?" Sis responded as she brushed some hair from her face before heading toward the coffeepot. "That's so cold. When I lost Sid, I picked up my life … I didn't move on … I *carried* on."

"Good for you, Sis, but for you, Lasik surgery is too big of a risk." Daphne lost her pleasant tone. "For me, I moved to California, married a creep, divorced the creep, and didn't look back. There's more to life than painting your house with leftover paint from the hardware store or singing in the church choir."

"Sis, Daphne means well, and I'm just trying to do something positive—for Becca." Carol's voice quaked, her coffee cup shook.

"Just trying to help, girls. You know we got to keep moving." Daphne held her cup with two hands and looked at Sis as she took a sip.

"Moving on is not an option for me," Carol stated.

Losing Becca and not knowing if she was alive or dead devastated her. Thinking about Becca being dead took Carol's mind to a very dark place. If she were alive … thinking about where she was, how she felt, if she was warm, if she was fed, if she was loved … all these thoughts exhausted her. But doing something about Becca's disappearance liberated her.

Carol rose from the couch and walked to the mirrored wall. "I gotta do something, even if it's wrong. That's what Daddy always said. I've searched through my old books—my Roman mythology books, and even books on the sculptor of and model for Lady Liberty. I backtracked each step from the dime's origins in New York to France and Rome, even."

"I hear those Italian men are pretty hot," said Daphne.

"Daphne …" Sis held her forehead.

"Oh, I kid. How about another cup?"

Carol loved Rome and always wanted to return but not without Maxx and not without Becca. Still … No, she needed to be here.

What would people say? Husband and daughter gone, and me in the Mediterranean?

"Don't you still have connections over there? Some old professor?" Sis asked.

"Oh, Dr. Lazarus? Yes, I emailed him. I guess he's still there. Can't imagine he's still digging."

"Well, old girl, I don't know what to say."

"Old girl? You're seven years older than me, Daphne."

Daphne poured herself some more coffee and then returned to stare at the timeline Carol had created. While stirring the creamer into her coffee, she pointed to one spot and asked, "What's this?"

Carol came to stand next to her and saw the date: June 20, 1998. "That's the date we got our Becca."

"Oh, right. I knew that. And October 6, 2002 is in red?"

"The day she was taken."

"Of course."

Carol and Maxx had tried for years to have a child. She'd taken Letrozole and Clomid but after two dozen ultrasounds and as many blood draws and doctors' visits, they hadn't been any more pregnant, just more broke.

Sis, on the other hand, had five kids, now grown, Maxx had thought she must be something of a fertility goddess.

For Maxx, sex became a job. Everything calculated, scheduled, and performed. The joy long gone, and the magic forgotten, but the remnants of a ritual remained. He became the donor, she the receptacle. They suffered together. They suffered alone.

They'd searched for a child from Russia to China. They'd even considered a surrogate but thought the process too painful, worse than a barren womb. Sis had connected Carol to an adoption broker—just a lawyer, really. They were told the mother was smart and professional but traveled often and had no time for a child. She was from one of those flyover states and had insisted on two things— no contact and they keep the name Rebecca.

Carol hated the name Rebecca and quickly shortened it to Becca. She also remembered the agent remarking about their names—Caroline and Maxim—when they'd signed the papers.

"Perfect, just perfect, what are the odds?" the agent remarked.

"Odds?" Maxx asked.

"Oh, just that you would have your baby after all these years. The one intended for you."

They were so happy they hadn't questioned her further. It didn't matter they'd never met the mother or that they were not coming home from the hospital but from a storefront lawyer's office.

None of these facts mattered when they'd laid Becca in her crib for the first time. After Becca came into their lives, Carol stopped the intrauterine inseminations, the trigger injections, the grant applications, and being a research pin cushion. Finally, they felt like things might return to some kind of normalcy.

The ping of Carol's phone brought her back to the present. Dr. Lazarus had replied to her. She'd sent him a picture of Becca's chifforobe and asked about the symbolism of the artwork on it.

"Whoa, this is interesting. Dr. L says the symbols are a series of hieroglyphics depicting a sacrifice to a Roman goddess, the Lady of Liberty. Her temple, erected in a site known as Seven Hills outside of Rome, is now the sight of a recent dig. They haven't turned up anything significant due to equipment failures, personnel setbacks, and government bureaucracy. Seems a few workers got hurt and some Romanologists have petitioned to have the site marked as sacred, and not to be disturbed."

"Carol, your house here is in Seven Hills Estates," Sis offered.

"Yeah, weird, right? We always liked the name of our development. It's one of the reasons we chose to live here. Listen, it gets weirder. The temple was erected on Aventine Hill." She looked up at both ladies. "We live on Aventine Hill Court."

Carol walked to the window and stared for a while at the clump of trees in the backyard. Any other person would think it a cute coincidence. Some might even smile. Few got goosebumps. But even fewer lost children and found significance in dimes, birds, and butterflies. God's creation continually cried out to them for connectedness. Now Carol felt like it was screaming, and she heard little else. Her anger had not abated but, she felt encouraged.

Carol walked to her computer and sent an email to Dr. Lazarus to arrange for an online meeting. Next, she thumbed through her books again.

Daphne stood still looking at the notes on the walls when Carol heard the doorbell ring and Sis letting someone in through the front door.

Carol walked over to greet the visitor.

"Ma'am, we haven't met before. I'm Detective Krinshaw, the Emerald Isle detective assigned to closing out your daughter's case. I wanted to reach out to you after the funeral, but I heard it was canceled. First, I want to say ..."

Carol knew the words without hearing them. "I am so sorry for your loss." It seemed they were always followed with some form of "but." "I'm so sorry for your loss *but* you can't put your poster here." Or, "I'm so sorry for your loss *but* my hands are tied." And now, "I'm sorry for your loss but the case is terminated." She hated those words more than she hated being called ma'am.

"I just wanted to go back over a few details so that we're all on the same sheet of music."

Carol nodded. "Fine."

"I'm a little embarrassed, but can I borrow a pen?"

The boyish detective seemed overdressed in a white and blue striped and collared shirt with French cuffs. A gold collar bar with matching cuff links completed his outfit. His thin neck and oversized shirt made him look smaller and younger than he was. He asked all the right questions and took notes in a notepad that fit in his inside coat pocket. Carol surmised they must get those pads in detective school and are told to get a pen wherever they can.

"I have the initial report here from the Morehead police department." He pulled some paperwork from a satchel. "As you know, the FBI stepped in when evidence pointed to your daughter leaving the state, and now it appears a serial pedophile inspired the incident."

"Inspired? Incident?"

Without looking up, Krinshaw continued. "It looks pretty complete, but you and Becca were ... are residents here, so Emerald Isle has its own file. Let's check for inconsistencies one more time—anything that may have come up since then. There were a lot of moving pieces, and I just want to tie it all together in a coherent narrative."

"You just want to cover your butt ... I mean close another open case."

The detective looked away, his mouth gaped as if to say something, and his eyelids fluttered.

"Excuse me, I don't want to be rude, and I will answer your questions, but aren't you a little late for this?" Carol handed him back the paperwork. "I mean, I've gone over this story with the Morehead City police, the FBI, and even with Channel 9 news."

He nodded. "Memory is a funny thing. Sometimes, due to the initial shock of the incident, we forget things and then fill in the gaps later. Then, after a long period of time, some details can come back to us, while other memories are degraded."

"Okay, do what you have to do."

The detective took out a larger notebook from his satchel, and Carol could see a page full of printed questions. Some even had answers already penciled in.

"I see your daughter was six when she was taken."

The detective's soft approach settled Carol's nerves. She took a deep breath and let him do his job, as painful as it was.

"Did you notice anyone suspicious beforehand—at your house or in public? What was the first thing that stuck in your mind after she was taken?"

As his questions continued, she nodded or made brief comments, but grew distant and transported herself to a safe place.

When he pulled out a series of photographs, she disconnected completely from the room. Voices became distant, and the pictures seemed to click by like an old film strip. She didn't think anyone noticed the change in her demeanor. She barely moved and held her head still as the detective held each picture in front of her line of vision. The photos caused a flood of painful memories Carol had tried to avoid for the last year.

Crowded makeshift booths lined the narrow road along the Outer Banks sound for the annual festival. The smell of salt water mixed with fried crab cakes and corndogs. Live music competed with the din of buyers and sellers haggling over arts and crafts. Ten minutes in line for food at the Seafood Festival seemed like an hour, but now, with hands full, they tried to make the best of it. The wind blew the wrapping away from Carol's crab cake sandwich, and Maxx stabbed at it with his foot but missed. Carol held Becca's hotdog with her other hand while Becca held on to her soda with both hands. Carol's bag acted as a counterweight, suspended in the crook of her arm between mother and daughter. They needed to find a place to sit soon. Becca was hot, Maxx seemed oblivious, and Carol steamed.

"Maxx, find a place to sit down so Becca can eat her hotdog." She felt Becca bump into her hip. "Yes, honey, Mommy has some ketchup for you. Just come with me."

"I want to go with Daddy."

"Whatever."

Sighing, Carol began to follow the pair. Before long, she lost sight of Maxx and Becca in the crowd. When she emerged on the other side of the mass, she found Maxx sitting alone in the grass.

"Where's Becca?"

"Isn't she with you?"

Panic rising and food now forgotten, they pushed back through the crowd, stepping on feet, and bumping into the backs of old people and cutting-off strollers as they searched for their daughter. Maxx almost got into a fight when an auxiliary police officer gave them a parental lecture on how to keep control of a young child in a crowd.

"Just find my little girl!"

After Maxx reported her age, sex, eye and hair color, the cop asked him Becca's height and weight. Maxx looked at Carol.

"About this high," she said, putting her hand to her side. "Forty-five pounds."

"And what was she wearing?"

Again, Maxx looked at her.

Carol shifted her weight from foot to foot and fiddled with her hair, her eyes darting around the crowd while the large police officer towered over her, blocking out the sun.

"A ... a pink tank top, jean shorts with some sequins on the back pockets, and a white zippered hoodie. Oh! And white sneakers that light up when you walk."

Carol clenched Becca's hotdog as she ran around the festival. After almost twenty minutes of searching, she collapsed on a bench and pleaded to God to bring Becca back.

He didn't.

Carol went to the festival's information booth and repeated her story. An older woman fumbled for paper and a working pen and raised her hand several times to stop Carol's ramblings to write down every word. Her methodical approach caused Carol to stammer.

"I am so sorry," the woman said.

Carol looked away. "Just find her."

The loudspeaker barked Becca's name and description. Maxx went to the police station while Carol continued to search as the sun set. She refused to leave the area until the last vendor shut their booth and the last tourist left.

Emptiness invaded Carol's soul as they drove away from the vacant festival in silence. The only sound came from her unbuckled seat belt. It was a quiet she'd heard only once when Joey died. She fumbled through her bag and then saw Becca's uneaten hotdog, crushed at the bottom, still in its foil wrapper. Her last words to Becca came back to her. "Whatever."

Maxx drove in silence to their house. He learned to remain quiet in the days and weeks that followed. Saying anything to Carol either sent her into immediate rage or, worse, deep withdrawal. Touching her was met with a frigid flinch. "Whatever" haunted her for months.

"Well, I guess that should do it."

Carol's focus returned to the detective who put his photos back into his satchel. The brass lock made a crisp sound of finality.

"If I have any other questions, I'll call."

Carol continued to stare at him blankly.

As he rose, he motioned to the timeline. "What's this on the wall?"

"It's a timeline," Sis said. "Carol thought she'd do some investigating too."

"That's odd, here you have Sunday for the day she was abducted."

"So?"

"Well, I have it here that she was taken on the fifth … a Saturday."

"No, it was the sixth." Carol pointed to the timeline.

"Ma'am, it's written in the initial report … the fifth." He held out the paper for her to inspect.

"No one ever asked me the day. I guess they all thought they knew."

"The first detective, Sanders, must have wrote down the wrong date and no one caught it. He's retired now. I imagine things were pretty emotionally charged. I mean, with it being a child and all. Well, that's why I'm here, to clean things up."

"To sanitize it."

"That's not what I meant." His eyelids fluttered making him look flustered. "This is important to all of us. Just because Emerald Isle's responsibility is closing, it will remain open for the FBI and for Morehead City, doesn't mean there is closure for you. I know that. I live in this community. I want to raise kids here. We even go to the festival. Last year when this happened, I wasn't the detective, but it's still important to me. I remember because I was at the festival with my brother's kids."

Carol nodded. "I felt guilty for skipping church that day. That was the first thing I said to our pastor when he came over that night, and he laughed. I'll never forget he laughed. He didn't know what to do. I just rocked back and forth all Sunday night. I sat by my phone. I opened the front door several times. I kept checking her room, I thought I heard her—all on Sunday."

"Well, at this point it may not mean anything."

"So, what now," Sis asked. "This has been so hard on everyone. Please tell us it's over."

"For the most part. I'll write my report, the higher-ups will decide when to close it, and, well, that's about it. But don't give up."

His little note of encouragement fell short. Maybe because it sounded perfunctory. Carol had heard false encouragement for a year—"God will work it out… just trust Jesus… hope springs eternal."

Krinshaw turned to the door.

"Thank God," chirped Daphne. "Don't you dust for fingerprints or collect DNA or something?"

"No, not at this point. We'll be in touch if there is more to this date thing. Thank you for your time, ma'am."

Carol felt as if she were looking right through him, as if he weren't in the room. She'd heard the "ma'am," but didn't acknowledge him.

Daphne smiled and walked him to the door. "I'll walk you out, I was just leaving anyway."

"That stupid hat."

Krinshaw stopped at the door. "What's that, ma'am?"

"That stupid hat," Carol repeated. "You asked what I remembered first. That hat. The one I saw in your photos."

Krinshaw knelt, popped the brass lock on his satchel, and produced the file of pictures once more. He riffled through them and then turned one out to her. "This one? This hat?"

"Yeah. The person wearing it was in line behind me … some girl talking, that's all I remember."

"Anything more? I mean, a name, anything?"

"She seemed rude, I didn't like her. 'Whatever,' I said and turned around."

"Whatever?"

Carol cringed, she wanted to scream, wanted to wipe the word from her memory. She closed her eyes. "Yes, whatever."

"Okay, Okay. Well, that could be something." He smiled at her while he put away the file of photos once more. "Thank you. It could be nothing, but if you remember anything else, be sure to call me."

Carol gave him a little nod and then turned back toward the house. She could hear a phone ring coming from her laptop.

"I have to take this, it's a call from Rome."

CHAPTER 5

"Hello, kid."

"Dr. L, you haven't changed a bit. Is that the same safari shirt you had when I was your student?"

The computer connection was delayed and went fuzzy when one of them moved too quickly but was clear enough to bring the two together.

"You should know, you gave it to me. I'm glad you got in touch with me. Some interesting developments have occurred on my latest dig. And some have to do with Lady Libertas."

"Why's that, sir?"

"Libertas lives!" Dr. Lazarus punctuated his statement with a finger raised in the air and a smile.

Carol waited. She knew there was more.

"Libertas was born about the same time the Roman Empire was born. She was immortalized in statue, poem, and coin. Despite her temple—which was dwarfed by Juniper's temple—it was Lady Libertas who found herself in the birth of modern France and America. She was emblazed on our coinage and on our shores."

"The Statue of Liberty. I know that, sir."

Dr. Lazarus's voice lowered. "But you don't know about her dark side. Libertas lives in the hearts and minds of pagans today. There have been reports about revivals. Pagan rituals beckoning back to a pre-Christian era. They want you to believe they are only interested in worshiping Mother Nature. In truth, they're interested in war. Call it fascism, terrorism, or radicalism, but call it for what it is—they want to wipe out Christianity, the religion that almost wiped them out."

Carol sat motionless and quiet. His conviction seemed unmistakable. Hearing her mentor talk in global terms briefly reminded her of her scholastic pursuits, but now she wasn't processing politics, movements, or religion. His words seemed too much to comprehend. Envisioning her daughter in the middle of that chaos overwhelmed her. Paralysis creeped in. Her nightmare was returning.

"Caroline, little girls over here are missing. They take girls from Christian families. I climbed Aventine Hill after you first contacted me. I dropped my clip-on sunglasses that you were always so fond of. And when I bent down to pick them up ..."

Carol watched her screen as he slowly stretched out his arm and opened his upturned palm.

As his fingers uncurled, she saw a Mercury dime. Carol gasped and drew closer to the screen. Her hands which had been folded in her lap, now held both sides of the monitor.

"What's the date," she asked, awaking from her nightmare.

"That's what I want to tell you. It's ... well, here ... Oh, that's strange, it's 1942."

"What's strange about that? That's what it's supposed to say."

"The thing is, Carol, when I found it, I could swear it said 1996."

What is going on with these dimes? Wrong dates, Becca's birthdate on old dimes, and now dimes with dates that change?

"What we think of as the symbol for patriotic liberty began in Babylonia with Ishtar. This pagan goddess promoted personal sexual liberty. Temple fees were paid to the priest, and young girls were kept for sexual pleasure. This appealed to the Greeks and later to the Romans. Aventine Hill was on the outskirts of Rome where immigrants congregated and practiced their pagan rituals. Sacrifice, sex, debauchery abounded. April 13 is the traditional date for the feast commemorating the joining of Jupiter with Libertas."

"Next week?"

"At night."

"Where?"

"No one knows, no one ever knows. But when I found the dime, I went back to Aventine Hill that night. I saw thirteen hooded characters come out of the woods. They talked among themselves as they pointed here and there and stepped-off an area. I don't know what they said, but they were planning something."

"A ceremony?"

"Maybe. After I got back to my office, I did some research and discovered information about a feast. I surveyed the recent news feed, and there have been a number of attempted child snatchings at hospitals in this area. All from Christian families. They caught a young woman at a day care before she almost drove away with a toddler. She told the authorities they could not be stopped and bragged about smuggling a child from America to stick a knife in the American religious movement. I saw her mug shot on TV. She had a small tattoo on her wrist of an eagle holding a thunderbolt."

"The symbol of Jupiter." Carol sat back once more in her chair. "I thought ancient Rome outlawed human sacrifice."

"They did. But remember, Aventine wasn't always part of Rome. Foreigners who settled there were rumored to sacrifice. Many foreigners were brought back to Rome as slaves. When they earned their freedom, they settled in Aventine.

"Anyway, there have been a rash of reports about human trafficking and the *polizia* broke up a child smuggling ring and found documents suggesting a link to the United States and now are on high alert for a little girl from the States. Carol, on the news, the young woman who got caught at the day care—as they carted her away— she held up her fist, the one with the tattoo and screamed, 'Rivka, Rivka.'"

Carol stared at the screen as her left foot twitched against the desk. Her right hand twisted through her hair.

"Carol?"

"Rivka is Hebrew for Rebecca."

"I know, Carol. It means 'fascinates with her grace.'"

"The ceremony is next week, you say?"

"Yes, what are you thinking?"

"I don't know ... I just don't know. Thinking is all I've been doing. Thinking is what I do best, but thinking is sending me in circles. For the first time in my life, I just don't know what to think. All I know is that Becca is gone, and the police botched the report since day one. I think Becca could be alive, but everyone here says she's dead. I have to stay put. She could come back any minute. I have to be here for her."

After she'd ended the call with Dr. L, Carol fumed for the rest of the day. Sis had gone out on a bike ride, and Carol relished the quiet. Questions about what she should do next cycled through her mind on a slow-moving carousel.

As evening wore on, Carol sat on her wicker lounge looking out into the backyard. The lounge used to mean so much to her when Becca was here. They'd sit on the bright red cushion and blow bubbles using a small wand and bottle of bubble mix, making each other laugh. Things could never be the same now. Her life had been stolen. Now she imagined Becca in a bubble.

She stared endlessly through the screen but barely noticed Sis getting caught as she came through the broke screen door.

"Maxx always said he'd fix that old door," Sis said as she emptied a yellow sugar packet in a glass of iced tea.

Carol's iced tea now sat on the painted pressure-treated porch floor, watered down and making a ring. Life was on hold.

"Well?" Sis asked from her spot beside her on the lounge.

Well, nothing, Carol wanted to say. Instead, she said, "That's a deep question."

"Seriously, maybe we should take all that stuff off the wall."

"Seriously? There are all these signs—the dimes, the jasmine—I saw her. I saw Becca. But it's just not logical. I have all this stupid information on this wall and none of it points anywhere. But a dime shows up and points me to Rome? It doesn't make sense."

Carol stood and stared at the surrounding trees, her arms folded. "Since she's been gone, my world has been turned upside down. I don't know who I am. I don't know who God is. I really don't know what this world is all about. I mean, should I trust you? Should I let it all go? Dr. L didn't even tell me what to do, but I feel like he was telling me something. Should I trust him? I don't trust Maxx. I don't even trust myself."

CHAPTER 6

The locked satchel brushed along Krinshaw's neatly creased pants. He shifted his lunch to his left hand and gave a casual salute to the sergeant behind the plexiglass. He straightened as he passed the flags on the police station quarterdeck.

Then he pushed on the metal-framed glass doors and responded to the hail of "Krinshaws" with a deep sigh. The hallway of offices always seemed too long to the back stairs where he descended to his "corner office." That's what he called the corner of the basement where an old oak desk and several metal file cabinets formed his makeshift outpost. He shook his head whenever he saw the stuffed cabinets knowing the phone clipped to his belt held even more information.

"So much paper, so little time," he said out loud. "Think of the trees—oh, the humanity." He laughed but it was his mission to bring his department into the twenty-first century. *Who keeps paper anymore?*

The old cases took the balance of his day, but he longed for something fresh, something that would make a difference. He didn't see how putting a dent into the towering cabinets mattered.

He had sought out his now retired predecessor, another repository of disorganized facts and historical anecdotes. Krinshaw had found him working on his skiff boat on the edge of the marshy sound. The older man had a few days growth, and an almost empty bottle of whiskey sat on a plastic table.

"Look, son, we're small here. Sure, our population fluctuates but it's mostly made of middle and upper middleclass folk on vacation. We have some drug issues in the schools, but we're free from murder and rape for the most part. So, no, we don't have the resources for those kinds of cases. Shoot, we didn't have the resources for new tires for my squad car."

Krinshaw had stopped listening to him at "son." His predecessor wasn't opposed to the new technology, he just didn't understand it.

Krinshaw spent his own money on training and software. His boss had recognized his new can-do spirit by finding a way to upgrade his computer system. Now Krinshaw had a case with a name and a face. Getting the date wrong bothered him, and his predecessor did little to inspire confidence. *And well, if something as simple as an incident date could be overlooked then what else did my declining predecessor miss?*

He loosened his tie, unclipped his collar bar, rolled up his sleeves, and sat down to work.

Hours later, after poring over screen after screen of local and federal reports, he lifted his bleary eyes when he smelled coffee.

Tomlinson—an aging corporal, set for retirement—had worked the evidence locker for as long as anyone could remember. He wasn't much for making friends, and several officers had warned Krinshaw not to mess with the guy. Rumors about why he manned the cage alone ran rampant in the department, but most people felt he must have done something really wrong to the wrong person to deserve the lone billet.

Any past attempt to talk to Tomlinson had resulted in Krinshaw babbling nervously. Every awkward conversation had ended with Tomlinson locking himself behind the gate of the evidence locker for the rest of the day.

While Krinshaw coughed and sneezed from the musty odor of the basement, Tomlinson seemed to thrive amongst the mold, a fixture in grey wearing a coffee-stained skinny black tie. He was a man who barely moved and was hardly noticed before. A few hairs grew out of the top of his head, and a few more out the top of his ears. A bulbous red nose and his red-pocked complexion earned him the nickname Santa ... but no one ever called him Santa to his face.

Now, this curmudgeon everyone had warned him about stood in front of him holding a steaming hot cup of coffee.

"Uh, thanks," Krinshaw said. When he'd turned back from setting the cup on his desk, Tomlinson had disappeared. "Weird."

He looked at the coffee and briefly wondered if it could be laced with something. He took a tentative sip. Double cream, no sugar, just as he liked it. He looked back to where Tomlinson had disappeared and then shrugged his shoulders.

Krinshaw heard nothing for the rest of the day except the distinctive sound of the slide bolt locking the evidence locker. Then Santa was gone. The detective checked his watch and slid a handful of manila folders into the faux leather satchel his wife had given him when he'd been appointed detective. He turned out the light, rounded the evidence room, and continued back up the steps and down the main hallway to the double glass doors flanked by traditional globed lights jutting out from the exterior front.

Another world awaited him behind apartment door 33b written in gold script. His beagle barked once before jumping off the couch and running toward him.

"Barney, you know you shouldn't be up there." The smell of spaghetti sauce heavily laden with oregano drifted through the studio apartment.

He spied his petite blond wife standing in front of a steaming pot on the stove. She didn't turn around when he reached around her with both arms.

"Detective Krinshaw, that better not be your gun sticking me in the side."

"What do you think?"

"I think you better lock it up if you want any of this pasta. And take off your shoes while you're at it."

"Right away, Mrs. Krinshaw."

He got out of his work attire and threw on some jeans and a torn college T-shirt before returning to the kitchen to help set the table.

After dinner, he sat surrounded by folders cluttered on the couch while watching the ACC game. He awoke when his wife turned off the television.

"I'm watching that, Julie."

"Sure you are. Come to bed. What are you working on anyway?"

"Remember the Davies child who was abducted?"

"By that psycho in Pennsylvania?"

"Not exactly, but he had something to do with it. Anyway, I visited her mother today to close out the report now that she was reported, um ... dead."

"That must have been difficult."

"Yeah, well, I found out today the initial report had the date wrong. Such a basic thing, it should have been so obvious. Turns out she was taken on a Sunday."

"The day we were at the festival."

"You remember that?"

"Of course. We had your two nephews. Wow, we were so close and had no idea."

As Krinshaw rose from the couch, two folders hit the floor and black and white photos spilled out.

"There's the gelato girl." Julie leaned over the back of the couch with a tea towel in her hand.

"Who?"

"Remember? We were in line with the boys for ice cream, and she kept saying how much better gelato was for you, and she was going to get the real thing when she got to Rome. Gelato this and gelato that."

Julie came to his side and sat down, picking up a grainy black and white taken from a security cam. The distinctive floppy hat with a chiffon scarf tied around its brim looked out of place in the southern town crowd. The woman's top exposed most of her back.

"Would you look at that outfit, so tacky," Julie continued. "Said she would never bring a child to such a dirty crowd and couldn't wait to get home. Oh, and that accent. I know it was fake. Just as tacky as her."

"Really? Where was I?"

"Next to me."

"I was probably paying. When I was leaving today, Ms. Davies was waiting for a call from Rome."

"Funny, huh?" Julie put down the photo and went back the hall to the bedroom.

The next day, a hot coffee sat on his desk. After putting down his satchel, Krinshaw raised the paper cup in a mock salute to the fenced-in Tomlinson. He thought he saw a slight smile.

Hours later, he interrupted his pecking away on his keyboard to enjoy a familiar paper bag lunch prepared by his wife.

After eating his sandwich, chips, and apple, he scrunched up the bag, imagined a shot clock, and made a one-handed, seated jump shot that landed on the rim before flopping into the trash can.

"Yes!" he exclaimed before heading to the restroom. When he returned, a folded scrap of paper sat on top of the folders and reports on his desk. On the paper was written "1 4 3" which was surrounded by a heart. *Hmm, must have been in my lunch.* He surmised Tomlinson must have seen the note fall from his lunch bag and put it on his desk while he was away. *Well, at least I solved that mystery.*

The "1 4 3" was his wife's code for "I LOVE YOU" and made him think of her and their conversation last night about his case. Krinshaw returned his attention to the mystery hat girl. Abductors go to great pains not to stand out, to blend in. *She's no pro, that's certain.*

He couldn't shake the image of the hat girl. *Maybe she'd been a plant? A distraction? Maybe a lookout. Or maybe nothing.* Krinshaw knew that many abductions utilized a team to get the job done. There was the primary abductor, sometimes two in case of a struggle. There is the possibility of a lookout, to keep an eye out for police, especially if they were in a public location. Some abductors staged distractions to be employed if the kidnapping is detected.

Krinshaw stared at his screen. His report just needed the chief's approval. The send button stared back at him. *Just get it done, make everyone happy.* But gelato girl kept interfering. *Darn it.*

He looked over at Tomlinson who was reading a newspaper. *I must be crazy.*

He had nowhere to turn. His boss wanted turnover, and his peers found him pesky, wet behind the ears. They were already jaded. Any attempts at friendship fell short. Krinshaw's knowledge of trivia made him come across like a know-it-all. Desperate and nowhere to turn, his veneer of independence was a thin façade shabbily covering a longing to achieve and be acknowledged.

He turned to yell to Tomlinson, but then thought better of it. He walked over to the cage instead.

"Hey. I'm working on closing this Davies case, and I can't get past this one thing. I don't have a partner so maybe I could bounce this off you." Tomlinson sat motionless, so he continued. "I mean before I go to the chief. You don't have to say anything if you don't want to." Again, silence. "Just, you know, a dry run, a rehearsal." Still nothing. "Okay, so here's the thing. First, Morehead got the initial report date wrong. Not critical, because it got corrected, but it makes me want to dig deeper, could be more, right?" Still silence. "Anyway ..." Krinshaw went through the chronology while Tomlinson sat quietly and without reaction.

After he'd finished, he looked up to see Tomlinson had not moved one muscle during this entire speech. "So ... that's about it. Except, the other day, the mother says something about a hat, and then that night my wife remembers seeing a girl, a young woman in the same hat. I mean, my wife and I were at the festival too. Are you with me so far?" Tomlinson barely blinked. "Anyway, long story short, the young woman who owns it, is connected to Rome somehow—something my wife heard her say. When I was leaving Ms. Davies' house the other day, she was getting a phone call from, you guessed it, Rome. Weird right? What are the odds? So, what do you think?" Silence. "You got anything?" Krinshaw heard nothing. "Well, okay then."

Krinshaw returned to his desk. Tomlinson remained quiet in his cage for the rest of the day until the gate rattled and then he was gone.

The next day, Krinshaw walked down to his office. Everything the same as it always was ... except Tomlinson wasn't at his desk.

Krinshaw heard grunting and saw boxes moving and dust dancing in the air around the florescent ceiling lights. Occasionally, he caught a glimpse of someone who must have been Tomlinson, but he just wasn't sure.

Santa must be spring cleaning.

No coffee awaited him today. As he set to work, the noise continued in a sporadic but non-intrusive way. Krinshaw turned on his computer and scrolled through a plethora of routine emails. Tryout reminders for the police softball team, an invitation to mandatory fun night at Chelsi's Tavern, the latest updates on policy, and, of course, the daily report.

The report showed a summary of everyone's activity over the last few days—mostly patrol arrests. At the end of the spreadsheet was a blank row where his progress should have been recorded. No one had said anything to him, but the blank space seemed to send a message: "Yo, Millennial, close the case." The space made Krinshaw squirm. He was getting pressured to move on, to finish what amounted to a bureaucratic function, so he could tackle more bureaucratic functions, then more after that.

Krinshaw keyed in the Davies summary report. *This gets sent today.* His lunch bag sat in his satchel, unopened, a folded scrap of paper, unread. Krinshaw buried himself into the Davies file. He poured back and forth through the background, evidence, and procedure sections until he came to the conclusion.

Maybe if I read it aloud.

"In conclusion, all evidence points to the victim, Rebecca Davies, being abducted on October 6, 2002. Evidence further indicates she was transported to Pennsylvania where she died of unknown causes. The abductor remains at large but was clearly influenced by convicted serial killer Harold Baker who remains on death row in Pennsylvania. All other leads, suspects, and motives have been systematically ruled out, leading to the termination of the active status of this case."

Krinshaw barely heard Tomlinson's commotion as he stared at the SEND button on his screen. It loomed large. *Push it, just push it. Move on.* He glanced at the files piled two feet high on the corner of his gray metal desk. Behind them stood the filing cabinets that cast a haunting shadow across his keyboard. "I need some air."

Becca was still on his mind as he headed to the station's locker room. After lacing up his running shoes with a tight knot, he headed for the open road. Running always cleared his head. At the three-mile mark, he stopped to soak in the setting sun on the other side of the bridge connecting Emerald Isle to the rest of the world. The tranquility lay in contrast to the ugliness that filled the basement files in his world.

A simple two-lane bridge that brings hope for many brought a murderous fool to kill a family's only dream. The thought stole the rest of his motivation and he staggered back to the station. This time, too depleted to endure any more comments from the locker room pundits, he headed straight downstairs. *Who'll care about more sweat? Maybe I am just an elf, and Tomlinson is Santa.*

A large paper bag sat on his desk. He thought maybe Tomlinson had made him lunch but realized how ridiculous that would be. He drew closer and noticed the bag was stapled with an official evidence form.

He grabbed a pair of latex gloves from the box on his desk and then tore open the bag. Reaching gingerly into the bag, he pulled out a plastic evidence bag containing a purple hat with a long sash tied around the brim.

"What in the world?" He took the hat in one hand and the paper bag in the other and strode to the cage.

Tomlinson stared at him from behind his desk.

"C'mon, man, talk. Where did this come from?"

Tomlinson stood, unlocked the cage, and then turned and walked to the back. Krinshaw walked past rows of stacked-to-the-ceiling boxes and finally caught up to Tomlinson. He looked over the old man's shoulder to where he pointed at the back wall.

"Back there. It fell from the top shelf and landed behind everything. Stuff is pretty crowded here. When you showed me that picture yesterday, I went home and told my wife about it. It got me thinking I'd seen that hat somewhere."

"Wait, you have a wife?"

Tomlinson glared at him before saying, "Anyway, I figured it must mean something."

"I could kiss you, man."

Tomlinson continued his glare and took a step back.

"Well, I got to take this upstairs."

Upstairs, the chief explained several jurisdictions had been called in to comb the area after Becca went missing. An auxiliary police officer had found the hat where Becca was last seen, bagged it, and, instead of turning it into Morehead City, must have brought it back to Emerald Isle where Tomlinson assigned it a ticket and put it up on the top shelf to be sent back to Morehead at a later date.

"I suppose it fell down behind other boxes and was forgotten. An easy mistake, even for Tomlinson."

"Chief, we have to send this to the state forensics lab."

"Close this case! That's your job, remember? Labs cost money. Besides, what's this going to do? Add more questions for these parents? Haven't they been through enough? Do you really want to do that?"

"The thing is, you weren't there, Chief. You didn't see what all these pictures did to that mother the other day. She was in a dissociative fugue."

"A what?"

"A fugue. Like, in her mind, she just wasn't here anymore. But the hat brought her back. Down deep in her psyche, this hat is very important to her. So, yeah, I do want to do it, but *for* her, not *to* her."

"Krinshaw, I don't know about that psychobabble stuff."

Instead of rattling on about analytics and statistics while the chief yelled, Krinshaw simply stared. Spending so much time with Tomlinson had taught him a new tactic.

Finally, the chief stopped talking and asked, "What?"

"Well, Chief, it's your call. What do you want to do?"

"For crying out loud, send it to the lab, then. But if it comes back negative, you owe me big time."

Krinshaw opened the door.

"And don't think that reverse psychology crap you learned in college worked on me either."

Krinshaw walked as fast as he could to express mail his package to Raleigh.

CHAPTER 7

Doing nothing killed Carol but kneeling among her flowers brought her life. Her roses were blooming, her chrysanthemums finally showed promise, and even the tree planted for Becca showed signs of life. *My babies*. Carol smiled slightly. A few bees and a yellow swallowtail butterfly brought her hope.

Her phone lit up and she answered.

"Ms. Davies, this is Detective Krinshaw. We found the hat."

Carol took off her gardening gloves as she pressed the phone against her ear. "What hat?"

"The one you mentioned the other day. They found a group of red hairs with dark roots in that purple hat. Anyway, it went through our databases and onto the FBI because, as you know, they have jurisdiction. Long story short, it got a hit on an international database. The woman had been arrested and released last in Italy. She has a list of priors, vagrancy, and some other small stuff. Plus, she was suspected of attempting to abduct a child from a day care. I'm probably saying too much but, well, you deserve to know. Her religion is listed as 'Pagan'."

"Where is she now?"

"Well, we don't know. I couldn't tell you if I did know. The address she gave was likely bogus, but like I said, her last arrest was in Italy just a few weeks ago. My guess is she's likely with people she knows, people who can give her safe haven. I'm thinking she's still in Italy."

"What happens now?" Carol asked as she stood up next to a volunteer tomato plant.

"The Italian police can keep an eye out for her. However, unless they have a lead, they are not going to search for her. I was instructed to send my report to investigators in Rome—Inspector Rizzo, but I have to stop my investigation at this point. I'm sorry, but until I have more there is nothing at my end for me to do. The police usually wait for them to slip up then arrest them. No telling when she'll slip up, though. It's a waiting game."

Carol's eyes darted back to the yellow swallowtail. She fidgeted with her shears, still pressing her phone so tightly against her ear it hurt.

"Ms. Davies, are you still there?"

"Yeah ... yes, I'm thinking, that's all."

"It's a lot to take in. I can't imagine what you're going through."

Carol thought about her conversation with Dr. L and about the ring of abductors. And about the woman who yelled "Rivka" at the news cameras. How the abductors said they wouldn't stop. She thought about the pagan festival Dr. L had told her about, which was now just three days away at midnight. She also thought about how she'd said she had to stay home for her daughter.

"So, do you have any idea where my daughter is?"

"Well, no, not really. Mind you, I'm not saying she's alive. I'm just giving you all I have, but all I have are a series of sightings of a significant person of interest. While it's not enough for the Italian police to investigate, it still makes the hair on the back of my neck stand up. I really want to know more about this person. I feel she's connected—I just don't know how."

Carol left her shears and gloves in her gardening basket and walked back to the house. *Maybe Dr. L will know what to do.*

She sent him an email with the new information and then, later that day, connected with her old mentor again online.

"Carol, I went to the polizia to see about your new information. It took a while, but I met with the detective who received your detective's report. He had some additional information. Your hat girl spent her brief time in jail proselytizing about her pagan religion. She told the others that pagans are worldwide and seemed proud that her group had direct connections to the States. She talked about children being the future, and that children have a special connection to the universe because they have not been influenced by religion."

"Sir, that's incredible. When you put this all together, it makes sense. Well, sort of. But is it enough? I mean, does it tell me where Becca is now?"

"No, Carol, we still don't know where Becca is. But we have a name—Starlite. At least that's the name she gave, and because she was never arrested before in Italy, they released her."

Dr. L leaned into the screen. "Listen to this, Carol. This info was buried deep in the jail's daily reports. Seems Starlite was a focus of attention because she talked so much, unlike other pagans who usually keep to themselves about their beliefs. Starlite must have been entertaining to them. Anyway, here's what it says. 'The prisoner had a visitor today and returned to her cell. She was agitated and taken to medical.' The medical report recorded her chanting, 'We have Rivka, we have grace, we have Rivka, we have grace.'"

Carol rose from the desk chair, walked around, and sat back down. Then she repeated the ritual several times. When she returned to the computer screen, Dr. Lazarus reviewed details with her. They discussed the cult.

"Starlite must be the young woman in the purple hat, and she's probably the woman from the daycare."

"The fact that she had been in the vicinity of Becca's abduction and later arrested in Italy is incredibly significant," Dr. Lazarus added.

Carol pulled her passport from the bottom of the drawer. She hadn't seen it since she and Maxx took their failed winter cruise to the Bahamas. When she hung up with Dr. L, she booked a flight and hotel for Rome.

Sis came in as Carol was cramming a nylon duffle bag with clothes and personal items.

"Carol, you're nuts."

"I booked two tickets."

"Oh. Well. Okay, then. I wouldn't have it any other way. Someone needs to look after you." Sis started packing her own bags.

"You have to understand, Carol, before I started coming down here to help you, I never missed a day at the hardware store—I know when customers need fine-thread nuts and when they need course-thread. I know how to start the paint shaker, and I know where the sandpaper falls behind the shelf. All they'll know is that Sis is gone."

Her sister did not have the sense of urgency that Carol felt. At the airport, Sis held up the line because she'd tried to bring a twenty-four-ounce bottle of skin lotion in her carry-on. Then she got into a genealogy conversation with the TSA agent.

"Why, we could be cousins, shug!"

Carol hurried ahead to get a spot in preboarding. Sis would have to catch up. When she heard her sister calling, Carol slowed on the gangway leading onto the Airbus.

"Wait up!" Sis chugged up to her, out of breath. She slung her large woven bag, almost as big as an artist's portfolio, over one shoulder. Around her neck she'd already fastened a horseshoe-shaped pillow she'd ordered from *Sky Mall* on her last flight six years ago. Earbuds bounced on both shoulders. With her other hand, she pulled a carryon. Her handbag had slipped from her shoulder and now hung by her wrist.

"Good thing I wore sensible shoes, right?" Sis said, trying to regain her breath. "Gotta great deal on these earphones."

This is wrong. I don't do things like this. Did I stop the paper? I hope the post office gets my out-of-town card. Oh, Lord, what if I'm wrong? Carol's mental carousel whirled at a dizzying speed.

While Carol walked past the flight attendant, Sis stopped to show her boarding pass, tucked between family photos. Carol was already seated with her carryon overhead when her older sister plopped into her seat, across the aisle.

"Hey, move your foot."

"Sis, I'm really not in the mood—"

"*Move* your foot."

Sis reached across the aisle and picked up a shiny dime. Roosevelt on one side, 1996 on the other.

Maybe things are working out.

Carol pressed the dime in her palm, and breathed in a new world, one she knew she had no control over but one in which she needed to act—no longer languishing on a lonesome beach waiting to be found.

She felt as if she were watching a movie of her life—like she wasn't really part of what was happening.

When the plane landed in Charlotte, she took one of her sister's bags, bypassed the moving sidewalks, and headed to Terminal A as Sis labored to keep up. There was no way Carol would miss their connecting flight.

Just a year ago, she'd had days when her legs didn't tire, her feet floated as if on air, and her movements appeared fluid. Those days seemed to have faded away until today. Now she felt like that person again. She pressed the dime tighter in her palm.

She could sense Becca.

She smiled when she heard the announcement for the Fiumicino-Leonardo da Vinci International Airport. Such a beautiful name for such a beautiful place.

"I thought we were going to Rome?" Sis asked.

Carol looked at her sister with raised eyebrows. "That *is* Rome."

"Carol, I'm kidding."

"Oh, right."

Carol seemed to hover above the crowded gangway. Inside the plane, she absently gazed at the ladies in first class who were hoping someone would see them sipping mimosas and dabbing their lips with real linen. She squeezed her slender hips between the seats and then side-stepped into her middle seat. The man in the window seat had already assumed the middle arm rest. She reasoned he'd be snoring in no time.

Sis flopped down in the aisle seat after engaging in a lengthy luggage discourse with the attendant—much to the chagrin of the passengers behind her.

"Such a nice man," Sis said. "Shame about his marriage. Must have been from losing his job at the mill. Poor thing, I hope this flying thing works out for him."

How does she do that?

Carol buried herself in her book, *Romanesque Ruins*. Her pasta meal in a tin canister covered with a plastic lid took the edge off the long international flight. She watched Sis fumble with the smaller-than-normal size silverware and then make a trip to the water closet.

"Water closet, isn't that quaint?" Sis remarked.

Hours later, Carol's nap was interrupted by streaks of light streaming through the small window as the sun came up over the Mediterranean. She strained to look past the man snoring next to her in hopes of seeing Gibraltar. Her memories of college summers in Europe came filtering back. Those days had been special in a time when nothing else seemed to matter.

At the first sight of Sicily and the mainland, tears began to roll down her cheeks. Were they of joy, relief, or a realization of freedom she hadn't felt in over a year? She wasn't sure. Sis laid her hand over Carol's but said nothing as they landed.

"I guess we'll be in Terminal C," Carol said as they taxied down the runway.

"No, B. C has had some construction issues," Sis said. "It won't be ready for at least another year. See, there's the elevated people mover, still being built."

Carol raised her eyebrows in question.

"Oh, I read about it in flight. I also ordered you an automatic feeder for your cat."

The line for customs snaked down the hallway and into a large area filled with kiosks that looked like toll booths. Airport polizia stood at a distance with short automatic Uzis strapped around their necks. A cacophony of languages mixed with babies crying and parents calling for their children surrounded Carol. If the melee of languages bothered Sis, she didn't let on, but she was noticeably quiet. Carol reveled in the confusion, soaking it up like wet pasta in the bottom of the bowl or sipping a bit of red wine at the end of a long day. Italian phrases came back to her. She knew her lira from the past, but now the euro proved even easier.

Even though the airport was one of the busiest in Europe, Carol navigated the construction with the ease of an experienced tourist. Sis strapped her bags together with a bungee cord she'd found between the terminal seats and fashioned her portfolio bag into a flat backpack.

"When are we going to get a bite to eat?" Sis kept up with Carol and mentioned the men primping like peacocks who sniggered like schoolboys when they passed.

Sis thought they were welcoming her when one of the men formed a salute with his hand and then brought it across his stomach and said to the others, "*Ho Fame.*" The group laughed.

Carol managed to get a hand free to touch her forehead with her index finger and addressed the group with distain, "*E'matto.*" The group erupted while the leader looked away.

"What did you say?"

"Oh nothing, I just said you're married." Carol couldn't tell her she chastised him because he was mimicking Sis, claiming to be hungry.

"They look so soft," Sis replied. "Definitely not my type. Bet they've never changed a diaper or a tire."

Carol flagged down a cab and they were off to Rome, thirty-five kilometers—or roughly twenty-two miles—away.

"We're making good time. Here, drink this water, you'll thank me. It helps with the jet lag." Carol handed Sis a bottle she'd bought at the airport. The ride and water revived them as they took in their new world of carved stone, motor scooters, and tiny cars.

Carol handled the fare after the driver deposited their bags in front of a long line of four-story row homes and then pulled Sis away from a flower and fertilizer discussion with a homeowner who didn't speak English so the two could check into their B&B.

After climbing the narrow stairs with their bulky baggage, Carol managed the skeleton key in the brass door plate. The elaborate doorknob turned loosely, and the door swung open, revealing a double bed, three large windows, and a porcelain sink. Sis fell on the overstuffed bed as Carol pushed the luggage into a small closet before they heard a knock at the door.

"Hello, *signora*, I'm Antonio."

"Yes, Dr. L told me you would meet us."

"Dr. Lazarus asked me to take you to the polizia. If there is time, I will show you some items of interest at the *museo*. You will like them. Dr. Lazarus told me they may have something to do with your daughter."

As he led them to his car, Sis pointed to his mismatched floral shirt and printed pants. When Carol pushed her hand away, Sis whispered, "He could use a haircut."

"Shush."

"I could help is all I'm saying."

At the police station, an older detective sat down with them with a large file. His office was separated by glass, framed in metal, cutting down some of the clamor of the surrounding department which sounded like an active beehive. He pushed his chair back to formally introduce himself as "Inspector Rizzo, at your service. I am sorry for your loss." His English was good enough for him to explain, "We have watched various pagan groups for a long time, but it's only been recently we noticed an increase in activity. This young woman you are interested in—we sent a car to pick her up, but she seems to have vanished. We contacted the American embassy. It is all we can do."

Carol talked about Becca. She talked about her pink T-shirt, her stuffed Pegasus horse, her sparkling blue eyes, and her love of the ocean. Carol hadn't talked about Becca like this since she'd been abducted. Maybe it was exhaustion, maybe dehydration, or maybe it was hope.

Inspector Rizzo's dark eyes saddened. "I am very sorry for your loss."

Carol nodded. "Yes, you said that. I know you are. Now you are going to say, 'But I can't help.'"

"Not true, my superiors told me not to open a new case, not at this time. For us, there is not enough new evidence. But we had already planned on having men watch out for this gathering tomorrow night and, well, I am—how you say—at your service."

"Oh, thank you, and please forgive me," Carol replied. "It's just that—"

"We have a saying here," Rizzo interrupted, *"Amor di madre, amore senza limiti.* It means a mother's love has no limits."

"Yes, yes, that's it," she replied, not caring her eyes filled with tears. She impulsively hugged the inspector. Carol clung to his stiff form, then gathered herself and said goodbye. A sense of peace and brief optimism fell over her.

Antonio took them to the Musei Capitolini as promised, famous for housing many of the antiquities of Rome. The buildings stood on the smallest hill of the city causing the sisters to pause as they climbed the steep steps. As they rested, Carol explained to Sis how the museum buildings themselves were an exhibit, dating back to ancient Rome when they served as the hub of government. Later, da Vinci had designed a massive remodel which included additions and a courtyard to house Roman art.

In the museum, the good Dr. Lazarus had asked Antonio to take them straight to the Capitoline Coin Closet.

"It's still a work in progress," explained Antonio. "The display was not to open for several months, but I have the museum privileges."

The sisters followed him through several roped off areas, down a darkened corridor to a series of staircases, and into the coinage room. Coins of all shapes, sizes, and materials—copper, bronze and even shells—lined the shelves and were embossed with birds, forks, men, women, and gods. Their guide led them to a display with mostly goddesses adoring the coins.

Then, they saw her—Lady Libertas.

"Libertas was a minor goddess but held a special place for the downtrodden. She was the goddess of the free, and the hope of the enslaved," their guide informed them.

"I like her hat. It looks warm and she doesn't have to do her hair," Sis remarked. "Didn't Becca have one?"

The guide smiled, seeming to warm up to Sis's down-to-earth view. She often had that effect on people.

"That's not a hat, Sis. It's called a *pileus*, a liberty cap. When slaves in Ancient Rome were granted their freedom, they shaved their heads to mark the occasion and were given a cap. That, I do remember."

"Looks like a beanie."

"Well, that beanie started out as functional and became a symbol of Libertas. The Romans didn't just cherish their freedom, they worshipped it. Freedom was a god to them."

Carol was the expert here, and it was her daughter that was lost. Yet her knowledge had gaps—her command of details no longer sharp. As they talked, she stammered with pronunciation and mixed gods and goddesses from different eras. Antonio politely redirected the conversation when Carol lowered her head and stopped in mid-sentence.

"I knew all of this—more—at one time," she said.

Sis was still pointing at the goddess's cap.

Carol envisioned Becca wearing the cap in the summer on the playground as she shrieked on the swings. "Higher, Mommy, higher! Someday I'm gonna go even higher."

She remembered Becca before her bath, protesting when Carol tried to take off the cap. When Becca climbed into bed and fell asleep, she'd been holding her cap and Peggy, her stuffed Pegasus.

Carol fixated on one coin. Centuries old, it was embossed with a woman's profile. Her pileus surrounded by a ring of laurel leaves. A cat sprawled at her feet.

"Why the cat?" Sis asked.

"Is it me or does the goddess look like Becca?"

Sis leaned in closer and then said, "No, I really don't see it."

Suddenly, they felt a whoosh of air so strong it caused the filaments inside the sealed incandescent bulbs to flicker and sent a chill throughout the room. The sisters turned to see the large bronze doors close as Antonio left them to peruse. The doors sealed them in a vacuum, created centuries ago to preserve the artifacts. They looked at each other and laughed.

"Spooky, huh?"

"Yeah, hope it's not an omen." Carol began to read from a book she'd brought along. "Seems that Lady Liberty has survived the centuries. Poems were even written about her. These days, she's a symbol for contemporary Wiccans and other pagans. She is a powerful and ancient goddess who can guide, inspire, protect, and comfort. Pagans have invoked Lady Liberty in rituals for personal liberation."

"Creepy." Sis shivered.

"Maybe."

"Carol, you wouldn't invoke—"

"There's nothing I wouldn't do to get Becca back. Nothing."

Sis raised one eyebrow and then turned back to the display. "What's with the cat then?"

"It represents independence—cats do what they want."

"Becca loved her Kelly ever since she found the calico kitten abandoned beneath our house. They were inseparable."

They took a few pictures and became enamored with the rich history. But soon, they needed to move on.

"Where to?" Sis asked as she put away her camera.

"Aventine Hill."

"Home?"

"No, Sis. Lady Liberty Temple. Tomorrow you get to meet the great Dr. Lazarus. He'll meet us where the temple used to be and show us around. He emailed me to say he has some critical information. He couldn't share it over the web."

"Wow."

"Yeah, it just doesn't let up." Carol took one last look around the expansive room and then turned back to her sister. "I'm hungry. Let's get something before we go back to the B&B."

"Let's go Italian. How 'bout pizza?"

Carol gave a short laugh. "Sure."

Sis and Carol managed to open the large brass doors to find Antonio.

"Please let me know, signora, if there is anything, anything I can do. I am at your service. Anything."

She felt a bit woozy—likely from the flight and perhaps from something she'd eaten in the airport. She touched a hand to her dated braids which had suffered from the nine-hour flight. An occasional errant wiry gray hair sprouted from the braids. As they left, she saw Sis motion to her forehead and say something to the guide.

"What was that, Sis?"

"Oh, nothing, I just told him you were married in Italian. Like you did at the airport."

Carol looked back to see the puzzled Italian guide, but then her thoughts refocused on the pagan rituals she'd been reading about. What was she capable of doing when it came to her little girl? The answer frightened her. She stood now against a growing force, sinister in nature, and undefined in form. She remembered a Bible verse from Sunday school.

For we do not wrestle against flesh and blood, but against principalities, against powers, against the rulers of the darkness of this age, against spiritual hosts of wickedness in the heavenly places.

Carol shuddered as she thought about tomorrow when she would be in a high place, the center for darkness and spiritual wickedness of a once mighty empire. Libertas.

CHAPTER 8

The sisters dined on salad, linguini, seafood, and wine for Sis at a street-side bistro. The streets were alive with couples, families, old people, and the young. Although nine in the evening, children were led by grandmothers as parents shopped for food and held hands.

"You know Antonio was flirting with you," Carol said.

"Me? He liked you."

"He was trying to make you jealous—it's how it's done."

"Yeah, right."

"Americans find it forward, but Italians consider jealousy flattering."

"Sure."

"Okay, Sis, but I bet we haven't seen the last of him. You know he's a bachelor? He told me." Carol smirked at her sister. "You tell me why he did that."

"Stop it. You're teasing me. I've had two glasses of delicious wine, I'm in Rome, and I haven't had a man since Sid. And I've just said too much." Sis laughed and put down her empty wine glass. "Let's get out of here. I'm beat."

The women strolled arm in arm, breathing in the culture. Carol felt free for the first time in over a year. The small cars, the colors of the night, and young people strolling past gave Carol a brief peace. When they returned to the B&B, however, her freedom unnerved her, and her dreams made for a fitful night. In the morning, flashbulb memories popped in her mind about Pegasus circling the Statue of Liberty. But Bellerophon hadn't been riding the flying horse. The rider had been slender and feminine in shape, her face shadowed by a bulky helmet with red hair cascading across her shoulders.

The next morning, as Sis lay in bed, Carol talked about the dream while fiddling with her hair and looking out the windows.

"I think the rider was Daphne."

Sis scowled. "No, that's wrong, don't give it another thought."

Carol raised an eyebrow at her sister.

"It must be a lot of work, carrying around all that stuff in your head," Sis said. "Once, I had a dream about a team of astronauts walking into the hardware store because they needed to fix their shuttle that was parked out front. Not everything means something."

Later, as they waited for their driver, Sis pulled out a pastry from their continental breakfast. Carol raised an eyebrow again.

"What?" Sis looked up from her wrapper full of crumbs.

"Nothing." Carol still felt perplexed about Sis's reaction to her dream but couldn't find the words to argue. She watched the Roman metropolitans sidestep Sis as they headed to another day in the Eternal City.

Their driver pulled up and both were glad to see Antonio, their guide from the day before. Carol reached for the back-door handle and nudged her sister to the front. Sis scowled for the second time that day.

"What?" Carol smiled and got in the back seat of the small green sedan while Sis got in the front.

"It's my day off at the *musei*, so I told Dr. Lazarus I was free," Antonio said.

Sis practiced saying musei as the three headed to Aventine Hill. They crossed the Tiber on the Ponte Palatino and Carol caught a glimpse of the Circus Maximus, site of ancient chariot races.

Antonio smiled when Sis said, "Spartacus."

They parked the Fiat near Saint Alessia which dated back to the seventh century and was now a cathedral and monastery.

Carol spotted her old professor first. Dr. Lazarus had changed little in ten years. Quick witted as ever, he entertained his former student and company with memories and anecdotes. Although now seventy, his mind still seemed sharp from years of study and observation.

"I'm a big fan of the Baroque architecture, so this is one of my favorite spots. I come here often to think and smell the roses," Dr. Lazarus said.

"You said you had something for us," Carol asked. *I must sound like an impatient child asking for ten more minutes on the playground.*

Dr. Lazarus turned and motioned for the group to follow him. As he walked away, the three worked to keep up with the bounding, balding professor. They walked past the Basilica of Santa Sabina where they stepped off the tourist path and ducked under some low hanging branches.

The group found themselves among an outcropping of ruins partially covered by ivy. The crumbling walls stood in contrast to the green lawns. Overgrowth and the walls separated them from the crowds. Carol walked close behind her mentor and turned to see Sis and Antonio lagging behind, taking pictures, and sipping bottled water.

When she turned back, she noticed the Tiber River lying below them with a panoramic view of Rome beyond. "What a view."

"Libertas lives," Dr. Lazarus said.

"That's what you said during our call."

"This is where I found your dime." Dr. L stretched out his hand once more to reveal the dirt encrusted dime imprinted with 1942.

Carol's breath shortened and she sat down heavily on the ground as Sis caught up to her.

"Antonio! Give me your water," Sis demanded. "Now back up. Give her some room. She needs space. Carol. Carol. Hey, lil' sis, it's me. Antonio, do something!"

"She's overheated."

"She's dehydrated." Dr. Lazarus stood next to her still holding the liberty dime.

"She's overwhelmed," Sis countered. "Maybe we should go back to the hotel."

"Carol, my dear, Carol, I am so sorry." Dr. Lazarus fanned her with a discarded newspaper.

Carol shook off Sis's offer of water. "No, no, I'm fine. This happens from time to time. My doctor says the worst thing is the embarrassment." She looked up at Dr. Lazarus. "Please, tell us more."

"Not now. Let's get you down the hill. You need food."

The group slowly made their way back to the sidewalk and navigated through the dwindling crowds. Sis walked in front while Dr. Lazarus escorted Carol until they reached the rose gardens. The quartet shared a bottle of sparkling water, and then Antonio spoke.

"We do not know how evil this group can be. When we went to the polizia with Dr. Lazarus's research, they laughed at us at first. This is an ancient branch of pagans who predate the birth of Christ. They are not a joke."

"Antonio, you're so smart," remarked Sis.

Carol looked at her sister with a raised eyebrow.

Antonio paused, and his eyes darted around for a moment before he continued. "We wanted them to surround the park and put this group under surveillance, but the government does not like to get involved in religion. It is a reaction to a time when the church controlled the government and later, when fascism controlled the religion."

"Well, the detective told me he plans on sending some men," Carol stated. "I think seeing a mother in pain convinced him."

"You already know that April 13 is the date for the feast commemorating the joining of Jupiter with Libertas," Dr. Lazarus said.

"Today?" asked Sis.

"Tonight midnight marks the thirteenth, the start of the ceremony when there's a full moon."

"What's the plan, Doc?" Sis asked.

Dr. Lazarus smiled nervously. "Get some rest and we'll meet back here later. Let's say ten when most Romans are out in the streets. That way we won't draw attention to ourselves, and we can slip into the woods to wait. The polizia have been informed, but frankly, they were skeptical. They really don't like to get involved with matters of religion, but in this case, with a child involved, I expect them to be there."

Carol and Sis retired to their room where they shared a double bed like they did when they were girls. Carol found it comforting to have her sister so close. Still, Sis fell fast asleep while Carol stared at the plastered ceiling.

She shut her eyes and, like every other night, saw Becca. She envisioned her girl riding her bike. She saw Maxx holding her on the back of a horse. She pictured the bag of green ashes they said was her little girl. Tears rolled down her cheeks.

"Green? Where does the green come from? That's not my little girl." She'd questioned the color then, but still didn't know the answer. "Mommy's here," she said before slipping into a moment of sleep.

Carol awoke to see a glow emanating from under the covers.

"Sis? What are you doing?"

"Oh nothing. Just ordering some more stuff on *Sky Mall*."

"*Sky Mall*? You're shopping?"

"Yeah, it's what I do. It helps me calm down. QVC helped deal with Sid's death."

Carol realized she never thought about Sis grieving— she'd always seemed fine, and Carol never asked. She reached over and hugged her big sister.

A few moments later, the pair rose for their ten o'clock meeting with Dr. Lazarus. They pulled on some warm clothes and began filling their packs with gear. Sis handed

Carol a small headlamp and put the other one in her cargo pocket. Carol smiled and wondered what else she had in that bag.

Sis is Mary Poppins with a touch of MacGyver.

They met Antonio downstairs. This time, Sis took the back seat. The four looked like casual tourists as they walked past the Basilica and ducked back into the trees. They split into two groups to get a better vantage point— the doctor and his old student, the guide and his new pupil.

Dr. L's instructions were brief. "Stay awake, and just watch. These people could be dangerous. They could be on drugs—mushrooms specifically—which act as a hallucinogen to heighten the sensory experience and free their inhibitions. We know they are capable of kidnapping, maybe murder."

Carol winced at his words but, after two years of wondering and waiting, words hurt less.

"Turn your phone ringers off. Alert each other by text only. If you see something that looks like someone getting hurt, don't worry, the polizia will intervene. I saw them already. Remember, the pagans may show up early to set up, so stay quiet and motionless."

"Shouldn't we wait here?" Sis asked.

"I want to watch," Carol replied. "I've come this far."

"Be careful. These people scare me." Dr. L said. "We need to stay focused on collecting information that could lead to Becca, but we need to stay safe. Meet back at the car when everything is over."

Sis knew how to walk through the woods quietly. She and Sid had hunted the woods behind their place in Pennsylvania. Bagging a buck and gutting it was what she did. She took two steps, waited, and then walked farther on soft feet. She thought she could hear her heartbeat and hoped the others couldn't. Antonio, on the other hand, was not as stealthy. His stylish leather-soled shoes snapped branches and crunched leaves.

"Here," he said, as he plopped down into a gully.

"No, up there." She pointed to an alcove in the stone wall. "You can't see a thing down here."

After several unsuccessful tries, Antonio climbed a tree and reached for the alcove. Sis was already there pulling out a four-color face kit. She smeared black, brown, and tan across her nose and forehead.

"Now you." She held out the camouflage kit. "It's fun—better than a facial." He kept his face still as Sis smeared his soft skin while looking into his dark brown eyes. "That's enough, I think. You know, you *can* get too much of a good thing," she added.

"You can?" he asked.

From her pack, Sis pulled a pair of nocturnal vision glasses. "NVGs," she explained.

"Who are you?" Antonio asked and then smiled.

He watched her in the moonlight. Her bangs that couldn't be caught by her loose ponytail, fell across her eyes. She smiled back. In the woods, she was home.

Opposite the new couple, the old research team found a small hill they could crouch behind and still have a view of the ruins.

"Based on last week, the pagan worshipers should come up over the ridge on a small animal trail," Dr. Lazarus said.

Both parties would have a view and an egress to the tourist path.

Carol hadn't prayed much after Becca disappeared but had found herself talking a lot to God. Those times weren't really praying, but more like quiet arguments. After the pain of trying to get pregnant, how could he have let her baby get stolen? She shook her head free of the thoughts. Not now. Now, she needed clarity.

She sat back and felt something sticking into her back. Carol reached in her kidney pouch and found a wrapped-up paper bag with the words, "For you, Lil' Sis" written on it. She pulled out a pair of NVGs. Smiling slightly, she put them to her face and looked across the field where she spotted Antonio and Sis sitting close together in their perch.

"Oh, my."

"Something wrong?" asked Dr. Lazarus.

"Oh, no."

"Shush, I think I hear something."

CHAPTER 9

Four figures emerged from the woods carrying what looked like slabs of wood, bags of varying shapes, and large backpacks. One figure carried less than the others but seemed to be directing them with hand gestures.

Dr. L pointed. "The director is the priest. The person to his left is the priestess."

The priest moved with quiet purpose. The priestess looked more emphatic at times and her directions to the other two seemed frustrated, even angry, especially when one of the workers seemed to be heading the wrong way.

Carol watched as they set up the wood slabs in a large square, separated by at least thirty-two feet. In the center of the square sat a large rock on which they set a candelabra.

Lazarus continued, "This is unusual. Maybe ..."

"What?" Carol asked.

"Well, sometimes, a candle signifies a sacrificial ceremony, usually animal."

Carol decided she'd keep her questions to herself for now.

Dr. Lazarus took out a compass and began pointing. "Over there is east, near the path. That altar represents air. Across from us, closer to Sis, is the northern altar for earth, and near the hill they climbed up is west for water, and closest to us is fire."

Carol could see the group had set up ornaments representing the elements at each location on tables. A lavish decanter—likely containing water—stood on one table, while an old bellows for air, a small pile of dirt for earth, and more candles— representing fire—stood on the other. The pagans had covered each table with an ornamental tapestry that depicted the elements. The workers dug a small pit next to the center rock and placed kindling for a fire. Then, two of them searched for larger pieces of wood to add.

"That rock formation—presumably the main altar—likely holds trinkets engraved with symbols of their gods, Jupiter and Libertas. Watch the priest. He's lighting the fire, signifying the beginning. See the priestess? She's meditating. They likely fasted and bathed earlier."

"What's over there?" Carol pointed to bushes rustling in the distance.

"I don't know, it looks like more worshipers."

First, only one, then two people emerged on top of the hill.

Dr. L checked his watch. "Three minutes."

Others joined the group, bringing the total to thirteen adults.

"Look," Carol pointed to one small figure holding the hand of a little girl.

"I see her. Showtime."

Dr. L and Carol watched as the group gathered in a circle while the priest rhythmically moved around them with burning incense dangling from a metal ball on a chain. In his other hand he held a ghoulish knife, bejeweled and twisted—an athame. He slashed the air with it as he outlined the ceremonial grounds. Then he and the priestess walked to each table and raised each of the elements in turn to the sky, offering them to the gods.

The followers now moved in a macabre dance—some beat drums, while others chanted. At the middle of the frenzy, the priest and priestess had returned from their offerings and were now locked in a long kiss. The old man and his young princess, her hair draped around her shoulders and falling to her waist, silhouetted in front of the fire.

The dancing continued and became more feverish, and the chanting grew louder until the priest raised his hands. Everyone stopped.

"Jupiter and Libertas, Jupiter and Libertas, Jupiter and Libertas," the priest chanted.

The small figure approached, wearing a dark crimson robe which the priestess deftly removed, letting the fabric fall to the girl's feet. The girl instinctively dropped her head and crossed her arms, clasping the straps of her slip on each opposing shoulder.

What Carol saw made her heartbeat faster and her jaw tighten.

"It's Becca, isn't it?" she asked.

"I don't know, all we can see is her back." Dr. L laid a comforting hand on Carol's shoulder.

"Are they going to hurt her?"

"I don't know."

Carol lay paralyzed behind her hill as if caught in a nightmare. She opened her mouth to yell but nothing came out. The priest now waved his athame through the air, at times coming close to the child's heart. The little figure never moved. Then, he handed the knife to the priestess.

"The priestess is now directing the followers with the athame," Lazarus whispered in Carol's ear. "She's prophesizing. It's hard to hear but she's predicting the rise of Jupiter and now that Libertas is united with him, true freedom will be unchained with the death of Christianity. The girl represents their sacrifice to show their commitment and to represent true freedom."

"We have to do something," Carol mouthed back to her partner and then looked away. Her eyes glazed over, and she saw only a hazy reflection.

Dr. L pointed. "Polizia."

As the priestess raised the athame over her head, Sis let out a shriek. Startled, she slipped on the loose rocks and began to slide down from her perch. Antonio caught her hand just as the priestess looked up. The candles on the west altar tipped onto the old tapestry and caught fire as the priest continued to wave his hands over the girl. Sis screamed. The coven broke and ran toward the woods. One member grabbed the little girl and disappeared with the police in pursuit.

Sis and Antonio ran to Carol who remained frozen on the ground. Dr. L grabbed one of the members, a female—as she tried to run past their hill.

"What's your name, girl?" he asked, pulling her close.

"I am Starlite." The brown-haired teen struggled.

"You were going to kill her—the little girl."

The girl shook her head and tried to break free once more. "That's ridiculous. We're not into that. We pretend, we get close, but we don't murder. That girl is now blessed. Someday, she will be priestess. Someday, she will marry Jupiter. We wouldn't kill her. She is special."

"Who is she?"

"I don't know her."

Carol began to stir.

"I'm here for the party," the girl said. "The priest was going to raise the cup of wine and marry the priestess. We were supposed to feast, eat shrooms, and drink ale. My boyfriend and I were looking to hook up. You ruined all that." She scowled at him and then said, "I'm hungry. You got anything to eat?"

"You're lying!" Carol screamed. "You're lying!"

Carol pushed Dr. Lazarus out of the way, but Antonio grabbed her as Sis reached for Dr. Lazarus. In the confusion, Starlite broke free and ran for the woods.

"Don't go after her," Dr. Lazarus said. "It's not safe. The polizia are in the woods. Hopefully, they will get her."

Sis hugged and shushed Carol while the men gathered their things.

No one talked as they walked away and back to their car. Antonio drove away in silence, past the Circus Maximus, and back across the bridge.

Carol had calmed enough to call Inspector Rizzo—hoping for news. He offered nothing over the phone but agreed to meet them.

Back at their familiar restaurant, they ordered salads and entrees with sparkling water. Sis refrained from wine—there was nothing to celebrate.

Carol pushed her salad around her plate with a fork. "What now?"

"I just don't know," replied Dr. Lazarus. "I really don't know. I thought I had something for you, Carol."

"The dime, the connections, it seemed everything was falling into place. Now I don't know what to think. It's all wrong. We're no further than we were. Becca is still lost and in the hands of a bunch of crazies." Carol's fork clattered to the table as she put her head in her hands.

"We don't know that for sure." Dr. Lazarus stared at his water. "What are we missing?"

"They're probably having an orgy right now," Sis said. The group looked at her. "Hey, I grew up on a farm."

"I'd rather be here," Antonio said.

The group laughed out of embarrassment, breaking the tension as the inspector entered the room.

"We'll get to the bottom of this," said Inspector Rizzo. "My men are on their trail. They have contacts. The streets are hot, I think you say, so something will turn up. This is progress, we saw Starlite, and we are getting somewhere."

"One step forward, two steps back," Carol lamented.

"Sometimes that is what police work is," Rizzo replied.

The inspector said his goodbyes and left the restaurant.

While Antonio and Dr. Lazarus waited for the check, Carol and Sis decided to get some fresh air. Carol couldn't help noticing when Antonio kissed Sis on the cheek. Her sister blushed and said, "Goodbye, Tony."

As the sisters walked past a darkened alley, Carol said, "Tony, huh?"

"What?"

"I heard you say 'Goodbye, *Tony*.'"

"It's how it's done, Carol."

Carol turned when she heard a scuffing noise on the pavement and saw Rizzo and a young man struggling in the shadows of a store entrance. The young man looked familiar. His jacket looked more like a cloak and his black jeans were unfashionably torn and had grass stains.

"He was at the restaurant. I recognize his torn jeans," she said to Sis.

The man burst free from the inspector, knocking Sis's purse to the ground. Rizzo took off after him and Carol took off after the detective while Sis gathered her gaping pocketbook.

Slowed by a crossing bus, the inspector leapt onto the young man's back and the two rolled in the street. Antonio and Dr. Lazarus saw the commotion, hurried across the street, and surrounded the stranger.

CHAPTER 10

Rizzo held the thirty-something-year-old's hands against his back, with his face planted in the asphalt street and his greasy died black hair spilling over his jacket.

Inspector Rizzo flashed his badge in the stranger's face. "You were at the ritual. Who are you? Tell me before I take you downtown."

Carol noticed the young man's black fingernails—from polish or damage it was unclear—and the silver rings on his left hand connected to his wrist by a thin silver chain. A small, silver earring adorned his nose, making him look like an aging punk rocker. Rizzo brought him to his feet.

"Starlite had a matching tattoo like this," Dr. Lazarus said, taking note of the crude half star on the inside of the man's wrist. "How do you know her?"

"I'm her boyfriend. How do you know Starlite?"

"You're too old for her."

Everyone, including Rizzo, paused to look at Sis.

"She's eighteen, and what's it to you, lady?"

Detective Rizzo looked back at the young man. "Why were you watching us at the restaurant?"

"I was told to follow you after Starlite got away, see what you're up to. I didn't think there would be cops here."

"Talk now or I take you downtown and you can say goodbye to your visa and Starlite."

"My little girl is missing," Carol cut in. "Becca. She's seven years old. Do you know her?"

Rizzo tightened his grip around the man's shirt collar and pressed him against the wall with a forearm to his throat. "Talk."

"She was supposed to be at the ceremony. Her mother—she's been in our family for years—lives in America. I was supposed to pick up the girl at the airport from an attendant, but her mother emailed and said she couldn't send her."

"Why not?" asked Carol.

"Said it was too dangerous. She somehow knew we might be watched."

"What about the girl on the altar—who is she and what happened to her? Is she alive?"

"We don't kill kids. Maybe others do, not us. That girl's mother is the priestess. Some of us are in it for Jupiter, some for Libertas. I'm in it for the hook-up. But all of us are family."

"What can you tell me about the American woman, the one who was supposed to send her daughter?"

"No one knows where she's at exactly. I think she wants her daughter to grow up to be a priestess."

"What else?" Rizzo tightened his forearm against the man's throat. "Tell us everything or we go downtown."

"Rebecca, the mother in America, her name is Rebecca. They gave me this picture to get the girl at the airport."

He reached a hand toward the pocket of his leather jacket. The inspector cocked his head to look but then loosened his hold as Carol, Sis, and Dr. Lazarus lurched forward to look at the wrinkled picture. Carol jostled the others to see first, causing the picture to fall to the curb, distracting Rizzo, who loosened his grip further. The man broke free and ducked back into the darkness of the alley with Inspector Rizzo in hot pursuit.

Carol picked up the picture from the gutter, now wet and soiled. She wiped off the computer-printed image with the sleeve of her coat and gasped. "Oh! My Becca!"

"Becca? It can't be. That makes no sense." Sis waved a hand. "Don't give it another thought."

"Look, lookey. Look!" Carol slumped to the wet curb, holding out the wrinkled paper.

The others gathered around to look. Now wet, the picture had faded and made identification difficult. But with one look, Sis gasped and put her hand to her mouth. The little girl stood against a plain white background, wearing a pink shirt embossed with a Pegasus in flight.

"What's that around her neck?" Antonio asked.

"It looks like a dime," answered Dr. Lazarus. "Libertas."

"Let me see that." Carol snatched back the photo. "She never had that necklace. Her birth mother—she must have given it to her. Of course, her birth mother must have wanted her back. Becca must be with her now. Of course."

"Maybe she wanted her daughter brought up to worship Libertas and to be priestess, or maybe she worried about getting caught with her in the States," Dr. L offered.

"But her mother has been out of her life for so long," Sis interrupted. "Carol, this is going nowhere."

"She covered her tracks. We never even thought about her."

"Carol, she's just a confounding variable. Isn't that what you scientists call it?"

Carol stood and looked at her sister. "Why can't you consider it, Sis?"

"'Cause you're ... you're just being emotional. Isn't that what you always tell me?"

"I'm not. Think about it. Becca's natural mother—her name must be Rebecca." Carol started to pace on the sidewalk. "That's why we were never allowed to change Becca's name. I'll bet she planned on getting her back all along—when she came of age."

Later, as both Carol and Sis lie in bed staring at the ceiling, the words the young man had said—*but all of us are family*—reverberated in Carol's head. Family must be the key.

I'm missing something, something big.

Her thoughts drifted to her own family as they often did, but now the memories came back with purpose. She could block out her past during the day but in the stillness of dark, there was nowhere to run. Thoughts of Becca brought quiet tears that dampened her pillow before she fell into a brief sleep.

Carol sat up, startled. Sweat cooled her body and she pulled up the coverlet. *Dreaming. Again.* Pictures of Daddy, Joey, Sis, and Mother surfaced. Now awake, she remembered being in her father's arms, of looking up at her mother, and holding on to Joey as they wound along Creek Road that last day of his life. Memories that made her warm and memories that made her sweat. Carol reached for a bottled water. Sis had bought a whole case.

Sis is always there for me. She picked me up at my lowest, and she's here for me now. She's the only family I can count on.

In the morning, the sisters took a taxi back across the bridge and to the ancient ruins. Antonio drove Dr. Lazarus who brought coffee, hot water, tea bags, and pastries. The group met at a small park adorned with flowers and lattice separating them from any tourists. They found a patio edged by the white lattice work and the sidewalk. Dr. Lazarus sat down on a wrought iron seat, too small for his girth, and produced a large book from under his arm.

Carol felt her stomach lurch as she looked at the sweet pastries but dipped a tea bag into a cup of hot water.

"What do you know about Adolf Weinman?" Dr. L asked and then bit into one of the sweet rolls.

"He was the sculptor who designed the Mercury dime, the one with Lady Libertas."

"Right, but what do you know of Elsie Kachel Stevens?"

"She was the model for Lady Liberty, incredibly attractive."

"Right again, but what do you know about Wallace Stevens?"

Carol put down her tea. "What is this, twenty questions?"

"Wallace Stevens came from a wealthy family prominent in the insurance business but was somewhat of a struggling poet and lived in a tenement in New York City. He and the beautiful Elsie were married when Adolf Weinman asked her to model for him. Her profile became famous while Wallace enjoyed limited success with his poetry."

Sis took a sip of her cooling coffee. "My brother was an insurance man."

"Your brother, Joey?"

"Dr. Lazarus, how do you know his name?"

"You never talk about him, Carol. You never talk about your family, so I did a little research."

"It's complicated," Carol replied. "I know this is going somewhere but I've been doing some thinking too. I'm thinking I may have been going at this all wrong. I'm missing something. Something big. Something that's been there all along."

Dr. Lazarus pulled a 1936 dime from his pocket and held it out for her inspection. "What do you see?"

"Lady Liberty," Sis replied.

Antonio sat by her side and nodded.

Dr. Lazarus looked at Carol. "Maybe we're looking in the wrong place."

Carol took the dime and turned it over. "The fasces."

"Feces?"

"No, Sis, fasces." Carol smiled.

"Fasces is a bunch of wooden rods bound together," said Antonio. "Used in Roman pagan times, fasces signified strength. Mussolini adopted the symbol for his fascist party."

"But you see it everywhere," Carol replied. "It's on the Lincoln Memorial, money, and state and federal seals."

"True," said Dr. L as he took back the dime from Carol. "Unlike the German swastika, the fasces never fell out of favor."

"And the fasces stand for the unity of family. Like the pagan family we watched last night. Like my family. There were fasces engraved on a monument in our county seat." Carol's jaw clenched. She had said too much.

"Oh, Carol, don't go there." Sis shook her head. "You've been through a lot. Finish your breakfast, hun."

The morning sun filtered through the lattice. She knew her face must be pale. Her shoulders carried the weight of being so close, but now, Becca seemed so far. She nibbled on some toast and sipped her tea.

"So instead of Lady Liberty, we should be following fasces, Dr. Lazarus?" Antonio asked.

"I'm not sure," he answered. "I wish I could protect you, Carol, but I'm not sure I can." His words seemed measured and his pace matched hers. Softly, the doctor said, "When I looked up where fasces could be found in the States, I came upon this picture of the square in New Bloomfield. Isn't that where you're from?" He held out a copy of a black and white photo originally printed in the *Perry County Times*.

The picture showed an unnamed soldier from the Civil War holding a musket by his side. After the war, grieving mothers had raised money to establish statues such as this as reminders their sons had stood and died for something. The statue stood on a square block of granite whose corners were adorned by four fasces in her hometown.

"I bet none of the people that drive by that every day even know about those fasces," Carol shrugged. "But I do."

"Carol, that's your home, your strength, your fasces. You and Sis are both from Perry County." Dr. L put his arm around her shoulder. "Walk with me."

Carol grabbed her bottled water and the pair walked through the ancient streets and past crumbling monuments while Sis stayed behind with Antonio. The grass looked exceptionally green sprouting up between rocks and ruins and laid a rich carpet for families to picnic, fly kites, and be together. The day was bright, the air clean—a morning for exploring. But Carol felt her world closing in. Her breath came in short gasps, her brow felt warm, and her gait slowed as she sipped water.

They walked among the ruins of the Forum Romanum.

"Carol, this forum is one of the largest in Rome. It's unique because it tells the story of Rome from its pagan era to Christendom. It developed as the Roman empire grew."

"Yes, I know that."

Dr. L held out his hands and looked around the forum. "But did you know that within this forum lay the temple for Vesta, goddess of hearth, home, and family? In a celebration to her, fasces were carried by the priests. These bundles of rods contained an axe head at one end and were lifted by a single pole at the other end. Similar to the fasces on your dime."

Carol shrugged. "Okay."

Dr. L and Carol walked side by side as if in their own procession.

"The priests were followed by six vestal virgins who left their homes willingly to serve at the temple and to be a human reminder to all of Rome of the morality of the basic family. Interestingly, they wore their hair in braids surrounding their head."

Carol touched her own similar braids as he spoke.

"You see," he continued, "Much like these virgins, you are held in high regard by those who surround you for your intelligence, your perseverance, and your dedication. Even the braids surrounding your head are a testimony to your virtue. You try to walk in perfection, but something is missing. I don't know what it is, but there is a hole inside of you no amount of research will fill."

Tears began streaming down Carol's face. Weakened by Dr. Lazarus's remarks, she no longer hid beneath her braids. She sat down on a piece of marble.

"You know nothing," she said. "You know nothing of what it's like to lose a child. To lay at night thinking you hear her on the deck. Or, when the wind blows, to hear her swing twisting in the breeze. You don't know. How could you?" Carol dropped her head and swiped at the tears on her cheeks. She felt him looking down to her. Her mentor placed his hand on his student's shoulder.

"You study the ancients," she continued. "You have no family, only the past. Do you know what it's like going to church on Mother's Day or waking up on her birthday and she's not there? She's not anywhere and, yet, she's everywhere, floating above, waiting ... waiting for me. How could you know?"

"I know that sometimes the greatest mysteries in life are not solved by reason alone. Some mysteries lie in the heart. Maybe what you're looking for is not in Rome. Like the coin, you've been looking on the wrong side."

"I can never go home."

"Because of the accident?"

Carol felt betrayed. *How did he know these things about her?* She got up to leave.

"After I found the fasces on the square in New Bloomfield, I did some digging. I found the local paper. *The Duncannon Record*, is it? I found this picture." He handed the photo to Carol.

The picture shook in her unsteady hand. She had never seen it before but recognized the scene immediately—wreckage of her brother's bike. The caption read, "Joseph Beck, local insurance man, died Tuesday morning after careening into the statue on the New Bloomfield square. His sister, Carol Beck, was airlifted to Hershey Medical Center where she remains in critical condition."

"This is how I knew your brother Joey's name," Dr. Lazarus confessed.

"The accident was my fault. Just days after Daddy died, I had to get out of the house. I made Joey take me for an ice cream. That's all I remember."

"That's all?"

"We don't talk about it—ever."

"Like a family secret," Dr. Lazarus added.

"Sort of."

Tourists who walked past became blurry images as she thought about that day.

"Years before, I'd left home for college and never looked back. My parents filled out the financial aid statement, helped me pack the car I'd bought, and waved goodbye. After college, I took the job with you as a research assistant."

"Here in Rome?"

She patted a fluted stone column. "Rome," she repeated. "I lived in another world. Nine years of reason and research replaced family and home until my mother called one day. 'Come home,' she said. 'Your father got caught under the tractor. He ... he's passed on.'

Dr. L nodded. "I remember you telling me."

"The words *passed on* echoed in my ears on the ten-hour flight home. 'Passed on? Passed on to what? Daddy's dead,' I told Mother when I got home. I saw the hurt in her eyes. I looked around the room as my whole family stared at me. Everyone. 'Joey, I gotta get out of here,' I said. 'Can you take me?' He looked like he didn't want to disobey Mother, so I said, 'Take me for ice cream like when I was a kid.'" Carol offered Dr. Lazarus a small smile. "Joey always caved to his little sister even if I was thirty-one. We took off on his Harley. That's the last thing I remember before waking up in the hospital staring at a cup of green Jell-O. They told me Joey had run off the road and crashed. Someone said he was going too fast, but Joey never drove fast, not with me."

Carol took a slow, shaky breath. Dr. L touched her hand, "You had no way of knowing."

"'Joey's passed on,' the doctor told me. 'No, Joey's dead,' I said and turned my back to him. After the funeral, I went back to my world of reason. I couldn't come back to you. You were like family and I stayed away from family. I worked for the Smithsonian and met Maxx. I got good at avoiding questions about home and family. I just said my parents were hard-working people who were too busy to visit whenever Maxx asked about them." Carol looked up at her mentor who also had tears in his eyes. "I caved to

Maxx when he suggested we move to the Outer Banks in North Carolina to raise a family."

Carol turned away then and stared at the ground in front of her.

Dr. Lazarus held out the photo once more. "Look at the fasces on the corners of the statue. They look like books bound together but they are separate rods, as weak as papyrus reeds. Fasces are a symbol of strength when bound together. Just like siblings bound together in a family. Torn asunder, they are fragile. Together is their real strength."

Carol sighed. "My brother was torn from me. Sis forced her way back into my life when I confided to her that Maxx and I couldn't get pregnant. Sis knew a woman who didn't want her baby. Sis always knows what I need."

Carol and Dr. L smiled knowingly.

"You followed the signs from one side of the Atlantic to the other. Yet you have a mother and a family you've denied for years. Maybe they are your real strength."

"And I have you, Dr. L. You're right about the coin, I've been looking in all the wrong places. But after Joey died, I felt like my mother blamed me. Joey was her perfect child, and I'd killed him. I know it was a vehicle accident, but it was all my fault. It was all my fault, but I couldn't take her judgment."

Carol's hands clenched into fists.

"Last night, all I thought about was family. It's been that way for a long time, but last night felt more intense. Back home, everyone knew who you were and what you did. They knew my daddy and my daddy's pappy. The thought of my family buried me. I never realized it gave me roots. Back home, we're proud of having only one stoplight in the whole county. Seasons are marked by chicken corn soup in the cold, corn on the cob on the Fourth, and sauerkraut on New Year's Day. But they are so much more. I quietly loved everything about it but felt like I'd ruined it all."

Dr. Lazarus fixed his gaze on Carol as she continued.

"Did you know I learned to swim in a pond? I can bait my own hook and know how to catch night crawlers in the dark after a rain. My daddy made me stack hay. I blew hay seeds out of my nose by pressing one nostril and kept the chaff out of my boon dockers by tucking in my dungarees. I tried to forget all that. Daddy was one of the smartest men I knew. He did all his figuring in his head, did all his own work, and helped anyone who needed it." Her hands were animated as they helped tell her story.

Dr. L kept his hands in his pockets. "What about your mom?"

"Mother? She drove us to school and slapped me for every wrong answer. Mother was half the size of Daddy and twice as menacing. She stood up for me at school but made me pay for it at home. Mother didn't wear the pants—just the belt. And she still blames me for Joey."

"Does she? How?"

Carol sat back down. "You can just tell. I felt it from the moment I woke up and saw her glaring at me in the hospital with those eyes that said, 'You killed my boy.' You're right, it became a secret—our secret. We won't talk about the accident ever, but the secret is, I killed my big brother. Joey could do no wrong. In school, he starred on the football team. At home, he raised a steer for 4-H. He never missed Sunday school at Christ Chapel, even when he moved into town and started his insurance business. Everyone knew Joey, and everyone loved him."

Dr. L shook his head emphatically. "For being so rational, you can be so irrational when it comes to you."

"What's that mean?"

He was now pointing his finger. "It means you've based your life on a feeling you felt when you woke up from a concussion and saw your mother."

Carol shook her head. "It's not that simple. It was so hard growing up in his shadow."

"I didn't say your life was easy, I just said it wasn't that complex. Life is hard. Seems like you made it complex to avoid dealing with how difficult it is."

Her tears had dried. "Dr. Lazarus, in all the time I've known you, you've never talked like this."

"Carol, don't be offended, but you just never took the time to listen."

People milled about the ruins unaware of the two and unaware of Carol's burden. Foreigners snapped pictures, bumped into each other, and climbed over artifacts like they were rides in an amusement park.

Two couples took endless pictures while a couple of backpackers sat down to eat their lunch. They spoiled any picture vantage of the photographers and caused a confusing exchange of three languages.

"I ... I have to go." Carol began to walk away.

"Where?"

"To find my strength. I ... Maybe I'm ready to listen."

Carol took out her cell phone, scrolled through her contacts, and then typed two words: *coming home.*

CHAPTER 11

In her short time in Rome, Sis had become accustomed to metropolitan life in a foreign country. As she flagged a cab for her and Carol, she thought about how good she'd become at ordering foreign food and asking for directions. Another world had opened for her. One that included Antonio, but also encompassed more than one friendly Italian man. She saw possibility in this new world. Growth felt good. Strange was not to be feared. Strange was to be embraced.

Growing up on their family farm in Pennsylvania, Sis had been no stranger to hard work, pain, and death. She had taken it upon herself to nurse any sickly animal.

"Don't forget, if you're gonna look after that one, you might have to put it down when it's time," her mother had often told her.

And she'd been right, but Sis soldiered on. Lambs, baby chicks, and even piglets could often be found under a heat lamp in her walk-in closet.

As a child, she followed her older brother into town. Joey would plead for her to go back but she kept on. Her big brother would first roll his eyes, then squint and stare unflinchingly at her. Sis talked through the silence but eventually people shifted their attention to Joey, and she was forced home and back to her menagerie.

While her older brother hung out in town and at school sports, Sis cleaned stalls and rode horses. For relaxation, she sipped lemonade while floating on an old inner tube in the small pond behind the barn.

"There's snappers in that pond," her mother told her one day.

"I know, but there's still room for me too."

Sis could hook a worm and cast as well as most boys her age and older. Her bedroom wall had been adorned with county fair ribbons, 4-H certificates, and a picture of her father and her sitting on the back of a hay wagon during better times.

Sis smiled as she paid the cab driver and the two sisters sat down at her favorite outdoor bistro. *Yes, change was good.* She looked past the young men and smiled gracefully at the old lady feeding her dog under the table. Sis ordered sparkling water *con ghiaccio* (with ice), and *piadino*, a lighter sandwich made with thin bread and heated. She'd managed to lose weight with all the walking and healthy meals, while still enjoying a selection of wines. She knew Carol would order a salad and water, no gas. Sis refrained from admonishing her to eat more, to try the bread, or to tell her to get dessert.

After eating, the waiter stood patiently against the far wall while the two sisters sipped their drinks.

"Sis, I have to go home."

"To the beach? I suppose it's time."

"No, I have to go *home*. I think I need to contact the lawyer, the one who helped with the adoption. She's still in PA, right? Maybe she can give me something on the birth mother. And well, I think I need to see our mother."

Sis knew that home meant *home*. Home meant family, Pennsylvania Dutch cooking, farm life, and, yes, Mother.

"Are you sure you want to do that? I mean it's been so long and we've ... you've been doing so good. I don't know if you're ready for that. I don't know if *she's* ready."

"I have to. I have to face her."

Sis shook her head and tightly clutched her linen napkin. "No, Carol. You don't."

"I thought you'd be happy for me. Don't you want me to go home? I don't get you."

"I've been there for you, Carol, from the time you hit your head under the shower stall. Shoot, from the time you got Becca. I've been there. I was there when you went away and when you came back. Then you left again. And now you want to go back? Again? You can't just walk in and out like a revolving door at a department store. It's not fair to Mother. It's not fair to me either."

Sis's voice naturally carried but now it grew louder. She pointed at her sister, then held her hand to her chest while Carol began to fiddle with her hair. "This has all been about you, I get it, but think about Mee-Maw. Think about me."

"What are you talking about?"

The waiter refolded his white towel several times, noticeably uncomfortable. He spoke little English but had picked up on their tone. He didn't interrupt them. A couple across the room looked over at them before leaving. They'd seen loud Americans before, but this wasn't an ugly American vacation spat—this was family.

"Nothing." Sis lowered her voice but leaned forward. "If you want to ruin your life, I can't stop you." She threw her napkin on the table, causing the glasses to chink together.

"I'm not ruining my life. I'm trying to get it back."

"What about Joey's life?" Sis asked, her voice rising more. "What about him? Did it ever occur to you what you did to this family? He didn't get a chance."

Sis had broken the rule and she knew it. They'd never speak openly about Joey's death. They both knew it. Sis had said too much. No one pretended he didn't die but no one talked about it either. He simply wasn't there. Gone. They never spoke about his motorcycle, the square, or anything remotely connected to his death.

"I think about him every day. I will never stop thinking about him." Restaurant patrons looked their way and talked quietly. "And I think about Becca."

Carol scraped back her chair and hurried to the restroom. The tiny bathroom had just enough room for a toilet and a white porcelain sink. A heavy machine with a rusty crank that turned a cloth towel hung by the door.

After she splashed some water on her face, she stared at herself in the faded mirror.

You do look tired. You look old. Maybe Sis is right.

When Carol returned to the table, Sis insisted on splitting the check, breaking their tradition of taking turns. As they left the restaurant, the two walked in silence for the block back to their B&B.

I guess this had been coming. We've been together twenty-four hours a day, and it's been all about me. No, it hasn't. It's about Becca. I can't believe she brought up Joey.

Carol felt her anger burning inside of her. She always kept her anger inside. No one ever saw the heat, only felt the cold. And the cold created distance. Over the years, the distance had created a void, a vast forlorn chasm with her family. Carol always swallowed her words to protect herself—a means of survival. She'd learned it at home. Saying how she felt made people mad. Saying what she wanted got people killed.

"I'm gonna' keep walking," Carol said when they'd reached the steps of their tiny room. She could no longer sit by the table reading while Sis laid on the bed shuffling through Roman pamphlets on the best restaurants, the best ruins, and the best night life. She needed some air without her sister by her side.

"Okay, *keep* walking," said Sis.

Something about the way Sis said *keep* stoked a flame that had been burning for a long time. The word spoke control and shouted judgment.

Carol turned on her sister. "No. Not this time. You're not doing this to me. You are wrong. It isn't about me. It's about my daughter, and I need to do this. I thought you'd be supportive. I don't get you. You've been there for me, but only when you could rescue me. Yet, every time you were wrong. I don't need rescuing, but I can't do this alone. Joey is dead, and I can't do anything about it. I need home. I need family." Carol's voice broke and went to another octave. "I hate to say it, but I need Mother."

Tears streamed down her face, but Sis's jaw remained tight. Carol never saw Sis cry—not when Daddy died, not even when Joey's closed casket had been lowered into the ground. Sis reached out and placed her hand on Carol's back. Carol flinched and stepped away. Sis's hand suspended in air. For a moment, she thought Sis might slap her. Carol took another step back. Sis's hand closed into a fist and fell to her side as a slow smile—smug, not happy—crossed her face.

They stood on new ground now, more foreign than the Roman ruins surrounding them. Neither knew what to do. Habit and routine didn't apply. Rules didn't work. Anxiousness filled the space that silent dysfunction once occupied.

Sis hurried upstairs while Carol turned and walked down the street.

Family secrets often scream the loudest. They cry out from under the surface, but the waters muffle their true meaning. Secrets become woven into the fabric of everyday life and no one notices after a while. They start as secrets but grow into "it's just the way it is" or "times were different back then." They stay silent through avoidance. The pain lessens and families survive—in a different way.

Secrets float in the air, are baked into holiday meals, and sleep in vacant beds. Secrets invade the senses. They are seen in the desperate sisters living crowded lives.

When Joey died, his accident became a secret. Not his life—his death. Sis and her mother held his death over Carol's head. She noticed it in their actions. In death, more than in life, Joey could do no wrong.

Why do I always go back to Joey? It's not about him, it's about Becca. I need the adoption agent to help me track down the birth mother.

Carol walked over cobblestone streets as a drizzle of rain began to fall. Soon, her hair became both matted and frizzled, her short socks damp, and her eyelashes held onto the wet for as long as they could. She no longer felt dazzled by centuries old apartment buildings that surrounded older ruins, or mesmerized by whirling scooters, Alpha Romeos, and Moto Guzzi motorcycles. Now, she walked with long strides, her shoulders back, her arms pumping—her pace had increased into a power walk.

When she wanted to set her problems aside, she walked fast to clear her head. When she was done, a warm shower, a cold drink, and maybe even a nap would right her destroyed world. Her workout wouldn't make things right, but it would make things work.

As she rounded a corner, a scooter whizzed by and splashed water across the sidewalk. She heard the girl on the back laugh and say something. Carol crossed the street and sat on a bench. Its wooden slats flanked by faux-Romanesque concrete columns looked inviting and she didn't mind the wet.

"Fasces even on the benches, really?"

The small park had likely cleared of people by the rain. She realized she didn't know where she was and didn't really care.

Does it really matter? I haven't known where I am for a very long time.

The drizzle mixed with her soft tears and reminded her of those moments of desperation in her outdoor shower.

This is different. I'm not that woman. Not anymore.

She looked up and saw a dimly lit neon sign: "Clarity Tourist Service" and "English Spoken Hear." She smiled at the misspelling.

Carol walked across the street, against the hurried traffic, and into the boutique service.

In broken English, a woman greeted her. "Welcome to Clarity. Good day to you. I have been expecting you. I am a Miss Clare."

Clarity Tourist. Miss Clare. Cute.

Carol used a combination of English and her rusty Italian to book a flight back to the States. She handed Miss Clare her previous plane reservation and her passport.

"And what about this other reservation for a Miss Sis?"

A heavy sigh belied her resolution. Carol felt unsure how to answer and sat patiently looking into Clare's eyes.

"You seem uneasy ... how you say ... anxiety?" Clare waved a hand. "We can make her reservation refundable, yes? She can go online, call, or come in to make the change, anytime up to two-four hours before the flight."

"Two hours?"

"No. One day."

"Oh, twenty-four hours. My flight leaves in twenty-eight hours, that gives Sis the next four hours to decide. That works for me."

"That is Clarity Travel, and I am Clare."

For the second time that day, when Carol stood, she felt more than a burden lifted, she felt a force propelling her. Not a force compelling her, but a wind of encouragement, a helper of sorts.

Clare stopped her before she got to the door. "You left this," she said, pointing to the chair Carol had been sitting on.

Carol looked. A dime. She picked it up.

"It's not mine," Clare stated. "I don't carry American money. Oh look, the rain stopped. *Dopo la pioggia, arriva il sole.*"

"Excuse me?"

"It means, 'After the rain, the sun comes.'" Clare smiled.

Carol turned and walked out the door and found her way back to the B&B. On her way back, she noticed gargoyles on the corners of store front edifices. She thought it curious to see lawyers' offices next to pastry stores, next to shoe stores. Now that the rain had stopped, and school was out, children in blue blazers and round white hats with matching ribbons swirled around the pastry stores. Some of the kids sipped from bottled sodas, a few licked gelato in cups.

Seeing children the age of Becca used to cause her pain. But now with children came hope. They were signs of new life. And with hope came joy. The grip on her dime tightened.

Her skeleton key jiggled in the worn lock before swinging open the oversized door. Sis came out of the bathroom from down the hall donning a T-shirt that had "Colosseum" written across the front in glitter.

"Like it? Got it downstairs at the boutique."

"Cute."

"I was thinking Spanish for dinner tonight. Word is the place on the little square has authentic *paella*."

Carol wondered how Sis would know authentic paella from any other but felt guilty being catty. She also wondered how Sis could be so chipper after their fight, but after a warm shower and a bright, smart sundress, Carol felt a little more chipper too.

They walked side-by-side to the square while talking about curios, custard, and a man they passed whose shirt was unbuttoned practically to his navel.

"Least he's not one of the men from the airport," Carol remarked.

They both laughed. They brushed up against each other as they passed a couple and walked through the wrought iron gate protecting the courtyard of the Spanish bistro.

Carol ordered for them.

"So, what did you do while you were gone?" Sis asked.

"Well, I power-walked."

"Go-od." Sis looked at her with raised eyebrows.

"And I stopped at a tourist office. I changed my reservation." *Rip it, Carol, like a Band-Aid.* "I'm leaving tomorrow night ... for home. You can go, too, if you want. If not, you can change your ticket as well, no cost."

"What do you want, Carol?"

"Well, it's not always what I want, Sis."

"Okay, I've been thinking too," Sis replied. "I want to stay, for a little while anyway. This is fun, and I'm learning things. Antonio is teaching me Italian, and I'm learning that Romans are a lot like Perry Countians."

"Oh, they are, are they?"

"Hear me out. They don't bother you unless you bother them. They help you, but you have to ask, and when you do, they become your best friend. Family is more important to them than anything, even work. They work hard but they value food, fun, old people, and babies. Maybe they're loud but they're really very private. Maybe they get too close to you, but they know to keep their distance too."

"I've spent years here, Sis, and never thought of it that way. I guess I never tried. I always looked at Italians and Perry county folk like they were from two different worlds."

"And they have their secrets too."

The word "secrets" stung Carol, but she said nothing.

"So, go home, if you like. I still think you're making a mistake, but it's your dime."

Dime? Are you playing a game with me?

"I'm staying."

CHAPTER 12

The next day, after a continental breakfast, Carol preoccupied herself with packing. She knew how to pack, knew how to stay organized in new places, and knew where everything was that she owned, and Sis's things too. Sis called it her intrauterine tracking device, but she pronounced it "inter-uterine."

Sis met Antonio in the morning to visit another museum and didn't return until it was time for Carol to leave.

"We can take you to da Vinci-Fiumicino."

"Wow," Carol exclaimed.

"What?"

"Nothing." Carol knew anything she would say about Sis's improved Italian dialect would sound patronizing. "I've already arranged for a cab."

"Not a limo?" Sis asked, and the sisters laughed.

While she packed, Carol avoided the wrinkled picture lying on the small desk in front of the only window in their room. Carol couldn't forget the photo—she wanted to keep it within reach—but she also didn't want to deal with it right now. It reminded her of the pictures she used to see on the side of milk cartons. Her heart ached for those children—torn from their parents, waiting to be found. Thinking about Becca being a milk carton baby made her die a bit inside.

She paced about the second-floor room, read through her sister's brochures, and stared out the casement window until she could take it no more. Checking her watch and looking for the cab became a compulsive ritual that was, at last, broken by a knock. Carol flung open the door. The elderly shopkeeper from downstairs looked up holding a small box in one hand and a flower in the other.

"Signora, your sister told me you are going home, and I wanted you to have this."

"*Grazie.*" She took the box from him and opened it. Inside was a stained-glass picture of a butterfly hovering over buttercups.

"Here we say, '*Chi si volta, e chi si gira, sempre a casa va finire.*' No matter where you go or where you turn, you will always end up at home."

The old man shifted his feet, and she noticed his hand had a tremor.

"When we lost our daughter thirty years ago, it seemed that a butterfly always came to my wife when she needed it the most. When she felt lost, it gave her direction. When she was down, it made her look up. And it reminded her that even though a butterfly has a short life, its purpose is to bring joy to others by sharing its beauty. All things are valuable in God's world."

Carol's eyes filled with tears, but she blinked them back, refusing to cry.

"I wanted to make you happy, Signora," he said. "I want you to have hope. Someday, we will find our children, no?"

"Oh, yes, you did make me happy, you did. You have no idea. Buttercups, butterflies … How special. Grazie, grazie."

The little balding and bespectacled old man reached out to embrace her. Her barriers of mistrust and suspicion broke down as she hugged this stranger.

"The world has become a scary place for you, I know," he said, releasing her.

"I don't know who to trust. I can't count on anything." Carol shook her head and gave him a small smile.

"I know, I know, but you will trust again. You must. You will reach out. Some will tell you what to do. Pay them no mind. A few will understand. Pay attention to them. Go with grace, it is your best friend now." He patted her hand.

"Sir, you are so wise. I don't even know your name."

"It does not matter ... Life"—he emphasized with an upturned finger—"life is all that matters. Everything else is, how you say, vanity. Search for life. And when you find it—when you find life—you will find your daughter. I found mine here." He tapped his chest. "I hope you find yours there." He pointed to the window.

Carol turned to look out the window, and when she turned back, the little old man was walking back down the steps.

He was part of the "club." She had heard about the club, the one no one wants to be a member of. The club of parents whose children go missing. It doesn't have a name, but when its members meet each other for the first time, they know what to do. They stop whatever they were doing. They lay down whatever is in their hands, and they ask the other person if they can give them a hug. Usually before the person says yes, the two embrace. For a moment, the pain is manageable because there is someone else in this world who knows.

But Becca isn't dead. She isn't.

And for everyone else in the club, their child is not dead either.

But I'm going to find her. I am.

And everyone else in the club will find their child someday as well.

She was still staring down the steps when Sis walked into view.

"Carol ..." She waved a hand in front of her face. "Carol, your ride is here."

Carol made an awkward move to hug Sis, but it ended up feeling more like a drunken lurch.

"Carol?"

"Oh, ah ... oh, nothing." Carol straightened her skirt, picked up her bags, and walked down the steps.

The cab driver put her bags in the back of his four-door Fiat. As he started to pull away, Carol shrieked, "Wait!"

She got out of the car, ran up the steps, and into the room past Sis. She grabbed her wrinkled picture and held it to her breast. Then she walked by Sis and back down to her waiting ride.

Mopeds, scooters, and bikes surrounded every cab and car through the streets of Rome like escorts in a motorcade, but it wasn't a dignified procession. The hustle and bustle seemed more like a circus parade with each act going its separate way. The lines on the road disappeared as they rounded the Coliseum.

"Did you enjoy your vacation, pretty lady?"

"Yes, well, it wasn't really a vacation, but yes, I love this city. You are lucky to be surrounded by so much history and art."

"Look at those young people. They don't see it," he said. "I'm glad you do. Most people who come here bury themselves in their phones, or they are so busy behind their camera, they never see. They don't become part of the beauty and don't care about the history. They just care about impressing their friends. You're different, I can see you care. History is important to you, no?"

"When I was younger, I studied the ruins as an American student. I dug for the details. When I came back here this time, I did the same thing. But now, when I step back, I can see the landscape. I never thought about that before. Now I am starting to see."

Just then a moped brushed against the fender. The driver honked, and the rider gave him the finger.

"They don't see," the cabbie lamented. "They are only interested in themselves. They ignore life. *Nient'altro questioni detti,* nothing else matters. You are growing old and your eyes are opening up."

Carol sighed and looked out the window.

"No, you are growing into your beauty, pretty lady."

She looked at her driver in the rear-view mirror. Aware that she was blushing, she looked down at her papers.

"Some ladies cling to their youth and lose it. Other ladies embrace their age and gain it."

"Sounds like you know a lot about women."

"Yes, I live with my wife, her mother, and five daughters. And one bathroom."

They were still laughing when he put her bags on the curb. He looked at her and whispered, "Four in Rome, one in heaven."

Carol looked at him, perplexed, as he drove away.

A porter wheeled her bags to the check-in, and she stood in line. She hadn't counted on the extra people and became swept up in the immediate blur. She reassured herself by checking and rechecking her bag, ensuring she had everything.

As she waited for her flight to be called, her eyes grew weary and her heart and mind slowed. No longer able to focus on reading, she milled about, sipped her last cup of Italian brewed coffee, and finally boarded her flight.

When they reached full altitude, the plane quieted, and she took out a small mirror from her pocketbook to see what the cab driver saw.

"Four daughters in Rome, one in heaven."

How did he know?

She put her compact away and leaned her head back against the seat.

Power naps revive and the routine eight help the body to survive, but Carol's body craved a real sleep, and her body took over.

She tried to fight it, but it seemed futile. Initially, the flight attendants became a bit hazy. Then, she no longer saw them but only heard them. She felt warm, as if her body was floating. She drifted away ... away.

Her body accepted the deep stage of sleep. The one she needed the most. She let go. Her mind as well. The day, the week, the trip's events faded into the background as she floated away.

Carol floated among the clouds outside her plane. A menagerie of animals, things from her past, and people swirled around her like a constellation of stars. Her father's casket draped with an American flag floated by and then her brother's Harley—its wheels looking more like those of a covered wagon. She saw her room where she grew up and saw Peggy the stuffed Pegasus, but the creature was now full-size and alive despite one wing being torn and its body spilling stuffing.

Carol watched her life move by in this cosmic movie show. An occasional steer or pig mixed in with her mother, who sat sewing under a wooden lampstand. Torn pages from a Bible littered the space all around her and cluttered her view. Libertas floated past, cast in cement, but alive with her crumbled eyes and rust-stained face. Her beauty no longer showed—she looked hideous, satanic.

They all have a place in this world.

Her brother Joey came by dressed in a tux, a bride standing next to him. A veil covered her face, but Carol could tell it wasn't his wife. Carol's outdoor shower came by with water running. Daphne stood in the shower with a man, both giggling until they noticed Carol. The water trickled through the floorboards and formed a river in the sand.

Sis, Antonio, and Dr. Lazarus floated by in a Roman slave ship. She could tell it was Sis because of her hair but the rest of her was but a skeleton. The trio rowed as hard as they could, but their boat tilted and bucked as if in peril. A bloody athame, that looked like the knife from the pagan ceremony, dangled at Sis's side.

She could hear Becca saying, "Lookey, lookey," but didn't know where to look or what she was supposed to see. She could feel her daughter tugging at her but didn't know how to respond.

When she awoke, she saw the child in the middle seat leaning over her mother. "Lookey, look, I see a city."

"We will be landing soon in Philadelphia," the pilot reported over the intercom.

"Ma'am, would you like a moist towel," an attendant asked Carol in a soft morning voice.

The eastern light flooded through the windows and washed away any lingering traces of her dream. Passengers began to stir. She took the towel and covered her face. She was almost home.

The landing gear opened with a thud and the plane came down hard.

"Navy pilot," she heard the old man behind her say. "Thinks he's still on a carrier."

When the plane came to rest at the gate, Carol stood and saw the old man who wore a blue ballcap emblazed with an outline of the USS Truman on the front.

Carol smiled at the man. "Thank you for your service."

"Thank you for paying your taxes."

His wife hit him hard in the side, but he barely flinched.

Carol grabbed her carryon from overhead and let the older couple go first. As she made her way off the plane, she noticed the pilot wore an Indian Sikh turban and had a dark beard. She thought the old navy man in front of her stumbled when he saw him, but she couldn't be sure.

The Philadelphia airport seemed to be in a constant state of construction. In the seventies, organized crime controlled much of the labor unions and contracts in this city. The mob was no longer in control, but the airport was emerging from bureaucratic overlays and work shutdowns. The passengers still walked through a labyrinth of boarded corridors and escalators to get to their baggage and find a way out.

Carol felt like a gerbil in a maze as she wound round and round seeking the exit.

When, finally, she sat in her rental car, she exclaimed, "Libertas at last!"

Her liberty was short-lived. After exiting I-95, she was slowed by traffic on the Schuylkill Expressway.

"The Sure-kill Expressway," she said under her breath as she came to an abrupt stop in a long line of cars. Looking to her right, she saw a rowing crew working out on the river, reminding her of her dream. Behind them on the bank of the river stood the Philadelphia Art Museum atop a wide stone staircase. The building could have fit into the Roman landscape with its massive columns. Pediments with multicolored polychrome sculpture adorned the gables. The structure now seemed small after being in Rome, but Carol appreciated it even more.

Decades before, she'd fallen in love with Roman ruins on a school field trip to the same art museum. She'd decided in the sixth grade she wanted to be an archeologist when she'd walked into one of the rooms that had been recreated from Roman stone to house artifacts from the third century.

Afterward, she'd sat on this same expressway in a school bus without air conditioning. While the other kids chattered away, slept, or played with the toys they'd bought at the gift shop, Carol read the book she'd bought about Roman civilization.

The car behind her honked and brought her back to the present. The driver swung his car to go around and then gave her the finger as he passed. Carol smiled as she thought about the girl on the moped in Rome just twelve hours before. The last thing she saw of the car as she exited onto the oldest turnpike in the nation was an old Flyers Broad Street Bullies bumper sticker.

I wonder if people know the word "turnpike" came from the log, known as a pike, across the road? It turned to let people use the road after they paid their toll.

She took her automated ticket and sped west on the four-lane highway separated by a narrow concrete barrier.

Her heart thumped. *Almost home.* Her phone now charged, she called home. She felt relieved to get the answering machine at the farmhouse when she called, but still struggled to let her mother know she was getting close.

After exiting the turnpike at Harrisburg, Carol paid her toll and headed up the side of another river almost as wide as the Schuylkill but only a few feet deep. The Susquehanna was navigable only by shallow boats due to the rock formations that littered the river floor.

She drove past the massive Rockville bridge, the longest stone arch railroad bridge in the world and thought it resembled the aqueducts. *The Romans perfected the arch and here it is in Perry County.* She noticed a miniature Statue of Liberty that stood on a stone formation in the middle of the river. Carol had to stop to take a picture before continuing her drive west on US Route 322.

Perry County has its own Libertas, how funny.

She recalled how the statue had been constructed years before when someone put up a facsimile of the Statue of Liberty made from venetian blinds. When the artist received such positive response to the sculpture, he'd made a more permeant replica. Normally, it took an act of God to build anything on the river, but officials had looked the other way knowing how popular the statue had become. When the statue was first erected, lines of cars would park on the side of the road to get a better view, and parents would bring their children out for a history lesson. Today, truckers used the road as a major artery and cars sped by on Fridays, barely noticing Lady Liberty on their way to the Penn State football game.

For Carol, Libertas called her home.

Maybe I have been looking in all the wrong places after all.

Carol passed over the Clarks Ferry Bridge. After the ferry system stopped in the 1800s, a wooden covered bridge had spanned the distance across the Susquehanna River onto a peninsula known as "the Island." Carol imagined two-thousand feet of wooden roof overhead and rattling planks underneath as she drove across. Now the bridge was built from concrete and steel.

Carol crossed the traffic to head over the Juniata river, a smaller tributary of the Susquehanna.

"I forgot how narrow this bridge was."

The bridge had been constructed almost a hundred years before, built for a much slower age. Concrete walls guarded the edge of the two-lane road.

Her heart pounded and her clammy hands pushed against the steering wheel as she passed the Dairy Bar. She'd forgotten the familiar spot lay along her route. Sis used to work there, and they scooped as-much-as-you-wanted ice cream cones. Carol had always loved it there but hadn't seen the place since Joey's accident.

She felt hot and worried she might faint. Her foot lessened on the accelerator as her heart rate sped up. Then, she took a deep breath, pressed down the gas once more and kept going.

After leaving town, she pulled over when a John Deere tractor hauling a load of hay took up most of Hunky Hollow Road. *"He took his half out of the middle,"* Daddy *would say.*

She noticed the erratic and fast pace of her heart once more. She turned off the car and dropped her head onto the steering wheel as sweat began to form on her forehead.

Flashes of riding on her brother's motorcycle flooded her mind.

Oh, God—please, God.

Carol started to count her breaths. *1-2-3-4-5—breathe—1-2-3-4-5—breathe.* She pictured the air filling her lungs and then breathed in some more. She had learned how to breathe to increase her endurance when running long distances, and now it helped her in the middle of another panic attack.

Time felt meaningless. She lifted her head and noticed her headlights reflected against the green brush edging the road. "It's getting dark already."

She restarted the car and debated her options.

I can't go there. Not now. It's too late. I can't. I could turn around. I could find a motel room in Summerdale.

Blue lights flashed in her mirrors before she could put her car in drive. She turned off the car once more as a police officer rapped on her window.

"Driver's license, ma'am."

"Is there a problem, officer?"

"You're parked on a road that has no room to park. I'd say there's a problem." The officer pointed his flashlight on her driver's license.

"Carol Beck-Davies." He shined the light at her. "Carol Beck? What do you know? It's Ralph … Ralph Peters."

"Oh my gosh, Ralphie Peters! I haven't seen you since graduation."

"*Ralph* Peters."

"Oh, Ralph." She squinted up at his light.

"How long you back in town for?" Before she could answer he said, "We should get together. Do you know Mum never took down our prom picture?"

"I don't know what to say to that."

Ralph's smooth round face matched with his tight-lipped smile created an illusion of innocence—making him look much younger than his years. But his shirt pulled against its buttons and his skinny necktie fought for a place under his overlapping neck. His crystal blue eyes shown past a naturally squinting brow.

"Are you here to see your mother? She'll be so happy to see you. I saw her the other day at the market." He paused a moment before saying, "She looked frail. Still beautiful, don't get me wrong, but not like the tough woman I remember. Wasn't she cleaning a shotgun when I showed up with your corsage?" He smiled.

"No. You're still funny, Ralphie."

He handed back her license and then turned to walk to his car. Halfway there, he turned back and shouted, "I'll let you go this time, but you still owe me that canoe ride."

He waved as he passed by in his squad car, and Carol's resolve returned.

"Okay, girl. You can do this."

She pulled onto the farm lane leading home.

CHAPTER 13

She eased her car along the dirt road, avoiding potholes created by years of frosts, thaws, and neglect. Volunteer sumac shoots and locust trees intertwined with fence wire along the lane. The wire bowed under the weight of the overgrowth. In the pastures, where steer once grazed, stood rows of corn.

The outline of the asphalt-shingled farmhouse soon came into view—a plain structure, sensible without waste or embellishment—an honest house, nothing pretentious. The rusted metal roof was symmetrical on all four sides and came to one peak in the middle. Everything about this house made sense, with no wasted space. *Frugal and functional, just like Mother.* Carol looked up at the attic, her respite whenever she needed space.

Her headlights swept across the barn now draped in poison ivy vines which grew as high as the tallest peak and wrapped around the concrete silo.

She turned into the drive and parked behind the old Chevy.

"Brownie, I can't believe she still has you."

The monstrosity boasted huge bumpers and room enough for six adults—or ten teenagers. Carol had needed those bumpers one winter when a curve on Creek Road came at her too fast.

Daddy had towed the car home with his International tractor. He'd welded new supports and pounded out the bumper, but a rusted dent and bent hood remained. He'd tied the hood down with bailing twine, but he'd never checked the oil, so it didn't matter much.

A motion sensor light came on at the porch.

"That's new."

Carol turned off the car and walked to the front porch.

I should have brought something. Should I knock?

She'd never knocked before, but she felt a stranger now.

She shook her head. Of course, she'd just walk in. *Slowly.*

The storm door bumped her backside as she turned the door handle. She could hear women's voices. The console TV blared the news in the room, and her mother's voice floated from the kitchen.

"I have to see the weather."

Carol stood in the doorway and waited.

She smiled at the sight of her mother's silver hair, long, classic, and never out of style. Carol noticed her makeup was as tasteful as always—whether staying in or going out. Her dress, just as classic and practical as the lady. Her beauty was authentic, with a quality that cannot be bought with money but by knowing who she is in this world.

Carol's mother had become more beautiful when other women her age had lost theirs to thinning lips, sunken eyes, and double chins. Time seemed to stand still on this sensible farm in the middle of Perry County. Carol used to believe life came easily for her mother. Now, despite her well-kept appearance, Carol saw how fragile she had become.

"Carol."

She could hear a bit of relief and a whole lot of worry in her name.

"Hi, Mother, it's me." Carol sounded like a kid who had come home too late on a school night.

"Yes, yes, it is!" Her mother dropped the tea towel she was using to dry her hands and wrapped herself around her daughter.

"I should have brought something."

"Carol, Carol ... oh Carol."

Carol closed her eyes and soaked in her mother's warmth while the weatherman forecasted a low-pressure system by the end of the week and advised farmers to get the last of their field hay into the barn.

When did she get so little? This can't be the same woman that chased me around the house with a spaghetti strainer when I cut my bangs. Or the same woman that marched me to Bobby's house after he took my Beanie Baby.

Carol opened her eyes.

"Mee-Maw." She dropped her arms and rounded the couch, as an even smaller woman entered the room. "Oh, Mee-Maw, I am so, so sorry."

"Shush now, baby, don't you cry."

Carol worried she'd suffocate the old woman as she pressed her against her chest.

"I am so ... so ... sorry." Her chest heaved with heavy sobs and tears streamed onto her grandmother's face whose wrinkles guided them away to a safe place in her heart.

"Shush now. You're okay. Shush. You're home now." Mee-Maw rocked Carol back and forth. "It's gonna be all right. Don't you cry. Momma's gonna buy you a mockingbird."

Carol laughed between her tears, causing her to choke.

"Now, child, you're going to hurt yourself. Come in here." Mee-Maw motioned her to the kitchen.

Her mother handed her a glass of tap water. The smell of sulfur, that her mother claimed good for you, filled her nostrils and reminded her of her childhood. Water had been Carol's mother's answer for everything. Headache? You're dehydrated. Dizzy? Drink water. Stomachache? Drink more water. Skinned knee? Here, drink this.

She sipped from the glass and then sat down at the oak pedestal table in the country kitchen.

"Your Mee-Maw made dumplings, honey."

"I see."

"And the beans are fresh, picked them today. Not like those beans you get in your city."

Mee-Maw added, "Bobby still farms the ground ever since your daddy ..."

"Does he still drink?"

"More than ever. Had to drive him home last month when he fell off his tractor. Don't know how he keeps his rows so straight, but he does. Still the best at farmin', and he's better drunk than most men sober. Not better'n your father, of course. Your father put love in his crop. Bobby puts Jack Daniels in his."

"Bobby wouldn't waste a drop," said Mee-Maw.

"No, but last week I caught him peeing on the field."

The three looked up at each other and laughed.

She remembered Bobby from school. He'd sat in the last row and never said a word—ever. His hair always looked greasy, his clothes dirty, and his homework never done. The other kids had made fun of him while he'd run to his wooden clapboard house.

"Hey, Bobby, I like the color of our house—termite brown."

"Hey, Bobby, is that your room, the one with no glass in the window? Is that your air conditioning?"

"Hey, Bobby, why's your washer on the porch—so it's closer to the clothesline?"

"It'd work better if you had electricity."

He'd never looked back at their questions or laughter. They never mentioned his drunk father sleeping off his stupor on the couch inside.

Her mother interrupted Carol's thoughts once more. "Mee-Maw made her rhubarb pie. Here, I'll get you a slice."

"Oh, I couldn't, maybe in a little while."

As her mother and Mee-Maw continued to finish the dishes, Carol wandered around the old house. Everything seemed the same including the gun safe still standing in the corner—only now with dust on the handle and hinges.

Carol walked through the living room and into the hallway. Her hands caressed the walnut banister. She remembered sliding down this antique and getting her foot caught between the spindles. Her toes had swelled up so big Daddy had to cut one spindle to get her out. No one else noticed but Carol knew which spindle was different— the one with the extra scalloped rung and skinnier than the rest. She used to think she was that spindle, different and trapped.

Carol walked up the wooden stairs, skipping over the one that creaked, and ran her hand along the family pictures hung on the wall.

On the landing, she turned and walked to her room.

She'd loved this room with the long, skinny closet that still held her old prom dresses, dance recital outfits, and Barbie doll case. The walls were still painted pink.

"Not much has changed, has it?"

Carol hadn't noticed her mother come up behind her.

"It's so dusty. I can't keep up."

"It's fine, Mother. It's ... it's perfect."

"I was gonna make the bed, but I didn't know if you'd stay."

"Well, I was kind of thinking I'd like to stay in town— with Mee-Maw. You know, to give her some company."

Her mother nodded and wrung her hands. "Sure, honey, sure." She looked away.

"I must have spent hours in front of this mirror singing John Denver songs."

"And Marie Osmond."

"Did you hear me?"

"Every word."

"You never said anything."

"Carol, there's only a door between your room and ours. And besides, I didn't want it to stop. It's so quiet now. I never knew how much I'd miss it. I didn't know how special it was. Like Joey—"

"Mother, let's go downstairs.

As they walked down the steps, Carol thought her mother looked back at her when she stepped on the squeaky tread, but she couldn't be sure.

Mee-Maw sat at the table with a slice of pie and a scoop of ice cream.

"I couldn't wait."

Her grandmother's pie crust had won nine straight county fairs. She could have won today even at the age of eighty-two.

"Still blue ribbon, Mee-Maw. You could still beat Mrs. Fletcher any day."

When the three had finished, Mee-Maw put the remainder of the pie back in her Tupperware.

"I thought I'd leave this here with you'ins," she said.

"Mee-Maw, if it's okay with you, I thought I'd visit you a spell." Carol heard her own accent.

Mee-Maw looked at Carol's mother who sat expressionless but nodded her agreement.

"Well, then, you can give me a ride home."

A few minutes later, as they turned onto Church Street, Carol noticed a state police car sitting in a neighbor's driveway.

"Ralph still lives with his mother."

"You're kidding."

"Never got married. Sometimes he drives bus for the senior citizens. He always tells me he's still waiting for you."

Mee-Maw had lived alone for the past quarter-century since her husband Bull had died. Carol loved visiting her. She'd run away once to Mee-Maw's when her mother told her she had to wear a dress for a party at the Legion Hall.

"Child, how did you get here?" Mee-Maw had asked.

"I ran. It was easy because it was all downhill."

Now, she walked around Mee-Maw's house and put her hands on every trinket, figurine, and the back of every chair. A flashbulb memory popped up each time she touched something.

When she touched the silver bracelet sitting in an oak chifforobe, she remembered holding onto Mee-Maw's wrist with one hand at Joey's funeral and a handkerchief her mother had given her in the other. She knew Mee-Maw wore that bracelet only on special occasions.

When she touched the figurine of a father and a girl from Holland, she remembered sitting in Daddy's lap on the big La-Z-Boy chair. Even after she'd entered college, she still found moments to curl up in his lap.

When she touched a chair in the dining room, she remembered bringing Maxx home from college to meet Mee-Maw. She'd made dumplings that day too.

"Here's something you might remember." Mee-Maw smiled.

"Skimpy!" Carol grabbed the stuffed doll Mee-Maw had made fifty years ago. Each grandchild thought they owned Skimpy, but she'd made the doll for a neighbor kid who'd forgotten to take it home one day. One of his button eyes and part of an arm that had been torn off by a pet a long time ago were still missing. The doll had survived three grandkids' births and three family deaths.

"I'm going to go to bed, dear. I sleep down here now, but you'll find everything you need upstairs." Mee-Maw ushered her toward the steps and then pecked her on the cheek.

Upstairs, Carol caught the scent of moth balls as she sat her bags down in the corner. The ceiling on the second floor of the bungalow sloped to waist high at the back. The bathroom at the top of the steps had just enough room for a claw tub, porcelain sink, and toilet, but she had to crouch—her head hit the ceiling light if she didn't pay attention.

She washed her face and crawled under the heavy comforter and into a soft mattress that settled around her. She looked out the window and saw a light on at Ralph's house. Someone sat on the swing at the end of his porch.

The light from the street below made her feel secure. She never liked how dark it got at the farm. In town, there was always light, always life. In town, there was always hope she would get away. At the farm, the only cars she ever saw were either lost or trying to sell something like aluminum paint for the rusty barn roof or freeze-dried beef for their already bulging freezer.

Carol's head sank into the pillow. "I never did like rhubarb pie."

In the morning, Mee-Maw already had a pot of coffee and fresh-baked scones.

"What are you going to do now?" Mee-Maw asked.

Carol pointed to the scones. "Are these white chocolate raspberry?"

Her grandmother nodded. "Your favorite. I knew you didn't like rhubarb pie, but your mother insisted you did."

Carol smiled as she took her seat at the small table in the sunny kitchen. "I love this kitchen, so many windows."

"It used to be a porch, but your daddy fixed it into a kitchen. I made him keep all the windows. He said it'd be too cold in the winter and too hot to cook in the summer."

"I love it."

Mee-Maw eased herself into a chair. "Me too. So ... what's your plan?"

"I really don't have one."

"You always have a plan."

Carol shrugged. "Well, I need to find the lawyer that handled Becca's adoption, for starters. I'm looking for Becca. I know she's alive."

Her grandmother sat back with wide eyes. "How do you know that?"

"I just do."

Mee-Maw nodded. "I do too. Look here."

She pulled back the checkered café curtains that covered the lower half of the double-sashed windows. Carol gazed out into the backyard that sloped down to the alley. A patch of weeds grew waist high where there'd once been a garden, but the lawn was freshly mowed. Jasmine flourished all along the edge of the yard. Orange, yellow, and black butterflies flitted across each yellow and white flower.

"Oh, my. How did they—"

"They bloomed on the day you let us know you were coming. No one else in the neighborhood has them—just us. And the fragrance!" Mee-Maw smiled.

Carol looked at the other neighbors' yards. Mee-Maw was right. They had the only jasmine on the block.

"They haven't bloomed for years ... well, I mean, we had them years ago before ..."

"Before Joey?"

Mee-Maw nodded her head.

"You know jasmine is Becca's favorite."

"Mine, too. Remember, I knitted her a baby blanket and stitched in pointed jasmine flowers. When I saw them, I knew it meant something special was going to come into my life. And now here you are."

"Mee-Maw, there is evidence that links Becca back to Pennsylvania and to a serial killer named Harold Baker."

Mee-Maw let the curtain drop back into place. "I saw his story on the news. He's on death row."

"I know. Maybe somehow I could talk to him."

"He's supposed to die soon. This month sometime."

"That I didn't know." Carol started to fidget with her braids.

Mee-Maw reached out and took her hand, a look of concern flashed across her face.

"I'm okay. I'm going for a walk. I need some of this Perry county air."

Carol walked down the streets she used to bike on as a child. A few businesses still operated but gone was Miller's Newsstand where you could buy the *Duncannon Record*, ammo, and a carton of cigarettes. Gone was the jewelry store where Carol and Maxx bought their wedding bands, and gone was the drug store where you could get a Coke after school.

One hotel had survived thanks to the Appalachian Trail hikers who would rent a cheap room and drink beer in the bar. The trail wound through Duncannon and across Clarks Ferry Bridge before heading back up Peters Mountain and into the woods.

As she walked up the alley past the old hardware store, she heard someone calling her name.

"Carol! Hey, Carol, come here."

She turned to see Mrs. Schwartz, the mother of her childhood friend, rocking in the shade of her porch that bordered the sidewalk. A thin oxygen tube crossed her face which now seemed etched with time.

"Mrs. Schwartz, how long has it been?"

"Your Mee-Maw told me you were coming back, but I just didn't know when. I'm glad I got to see you. I remember when you and Donna used to play together. You know she caught the cancer?"

"Yes, I am so sorry. I wish I could have been here."

"She was a good girl. You were a good girl too. I have something for you. It fell out of an album the day I heard you were coming back. Go right inside my door and grab my purse."

Carol did so and then watched as the older woman rummaged through her purse. After a moment of digging, she pulled out a picture and handed it to her.

In the photo, Carol and Donna were trying to sit on Joey's lap on some swing—she couldn't remember where. A chubby little body in overalls and long, red, wavy hair pushed the swing.

"Who's this girl, she looks familiar?" Carol pointed to the girl with a rounded face and large eyes.

"I don't know who that is." Mrs. Schwartz handed back the photo. "Here, take it."

"I couldn't, it's a picture of Donna."

"I know, that's why I want you to have it."

The picture was grainy, and the lighting washed out much of the detail. Carol wasn't sure if the mystery girl wore a necklace or the picture had been overexposed. The girl's fingernails looked painted.

Odd for a child back then. Kids just didn't wear necklaces, not for play. We didn't have the money. Maybe Mee-Maw will know.

Her focus came back to the neighbor. "Thank you, Mrs. Schwartz." She bent down to kiss her cheek. "You were always special to me."

"You were always special to Donna." She patted Carol's hand. "Seeing you is like seeing her."

Carol hugged her again before hurrying back to Church Street.

As she neared Ralph's house, she saw him washing his police car in the driveway. Before she could cross the street to avoid him, he called out, "Hey, Speedy, where you going?"

"Ralph, I didn't see you."

"Yeah, right. Carol, remember, I'm a cop. Are you staying at your grandmother's? I saw your car parked out back." Ralph set his hose down in the soapy bucket.

Carol could feel her palms start to sweat and felt the old picture slipping in her fingers.

"Hey, I told you, I'm a cop, it's what I do. I was talking to Mum. She'd like to see you."

His springer spaniel barked incessantly behind a chain-link fence as she stepped closer and held out the photo.

"Do you know who this is?"

He looked at the picture quickly and then handed it back. "No, but I'll bet Mum does. Back then, she knew every kid. Come on up."

Carol started to back away. "I can't. Not now. I gotta go."

"Okay. I'll stop by later. Maybe you'd like to go to the pub tonight?"

The water from Ralph's hose had filled his bucket and now streamed around his feet and down the driveway. He didn't seem to notice.

Carol spied Ralph's mother peering out from behind yellowed lace curtains in her living room as a couple of kids riding their bikes on the sidewalk came closer.

She sensed the pressure in Ralph's voice, heard the kids getting louder, and smelled someone burning trash. She began to feel hot and her heart started to race.

"Gotta go."

She hurried across the street, not stopping until she stood safely back inside Mee-Maw's bungalow.

"Saw you talking to Ralph. What did he have to say?"

"Nothing, but ... something."

Carol ran up to her room, shut the door, and flopped down on the bed.

What is happening to me? He's gonna think I'm crazy, running away like that. I gotta get hold of myself. I gotta get control and stop this thing before it kills me.

As her panic attack began to subside, she drifted into sleep.

CHAPTER 14

Carol awoke with a start to a dark room. She felt Skimpy by her side and remembered where she was. She rose, threw some water on her face without hitting her head, and walked down the stairs to the living room.

Mee-Maw sat in the living room crocheting—her bifocals making her eyes look larger than normal.

How does she do it? Grandpa has been gone for years, she's lost a son-in-law, a grandchild, and maybe a great-grandchild, but there she sits, knitting away for some missionary project or some charity drive. I wish I could be her.

Carol sat down in the recliner next to Mee-Maw, and her grandmother startled.

"Oh, child, I didn't hear you. You were out like trout. It must have been that long flight from Italy. I'd like to hear about it some time."

"Maybe later."

"You just missed Ralphie. Good boy. He said he wanted to take you to the pub tonight. He shoots pool in a league."

"Seriously? Say, do you know what happened to the lawyer's office on the square?"

"No, but Ralphie probably does."

Carol nodded. "Okay. Guess I can ask him later then."

She remembered the pool players from her youth—cigarette on their lower lip as they sipped beer from a bottle at the corner of their mouths. Somehow, Ralph didn't seem to fit into the memory.

"Said he'd stop by again before eight. Oh, he stopped by to give you this. Said you dropped it in the street."

Mee-Maw held out the picture of Carol and Donna Schwartz.

"Mee-Maw, do you know who this is?" Carol pointed to the chubby red head.

"Yes ... no, no, I don't." She gave the picture back to Carol.

"Yes or no?"

"At first, I thought ... but I'm wrong. No, I don't think so, not that I can remember. Who is she?"

"I don't know, that's what I'm hoping you could answer."

"Don't know."

Carol stared at Mee-Maw a moment as she went back to her crocheting.

"Darn, missed a loop." She began unraveling a row. "Anyway, Ralphie will be here in a few. He's never late, that boy. Peterses never are. You better go get ready."

Carol went back upstairs and pulled on a pair of jeans, a sleeveless raspberry-colored top, and some earrings. She wriggled a bit as she looked at herself in the mirror.

Jeans are a bit tight. Ah, who cares?

She heard Ralph at the front door and made him wait until she'd put on the sandals she'd purchased in Rome. When she finally came downstairs, Mee-Maw held out a single key on a crocheted chain.

"Here's a key for the front door. Don't worry about me. I'll be in bed shortly. Thank you for the tomatoes, Ralphie."

Ralph smirked at Carol. "She still calls me Ralphie."

"Tomatoes, huh?"

He shrugged. "Mom has a greenhouse."

Carol hugged Mee-Maw and then let Ralph lead her out of the house, his hand on the small of her back.

"We could take Dad's old truck, but I usually walk. The owner asked me not to park my cruiser out front, said it's bad for business. I probably go there too much, but I forget I'm a trooper when I do."

As they turned the corner on Market Street, Carol saw the lighted sign and some people smoking outside.

Inside, they maneuvered around other patrons and found a table by the window. Ralph leaned his pool stick case in the corner before pulling out Carol's chair for her and then pushing her in. It had been a while since a man treated her with respect. The act unnerved her, and she grabbed for her water.

"This place hasn't changed much."

In the corner sat a stool, an amp, and a mic. The U-shaped bar seemed too big for the room and, behind it, she could make out a lighted pool table. There was enough light to read the one-page plastic menu.

After they'd ordered, Ralph caught her up on all the news he knew about their classmates.

"Bobby still drinks, which I'm sure you've heard from your grandmother, and Bob Jones took over his dad's service station. Ginny Zellers got married and moved to Lemoyne with a guy who works on the railroad. Alma Kernsey—remember how shy she used to be—is a stripper now."

"No!"

"No, I'm kidding. Just seeing if you're listening." He smiled. "Nothing's new with me as I'm sure you know from your grandmother. Mum lives with me—I own the house now. I get a lot of kidding about that, but after Dad died, it just seemed like the right thing to do. I'm the only family she's got. Family is everything."

"I think it's sweet." Carol knew she sounded patronizing. Perhaps because she could never imagine living with her mother. Ever.

Ralph simply shrugged and said, "What about you?"

"Well, you know about my daughter Becca—she's been missing for a year now. The police want the case closed. Maxx left a while ago. Her disappearance was just too tough on the both of us. We don't blame each other, but we both feel so guilty so it seemed like we did. Neither of us could take the quiet condemnation. I'm still living at the beach in North Carolina and love it. Well, I did."

"You always were a beach rat. In school, you made friends with anyone going to the shore."

"Remember walking along the Jersey shore all day and hitting the boardwalk at night? Anyway, I was content taking care of our daughter, and Maxx has a good job. I keep thinking I'm gonna get a job, but I never do. I write for some journals to keep active in my field, and I'm on the historic committee in town. I couldn't turn them down after they heard I was an archeologist. They think I'm Indiana Jones or something. I can't even find my own daughter."

Ralph placed his hand over hers. "You will. Maybe I could help."

Their food came and Ralph ordered her another Diet Coke.

"Do you know what happened to the lawyers on the square?"

"Kinkade and Foster? Kinkade retired, Foster moved the practice to Lemoyne, one of those old houses along the river."

"Mee-Maw said you'd know. You're not having another beer?"

"Tonight's tournament night. Gotta stay focused." He smiled and then his face turned serious. "Carol, you dropped that picture after asking me if I knew that girl. I showed it to Mum who never forgets anyone. She remembered you going to the Lutheran church. Mum helped run the summer church camp program for all the churches back then."

Carol chewed on a bite of her burger and nodded for him to continue.

"Mum recognized the swing set that used to be next to the Lutheran church. So, we went through her pictures of church camp. We had those dang things all over the floor, but we think we found her. Her name was Rea Billingsley."

Carol shook her head. "Rea Billingsley? I don't remember her."

"Turns out she never went to school. Her parents homeschooled back when no one was homeschooling.

Well, except for her, of course. So, I called into the station and did a quick background check on her family."

"Why?"

"Because you asked. It seemed important to you." He looked at her a moment and then continued. "Anyway, I don't know if I'm allowed to share this with you, but most of it is public record. Seems her father was a ne'er-do-well who was in and out of jail for different things—fighting, intoxication, check fraud. Her brother ended up in juvenile detention after beating up a boy scout on a camping trip."

"Wow."

Noise from the crowded bar made talking difficult so Ralph moved his chair closer to hers. A lone singer tuned his guitar in the corner, adding to the clamor.

"I know. The family is a hot mess. Seems her brother is in prison. Her mother was a quiet lady who tried to keep Rea on the straight and narrow, but she was pretty rough too. Guess that's how she got to camp."

Ralph checked his watch and looked back at the pool tables. Carol saw his age and realized she'd never taken him seriously before, but now he talked with authority.

"Where's the mother now?"

"Same place she's always been. Turns out I know her. She lives in one of the hollows out in the township. Anyway, her father died when Rea was about twelve. It seems like he drank himself to death. I found out she was in and out of foster care. Eventually, she got her GED and even applied for a state cosmetology license."

"Married?"

"Not that I could tell."

"Work?"

"I didn't get that far. She seems to have disappeared. Really, it's more like she was never here."

"Sounds like you're telling me a ghost story. You think she's not real?"

"You're making fun of me. No, not a ghost, more like a vapor."

"Aren't you being a little dramatic, Ralph? I thought you were a cop."

"Well, maybe I am, or maybe I'm not cut out for this line of work. It's just that after years of dealing with these so-called hardened criminals, you start to find out what crappy families they came from and you start to feel sorry for them. At least, I do. I guess I'm too sensitive, because it hurts. Every time I put the cuffs on someone, I want to slap their parents. And I want to slap them because now some other kid is going without a parent. So, yeah, I'm a little dramatic."

"You sound like Joe Friday—from *Dragnet*." She teased him but quickly realized he was no longer just the nerdy kid down the street and wanted to apologize. He seemed so sensitive to Carol. "Sweet" was the only word that came to mind.

The bartender shouted across the room, "Hey, Ralph, you're up."

"I gotta play." He slid out of his chair and held out his hand. "Come watch me, just one game, okay?"

She nodded. "Okay."

They walked around the bar to the back room. Several people stared while Ralph found a stool for Carol in one corner. A pimply-faced, twenty-five-year-old racked the table. Long greasy hair stuck out beneath his frayed camo hat with a large fishhook on the brim. His beard came in patches, and when he passed by Carol, she smelled wet cigarettes. But he could shoot. He shot fast, maybe to intimidate his opponent, or maybe because he did everything fast. Ralph got one chance in the middle of his run and sank two balls before the kid ran the rest of the table.

"Well, I told you I wouldn't be long," Ralph said as he returned to her side. "But that's not what I meant."

"You'll get him next time." She patted him on the back. "I bet he doesn't have his own police car."

"No, but he's been in the back of plenty." Ralph packed away his stick and gestured to the door. "I have time to walk you home before my next match, if you want."

"Yeah, I probably should."

They shuffled sideways past the busy bar patrons, their feet sticking to the beer-stained floor. A large, bearded patron shouted at Carol. "Hey, I know you. Let me buy you a Bud."

"No, I don't think you do," Carol answered.

The man in bib overalls put his arm around Carol's waist and corralled her closer to the bar.

Ralph reached out and grasped the man's elbow. "Hey, friend—"

The man spun around and took a swing at Ralph.

Ralph ducked, but the punch clipped Carol's jaw, and she yelped. Ralph pulled the man's elbow down and brought his wrist behind his back. He wrapped up the man's arms behind his back and pushed him against the bar.

"Now, what you're going to do is turn around and tell the lady you're sorry."

"Ma'am, I'm sorry."

Ralph's eyes widened before pushing the man away and moving toward her. "Let me see your cheek."

She held her cheek and shook her head. "No, just get me out of here."

Ralph led her out of the bar with a firm grip on her elbow. "I can take him in."

"No, I just want to go home."

When they got outside, Ralph took a closer look under the lighted neon sign.

"It's red, all right. It's gonna leave a mark."

"Oh, no." She touched her cheek again and stepped away.

"Just for a little bit." He smiled. "You're gonna have a story to tell."

"I already have plenty."

"You're never gonna take that canoe ride with me now."

Carol took out a pack of cigarettes from her purse, and unwrapped the pack while Ralph watched.

"I didn't know you smoked."

"I don't. Not for a long time, anyway. Not since I left here. I bought them at the Handimart today." She struck a match and then looked at him. "There's a lot you don't know about me, Ralph."

She lit the end of her Newport but then didn't know what to do with the match. For Carol, the worst part about smoking, besides the nasty looks from nonsmokers, was the littering. She breathed in the nicotine, shut her eyes, and blew out smoke through her pursed lips. She felt a false sense of control that let her go on with life.

As they turned to walk up Anne Street, someone called out her name.

They turned to see a tall figure standing in the shadows of an awning. The cold match fell to the ground.

"Maxx? What are you doing here?"

"Carol—" He frowned at the cigarette in her hand. "We really need to talk."

CHAPTER 15

Carol stubbed out the cigarette under her sandals. "What are you doing here?"

"I came up to see you. Carol, I ... I found God."

"You what?" She shook her head. "Whatever. I really need to go home."

Ralph reached out to touch her on the shoulder. She turned away, but Maxx touched her other arm. "Could we talk for a just a few minutes? Please?"

Carol looked from Maxx to Ralph and back again before saying, "I'm okay, Ralph. I'll talk to Maxx, then I'll get back on my own. I'm fine."

She could see Ralph's concern. He looked down and then turned and walked back toward the pub. Carol headed the other way down Market Street while Maxx tried to keep up.

They walked to the square where patrons milled about outside the hotel. The smell of cigarette smoke mixed with spilt beer seemed caught beneath the once impressive fake stone columns. Carol and Maxx walked single file through the crowd before crossing the street and ending up in front of the bank with its own stately columns.

Carol turned. "How could you? After all this time, how could you just show up like this? You found God. Great. Good for you, but what about me? What about Becca? You left us. And guess what? I don't need you. I hardly miss you. I don't love you. Not anymore ... I'm done."

"I know I don't deserve to have you back." He reached out to touch her arm, but she stepped back. "I know I hurt you. As hard as this has been on me, I know it's been even harder on you. I can't take back time. I wish I could, because I'd go back to that day. We've never talked about it. It was all my fault."

She waved her hand at him and looked out across the street. "I don't blame you, Maxx."

"But you kept asking, 'How could you? How could you?' And Carol, that look ... I couldn't take that look that said the same thing over and over. I couldn't take it anymore."

She turned back to him and frowned. "What look?"

"That look." He pointed to her face. Then he sat down on the massive stone steps while Carol stood resolute. "I don't get it," he said, "you always were ... accepting."

"I always *settled*."

"I don't know what to say." He stared at his running shoes.

"You're right about one thing—it is harder on me," she said.

"Is that where you can buy a hunting license?" Maxx pointed to the empty store on the corner.

"Yes, but what's that got to do with anything?" Carol wouldn't be distracted. Not anymore.

"Oh, nothing. I guess this isn't going too well." Max smiled sheepishly.

"Well, what did you think would happen?"

"I thought I'd tell you about God, and after that, I really didn't think."

"So?"

"So..." He hesitated. "I ... I said a prayer and felt a weight lift off my shoulders. I changed, I think. I feel right. Not good. Well, sometimes, but I feel *right*. Man, this sounded a whole lot better in the car on the way up. I know you feel bad, but we both lost—"

"Stop right there." She shook her head. "You don't go there. You have no idea how I feel. You have no right!"

Even in the dark she could see his eyes grow larger.

"Carol, when I left, I took some time off from work. I was a wreck. I called the house a lot just to hear the old answering machine. I'm glad you never changed the message. Just to hear your voice and Becca giggling in the background meant something. I hung up and never left messages—I didn't know what to say. During the day, I put on the TV and stared at my computer." Maxx stared once more at the ground. "By night, I'd go through a drive-thru for fast food, and then I'd go back to my rented room and watch TV again until I fell asleep on the couch. That's what I did."

He stood up and moved closer. Carol looked back at the hotel.

"Barry from work called after a while and said they needed me to finish one of the projects I was working on. So, after a month, I went back. I hadn't shaved, I needed a haircut, and I probably smelled. It just didn't matter. I stayed in my office and I worked. I got there before anyone and left after everyone. I avoided everyone."

"That doesn't sound at all like you." Carol still did not look at him, but her voice had softened.

"Then I got this crazy idea to hike the trail—the AT. Remember when we would see the hikers coming through here and just laugh?"

"You would laugh, Maxx." Her anger flared. She started to walk away, and Maxx followed.

Carol stopped at an intersection and Maxx caught up. There were no cars moving at this time of night, but Carol couldn't look in either direction—she didn't want to look at Maxx. They walked further before stopping under a streetlamp. A concrete bench under the light looked out of place for the tight corner.

"I stood on mountain tops and looked across miles of wilderness for as far as I could see. I felt so insignificant, but at the same time, when things started working out for me, I began to realize I was in the center of God's creation. I'd see the littlest bug and the biggest tree, and they were all connected—they all had a purpose."

Maxx's voice grew stronger. "One time, I walked up on a fawn just lying in the grass—it must have been about a day old. I thought, if God was taking care of this little fawn, maybe he was taking care of Becca too. There is a place and purpose for all God's creatures. I had started praying. I started thanking God for my life, for you, and for Becca."

"Sounds good for you, Maxx." Carol didn't mean to sound dismissive, but his story hurt. She looked out of the corner of her eye to see him looking down, both hands in his pockets.

"I went back to work after that. A secretary saw me early one morning and told me she attended this Bible study that met before work on Wednesdays. She gave me a donut."

"A donut? A donut made you a Christian?"

"Well, one Wednesday, I could hear them down the hall, and I could hear my stomach growling. I thought I'd just get another donut and leave, but I didn't—I stayed. I asked them how God could be so loving if he'd taken our little girl. Why hadn't he taken me instead? I asked if Jesus died for us, then why couldn't I die for her? That's what I wanted to do. I wanted to die, and I wanted Becca to live."

Maxx sat down on the bench and clasped his hands together.

He looks like he's waiting for the principal. I hope he doesn't start to pray.

"I've been asking that a lot too."

Maxx continued, "I was angry, so angry. They told me to just trust Jesus. I said, 'Oh yeah? Well, where was Jesus at the festival when Becca needed him?' We were in the crowd. I saw her looking at me. People were everywhere and then I never saw her again. 'Where was your God then?' I asked. I'm her father, I'm supposed to protect her. I didn't. Neither did God."

Carol took a seat next to him. She'd never heard Maxx talk like this before. He'd always seemed so confident. *He's always been so strong. Now he looks like a little boy.*

"I don't know if I can get Becca back, but I'm gonna try." Carol looked right at Maxx. "It's not your fault."

He looked back at her with a pinched brow.

"Maxx, it's not your fault. I blamed myself too. I couldn't take it either. But this past month I've been doing something about it. And I found out that what most people call guilt, we call parenting."

Maxx laughed. "Parenting. That's funny. I'm not guilty—I'm a parent."

"I know it sounds funny, but it's true. Maxx, we were ... we *are* good parents. Good parents do everything they can for their kids, and even when it's just not enough, it might be good enough."

"You know that doesn't make sense."

She shrugged. "Not everything does. I went to Rome, I started looking at all the evidence ... I started doing something. I needed to come back here—to family. I felt this pull, I had a sign, a dime, it pointed me here. But now that I'm here, I just don't know where to turn. Ralph wants to help. I need to track down the adoption lawyer. Also, there's evidence to suggest Becca may have been in Pennsylvania. Harold Baker is connected to her. Maybe he has some information." She put one hand on top of his. "And I'm changing too."

"I can see that." Maxx had tears in his eyes. "You don't have to take me back. I don't know if that's even what I need. I just want you to know I'm changing. I guess when I realized God lost a child maybe he understood. So, I started talking to him. Carol, I believe God is protecting Becca. I think she's alive."

"You believed the police reports that said otherwise," Carol countered.

"I didn't know what to believe. But now it's more than a feeling. If I'm wrong, at least I tried being right. When the funeral was canceled, I still went to the funeral home and just sat there. No one was there, and there was no casket, but the flowers were there. I could smell the jasmine."

"Her favorite."

They looked at each other.

"Right. I searched through the vases, but there were no jasmine flowers. What do you think that means? I think it means something. You're going to think this sounds funny, but some pretty weird things have been happening to me."

Carol smiled. She thought about digging underneath her outside shower, then staying up all night to watch a pagan ritual, and the old Italian cabbie whispering in her ear.

"Try me."

"Well, I flew to New York just a few days ago for a business trip, but because of weather, our plane was diverted to Philly. We were supposed to get on shuttle buses that would take us to JFK. But when I walked through that maze they call an airport, I thought I saw you with Becca."

"Really?"

"I called your name, but you didn't turn around, I mean if it was you. So, I bumped through the crowd, and, yeah, I got some pretty choice words, city of brotherly love and all, and I got up behind you or whomever it was. I reached out to the little girl, but she was gone. Right before you got on the escalator, a bunch of change fell out of your purse. I bent down to pick it up for you, but it all fell through the cracks. Except for this." Maxx reached out to press something small in her hand.

Carol looked down at her palm, then looked at him, and then down again. Her forehead felt hot and her chest felt like it had a band twisted tight around it. She couldn't see Maxx now even though she knew he was there. She felt 1,000 miles away but heard his voice in the distance.

"No. No. Not now. No."

"Carol? Carol, what's going on?"

She felt Maxx touch her shoulder, but her chest pain tightened and her breathing worsened.

Just breathe, just breathe.

She reached out to him. "Maxx, help me up. I gotta go. Mee-Maw will be wondering where ... where I am."

Maxx held her arm as she stood. "What is it? You can tell me."

"Later, I'll call you."

"Okay, I'm staying in Summerdale. Just call my cell—it hasn't changed."

Carol headed up Anne Street, gasping for air. She reached into her purse and fumbled with her Newports. She pulled one out but found no matches.

"Dang it." She dropped the pack back into her purse and walked up onto the porch where Mee-Maw sat on her porch swing.

"Carol, dear, come here."

She sat down and rested her head on her grandmother's shoulder. Her ear pressed against the soft ruffles on her nightgown and looked down at her grandmother's exposed arms, now dotted with age. Mee-Maw's fresh smell brought back a sensibility to Carol that she hadn't experienced since she'd been a child.

"Oh, Mee-Maw."

"I know, dear, I know. Maxx was here, looking for you."

"I'm so confused. I'm so lost. I don't know where to turn."

"You're fine, dear. You know where you are. You're home, it's all that matters."

Carol's chest heaved as she tried to calm herself.

"You know, you did this as a child sometimes. You did it in kindergarten one day on the playground, so you just left, just like that, and walked away. Everyone was worried about where you were, but I found you right here on my swing."

"I remember. My glasses got broke playing kickball. I couldn't see."

"Couldn't see? You got here, didn't you? You could see just fine. You see what you need to see."

The woman who'd never left her small town knew more than any Egyptian archeologist ever could. Her soothing words felt real, spoken from a real life. She was so different than Dr. Lazarus. Carol wondered what the two might talk about if they ever met.

She sat up. "You're right, nothing else matters. I just can't believe he came back now. I thought I was getting somewhere."

Mee-Maw patted her hand. "Oh, but you are, dearie, you are. When your mother was a girl, your father showed up here after his stint in the army. I told him she was working down at the diner. Well, that night I sat right here on this same swing, and she buried her head in my shoulder just like you just did. She said her boyfriend had been eating his dinner at the counter when your father walked in wearing his army uniform. She told me she couldn't stop staring at him.

"Anyway, her boyfriend got so mad he left without eating his pie or paying for it. Your daddy just sat down and said, 'Mind if I get a scoop of ice cream on this?' He knew what he was doing. You mother felt so nervous she covered the plate with ice cream. And he ate that boy's pie, ala mode."

Mee-Maw brushed a bit of Carol's hair back behind her ear.

"Your mother said she didn't know what to do, and she was so confused. 'I can't see straight,' she told me. But I knew."

Carol looked up and smiled. She held onto Mee-Maw's hand. "I never heard that before. I mean, Daddy liked talking about the best pie he ever had, but I didn't know Mother ended up here on your swing."

"Yes, that's right, and I'll tell you one more thing. When you brought Maxx by for the first time, I made him chicken and dumplings. He wasn't like your daddy, but I knew then too. Seems you and your mom are a lot alike."

Now Carol straightened up and looked into Mee-Maw's eyes. They drew her in. "I'm not sure I see that."

"That may be one of those things you need to see. Maxx is a lot like your daddy, he just doesn't know it yet. Like I said, sometimes you see what you want to see."

Carol listened to the creak of the rusty chain holding the swing, rocking her into a calmer state.

"Child, your one cheek is red, and you've been holding your hand in a fist like you want to hit someone since you came home tonight."

Carol hadn't noticed her other hand. It had stayed tight since she'd left Maxx. Now, she noticed the cramped fist while her other hand relaxed inside Mee-Maw's hand.

Mee-Maw pushed her foot against the porch floor, making the swing sway once more. "Some things you can't make go away. Like sand, you have to open your hand and let it sift through your fingers."

Carol unfolded her fingers and saw the dime.

"Maxx must have put this in my hand."

Mee-Maw looked down at the coin stamped with 1996.

"Maxx didn't know what it meant, but he knew he had to find me." She paused. "He says he found God, and now, he wants to find Becca. He doesn't know if she's dead, but as long as I believe he says that's enough for him. But I don't need him."

Mee-Maw shook her head. "No?"

The two sat a few moments in silence as the lightning bugs flickered about the yard and the crickets chirped their mating calls. An owl hooted somewhere in the distance. Maxx's words came back to her: *There is a place and purpose for all God's creatures.*

Carol stood and took a few steps to the wooden screen door.

Mee-Maw looked up. "But do you *want* his help?"

Carol held onto the small brass handle worn away from kids and grandkids but still strong and proud, still doing its job, still needed.

"I don't know."

"Do you *love* him?"

Carol said nothing, but looked back at her diminutive grandmother, now no more than a silhouette in the night.

Carol sighed. "I know I love you." Then she went inside to get some ice for her cheek.

"No more smoking, honey, promise?" her grandmother called.

"I promise."

CHAPTER 16

As Carol walked down the steps the next morning, she could hear voices coming from the living room. When she turned the corner, she saw Maxx and Mee-Maw sitting on the couch looking at picture albums. They grew quiet as she entered the room.

"Don't let me interrupt."

Maxx smiled. "Look here, Carol, here's a picture of you on Joey's shoulders."

Carol could see the sharp creases in Maxx's pants and that not a hair seemed out of place.

"Coffee." It was all she could say as she shuffled toward the kitchen.

"Good to see some things haven't changed. We finished a pot a while ago, but I can fire up another. Remember, level-five coffee?" Maxx stood.

Carol picked up her purse. "Joey used to say that." *Some things haven't changed.* "Maxx, would you mind taking me up to the Ranch House?"

Maxx grabbed his keys without hesitation. As he backed the rental car out of the concrete ribbon drive overgrown with short weeds and grass, Carol grabbed her door when a neighbor kid rode by too close on a bike.

"I saw him," Maxx said.

Carol looked out the window as they crossed the bridge. The rivers seemed high, but several rocks remained and most provided a perch for the birds to fish.

So different than the ancient bridges of Rome.

Soon they passed a sign for the Appalachian Trail.

Maxx shook his head. "HYOH."

"What?"

"Something I learned on the trail. It's important to always hike your own hike."

Maxx turned into the parking lot of the Ranch House restaurant. Several tractor trailers lined one edge of the lot while pickup trucks and sedans surrounded the restaurant. Maxx held the door for Carol and a group of older women followed.

"Such a nice young man," one said.

Carol smiled.

"Just sit anywhere." The waitress's smile and invitation made her seem familiar.

Carol sat in the warm light at a window seat.

"What can I get—"

"Coffee."

"And water," Maxx said.

The waitress gave a curt nod, scribbled on her pad, and walked away.

Carol fiddled with her phone, and Maxx read the local sales paper while they waited for their order.

"Says here I could buy a pair of Nubian goats."

"You raise goats?"

"No, but they come with a sack of feed. Hey, here's an '82 International hay tedder for sale. Need one?"

"I don't know what one is." Carol put down her phone. "Maxx, why are you here?"

"Coffee, remember?"

Carol raised an eyebrow and continued to stare at him.

Maxx shrugged. "I just want to do something. Same as you, I *have* to do something. I know you don't trust me. Don't know why you would, and I'm not asking you to. I guess I'm just asking to let me help. I want to believe she's alive. I want to believe in you. I've been thinking about this for a while. I thought we'd talk at the funeral."

"After all this time with not a word and now this? What am I supposed to say? I know you're still her father, but I can't trust you."

"Just let me help. That's all, just help."

Carol shifted in her chair and put her hand up to her forehead to block the sun. "I came here to find my missing daughter, not my lost husband."

"I'm not lost, not anymore. Oh, I talked with Ralph this morning."

"You hate Ralph."

"I don't. I made fun of him, but I never hated him. Besides, I got you and he didn't. Ralph's had a pretty tough go of it. Did you know he was on duty when he got the call about his father?"

Carol had heard about Ralph's father's suicide. She had been in Europe at the time, but small-town news travels far. The waitress brought their drinks and left quickly. Carol reached for a creamer. "I didn't know that."

Maxx continued, "Ralph's dad had been the town police chief. There were rumors about another woman. There were also rumors about some work irregularities and an ongoing investigation by the state's Attorney General. Ralph never believed them, and he doesn't think his father committed suicide either. His father was the reason he became a state trooper."

Carol stirred her hot coffee. "Wow, you two talked a lot."

"He was out at his patrol car this morning, so I went over. I saw a picture of Ralph and his dad in uniform taped to the dashboard. That got him started."

Carol shrugged as she placed two small ice cubes from her water into her hot coffee cup. "He does that—talk, I mean."

"We kind of bonded because of our loss. He gave me a copy of a picture of that girl, Rea Billingsley. He told me what you thought about the fingernails and necklace. He sent a copy of it to my phone, and I sent it down to my office. We have a great graphics guy. He was able to clean it up with some computer enhancements. Here, take a look. You were right."

The late morning light filtering through the streaky window glinted off the screen of Maxx's phone, but Carol saw what he meant—a small, metal, circular shape on the girl's neck.

Carol looked up at Maxx. "A dime?"

"I think it is. I just can't be sure."

The dime. Maxx had one and now this. Carol struggled for air. She saw the concern in Maxx's eyes and tried to look away before he noticed the same.

"Carol, Ralph knows where this girl once lived. If you want to go out there, we could call him. He said he wouldn't let you go alone."

On the way back to Mee-Maw's, Maxx called Ralph and asked him to meet them back on Church Street.

Carol got into the front seat of his squad car and said to Maxx, "You're coming too."

Maxx nodded and got into the back seat without saying a word.

They drove along the winding roads separated by farms, streams, and abrupt hills. Carol had never spent much time in the western part of the county. She noticed Amish families had moved into some of the dilapidated farms and fixed them up. Hunting cabins, mobile homes, and shacks lined the road where once there had been only farmland. Occasionally, they'd pass stone homes fronted with stately wood columns, a reminder of the past. At some of the larger farms, huge metal sheds covered farm equipment and massive round hay bales stood in the fields, each almost as big as a small bedroom.

"Kind of like stepping back in time, huh?" Ralph said.

"Yeah, in a good way," said Maxx.

They crossed a rusted metal bridge with wooden boards laid down to soften the ride. The bridge seemed just wide enough for the cruiser to pass through. Ralph maneuvered the car through a dip at the end of the short bridge and then down a hill and around to the left. They almost missed the drive overgrown with trees and brush.

Ralph brought the patrol car to a stop, but none of them rushed to exit. A dog on a chain snapped off several ferocious-sounding barks then laid down in the dust. Three more dogs inside a chain-link kennel barked and ran back and forth.

The doublewide trailer once white but now was grey. The crusty aluminum clad windows were covered with faded fabric, and a worn blue plastic tarp covered part of the flat roof. Metal lawn chairs rested under a large oak tree, and the remains of a wooden swing hung by one rusted chain. Cars and appliances long abandoned now gave birth to small saplings. Two propane tanks stood against the side, and green moss grew on anything that didn't move.

Something scurried beneath the wooden porch as Ralph knocked on the door. After several minutes of knocking with no response, he used the butt of his flashlight to knock again.

After several more raps, Carol touched Ralph's shoulder, and reached out to turn the door handle. The door opened.

"I can't go in there," Ralph said.

"I can." Carol walked through the doorway, followed by Maxx.

The fake wallpaper paneling held by ringed screws looked warped from moisture. A kerosene heater sat dormant in the corner while a window air conditioner filled a hole in the wall and spit out noisy air that was neither cool nor conditioned. Carol noticed cigarette butts in the ash tray and the burns in the carpet. Someone was living there. Some jeans and flannel shirts lay in a basket, and a few pieces of fruit sat on a 1960s-era Formica table clad in aluminum. Three torn vinyl chairs surrounded the table. Carol wrinkled her nose.

"Cats."

Maxx nodded and they backed onto the porch.

"No one's here. Let's go," said Carol.

Ralph touched her arm. "Not so fast." He nodded toward the row of trees behind the house.

Just then, brush moved, a branch snapped, and a mass of camouflage on two legs walked toward the trio. The person held a shotgun cradled in one arm and a bag over the other shoulder. Carol saw matted hair underneath the camouflage hat and studied the fat cheeks and rounded body held together with suspenders.

"What you doin' on my porch?"

"We're looking for a girl," Ralph said, stepping to the edge of the porch and in front of Carol. "We think you could help us, Miss Reba."

Miss Reba? Carol tried to move around Ralph, but he put out one hand to keep her back.

"I don't know nothing about no girl."

"We're looking for Rea."

"Rea, shoot, she ain't no girl. Been a coon's age since she was 'round here."

The three moved closer to Miss Reba.

Ralph nodded. "No, ma'am, but she may know where these folks' daughter is. Any idea where we can find her?"

Her reply sounded more like a grunt than a word.

"How about a recent picture of her?"

"Only pictures I kept of her was when she was seven. My world stopped after that. Ralphie, I've known you since your daddy would bring home our pappy. He was the only one I let take my Rea away from me. They didn't think we were fit to raise her. You're the only one I wouldn't have shot at from the tree line."

The woman rested the butt of the shotgun on the ground.

"Rea came back a few times, but it was only to show off what her new boyfriend got for her. Seems like she always had money. Rea had a mind of her own. She had looks, so she didn't have to skin squirrels." The hunter dropped her bag on a plastic patio table on the edge of the porch.

"Can you tell us anything, ma'am?" Carol pleaded.

"You missing family?"

"Our little girl. She's seven."

Ralph motioned to both. "This is Maxx and Carol Beck ... I mean Davies."

Miss Reba squinted at Carol, then at Maxx, and then back at Ralph.

"I know what you must be feelin'. That's how old Rea was when they took her. She lived in foster homes 'til she was old enough to run away. Seems like she was always running—grew up wild, that one. I never got her back. I know I wasn't much of a mother. I know I couldn't have given her much, and her father was a drunk, but we always had food, and we always had pride."

Miss Reba stood up a bit straighter and pulled on one suspender. "I heard Rea got mixed up with some married man and disappeared after that. She had a temper, that one. Sweet as pie one minute and ravin' mad jealous the next. I never gave up on her though. When I saw you here, Ralph, and I saw you here, Miss, I thought maybe you were my girl come back to me. You never stop hoping, never."

Miss Reba's face had softened. Carol looked into her light blue eyes and saw another mother missing her child. She stepped forward and wrapped her arms around the woman. Miss Reba tensed, and Ralph stepped forward but then Reba closed her eyes and returned the hug. The two mothers stayed like that for a long minute. When they stepped back, Carol used her sleeve to wipe away her tears.

She didn't know what to say.

"Well, we'll leave you be for now, Miss Reba," Ralph said, taking hold of Carol's elbow and turning her toward the car.

"Wait a minute." Reba reached around to the back of her neck and pulled a charm on a thin chain forward. A dime.

"Oh my ..." Carol said, moving closer once more.

"I gave one to Rea the day they took her, and I kept this one. Her daddy made 'em both from his coin jar. Here. You take it."

"Oh, no, I couldn't, no."

"Yes, you can." Reba reached up and secured the clasp at the back of Carol's neck while Maxx held her hair to one side. Carol pressed one hand over the charm, holding onto her silver bond.

On their return trip, Carol sat in the back of the car. She studied the same farms, trailers, and shacks, but now recognized them as homes, lives, and real people who were just trying to make their way in this world. They asked for little, just a patch to grow some kids and a porch to sit on.

It's all anyone ever really needs, just a place in this world.

Despite their being two very different people, she felt connected to Miss Reba.

"Wow, that was something," said Maxx from the front seat. "Good police work, Ralph. What's next?"

"We gotta find that woman, now more than ever. Miss Reba said she gave Rea the same necklace when she left. Carol, didn't you show me a picture of Becca with a necklace?"

Maxx asked, "That's too weird. You think Rea has Becca?"

"I think it's too much to be just a coincidence," Ralph replied.

"But what are the chances that some girl Carol only briefly met when she was a child would someday take our child from us? And why? It just doesn't make sense, Ralph."

"No, it doesn't, but it's our only lead. That's what police work is, you follow a lead 'til it dries up or a better one comes along. There's a lot more to this we don't know."

Carol clutched her necklace and stared out the window.

Ralph looked up into the rear-view mirror. "Carol, what do you think?"

She shook her head. "Nothing."

Ralph looked at Maxx with a raised eyebrow.

Maxx shrugged, then said, "You know something that's always bothered me? Becca's DNA showing up in that burn pit. They told us they found a pit based on an anonymous tip that had the remains of several people.

Some were never identified, and some were traced back to that serial killer. Thing is, he was already in jail when Becca was taken. They found a bracelet and some hair on the edge of the pit they matched with Becca's DNA. When they questioned Baker, he didn't disagree Becca was dead, and they stopped looking."

"It's not over yet," Carol said. "It's always bothered me too. Harold Baker is on death row for other murders. They find his burn pit, and they find Becca's bracelet and even some hair. How did he know she was dead?"

"I guess he was using his *expertise,* or maybe he was trying to ease his conscience," Maxx said.

"Psychopaths don't have a conscience." Ralph drummed his fingers on the steering wheel. "The investigators assumed it was some copycat, trying to make a name for himself or maybe trying to impress Baker. Sounds crazy but we're not dealing with normal people. You know they're executing Baker in two weeks at Rockview."

"What's Rockview?" Carol looked intently at Ralph.

"It's a medium-security penitentiary about two hours from here near Bellefonte where they do all the executions."

"I'd like to talk to Mr. Baker," Carol said.

"He's over seventy years old." Ralph glanced again at her in the rear-view mirror. "Some say he's senile, others say he acts that way to avoid execution. I don't think it's a good idea."

She held her new necklace tightly. "Ralph, I want to talk to him. Don't you see, this is why I'm here. The dime ... the dimes ... we're on the right path."

"Ralph, Carol wants to talk to Mr. Baker."

"Well, I know the state's been letting victims confront him now that the date is set. I'll see what I can do."

When Ralph pulled into the driveway, his mom stood by the window once more and Carol met her eyes for a moment. Then, Carol turned and crossed the street.

As she entered Mee-Maw's, Carol smelled the chicken corn soup simmering on the stove and saw her grandmother shifting pots and moving plates.

"Come here and eat, child."

"No, thanks, Mee-Maw. I'm kind of tired. I'll eat later."

Mee-Maw gave her a worried look and started to protest, but, despite the pleas, Carol continued upstairs.

She could hear the TV blaring in the living room and pictured Mee-Maw watching *Judge Judy* while crocheting another blanket for the needy. *How does she do it?* Carol thought about this little woman who'd survived every war since the depression. She knew her grandmother's losses and knew, like most nights, the quiet little senior citizen would soon turn off the TV, put her teeth in a glass, and go to bed.

CHAPTER 17

The next several days drifted by in a haze of humid summer air. Simply walking to the corner worked up a sweat and sitting on the porch sipping unsweetened iced tea wouldn't quench a thirst. Carol's back stuck to her car's leather seat despite blasting the AC, and everything felt sticky. Glasses left rings on countertops, and even the salt stuck in the shaker.

Ralph tried to find out more about Rea Billingsley but kept running into dead ends. It was as if Rea stopped living when she left Perry County ten years before. But Carol had found the adoption lawyer in Lemoyne and made a call to set up an appointment.

"Yes, Ms. Foster? This is Carol Davies, we adopted Rebecca in 1998. We're attempting to find her birth mother."

"I see. Well, I will have to pull the file, but this is highly unusual. Typically, we don't release any information unless there are release forms on record which would also be very unusual. I'll get back to you."

"There are extenuating circumstances you need to know about." But Carol's explanation came too late—Ms. Foster had already hung up.

Carol didn't know how long she would have to wait for a return call so she used her computer to find out everything she could on Harold Baker and focused on how she could find a way to question him. She had little energy to make small talk or reminisce, but Maxx still called her every morning. She couldn't bear to think about life before Becca. That life was gone. Now, after traveling the globe, spending thousands of dollars, collecting books and newspapers about possible leads, all Carol had was a wrinkled picture and a few dimes.

While he waited for Carol to let him in, Maxx had fixed Mee-Maw's squeaky door, her dripping faucet, and turned over garden dirt for a second planting. He'd changed the filters in the furnace, repaired a broken screen in the porch door, and even got the door to slow down before closing. The three often ate dinner together.

"Did you hear back from the lawyer?" Maxx asked a few days later.

"I had to call her and eventually reached her, but she refused to give me any information. She said she'd have to see if there were release forms."

Maxx shook his head. "Lawyers."

Mee-Maw reached across the table and patted her hand. "Your mother called again. She says she got a letter addressed to you from Italy."

"I know. You told me." Carol picked at her food.

"She says she's not going to bring it down here."

"I know."

"Says you gotta come get it."

"I will. I just got a lot going on."

Carol heard someone on the porch and then a knock. She looked up to see Ralph on the other side of the screen door.

Before anyone could invite him in, Ralph stood on the braided rug in the living room. He still had on his grey uniform and held his wide brimmed hat with both hands. The knot of his clip-on tie hid safely behind his chin.

"Want some strawberry shortcake, Ralphie." Mee-Maw didn't wait for his reply but prepared the cake with some of her homemade whipped cream.

Ralph sat down and looked at Carol. "I got you a date at the penitentiary to see Baker." As the others stared, he swallowed a bite and then wiped a smudge of cream off his lip before saying, "Tomorrow." Then, he went back to his remaining strawberries left soaking in the sweetened milk.

"Tomorrow?" Carol exclaimed.

"That's incredible," Maxx added.

Mee-Maw looked at Carol.

"It's so soon, it's what I've been waiting for but now that it's here, it's a lot. Thank you, Ralphie, thank you so much."

Ralph beamed.

"My man," added Maxx, "My man. I guess I'll stay here tonight if it's okay." Maxx looked at Mee-Maw who nodded her approval. "Just seems silly to drive all the way back to Summerdale for a few hours. And I have my bag in the back of the car."

"You can stay in the room next to Carol's," Mee-Maw said as she cleared the table.

"Well, we have a big day tomorrow then." Carol rose from her seat and turned toward the stairs. "Goodnight, everyone."

As Carol lay in bed, she could hear Maxx going through his nightly ritual—their two rooms separated by only a folding vinyl door. She knew he would place his shoes by the door, his keys on the nightstand, and any loose change would be stacked on top of the others. She knew he would pull up the sheets on the bottom of the bed to free his feet. After folding his pants across the footrail, he'd get into bed wearing his sloppy boxer shorts and a faded T-shirt from his college years.

She could see him as if she were next to him, and she fell asleep wishing she were.

In the morning, Mee-Maw made pancakes and bacon and smiled while her three "kids" sat around her table, spilled maple syrup, talked with their mouths full, and forgot to use their napkins. But no one put their elbows on the table. They offered to help clean up, but she wouldn't have it as she ushered them out the door and to Ralph's cruiser.

"Are you going to get in trouble for this, Ralph?" asked Carol.

"Forget about it."

"Ralph, could you swing by the farm, Carol has a letter she needs to pick up."

Carol shot Maxx a look. "No. Straight to Rockview. I don't want to be late."

This time Ralph didn't listen to Carol. This time, he made a left, drove out to the farm, and down the lane to her mother's house.

The three sat quietly in the car until Ralph said, "Well, I'm not going to get it."

"Me, neither," Maxx said.

"I'm going." Carol unbuckled her seatbelt and walked up to the door, hesitating in front of the screen door. Flies crawled across the screen, stuck to the tape hanging from the ceiling, and lay dead at her feet.

Carol raised her clenched hand, but then saw her mother's form through the dark screen.

"Well, I'm glad you remembered where I lived."

"Ralph knows where everyone lives. I heard you have a letter for me."

Her mother opened the screen door and handed out the letter. "Here." When Carol reached for it, her mother wouldn't let go. "Can we talk?"

"We will. Just not now." Carol pulled the letter from her mother's grasp and stepped back to the wooden steps. She looked at the envelope now emblazed with postal stamps and markings. "Sis is the last of the letter writers."

"Your sister always took pride in her penmanship. Carol, I always pray for you."

"I'll need it today. I gotta go." She scooted off the wooden porch to the waiting patrol car. Carol slammed the car door shut. The force of the slam startled her. "Oops, sorry." She turned to Ralph but neither he nor Maxx said a word.

At last, Carol broke the silence. "Listen, I know you guys agreed not to say anything when I came back to the car, but your silence is creeping me out."

Maxx said, "Okay, okay, what did your mom say? How was it?"

Carol shrugged. "Fine. She wants to talk. I told her I will. That's it."

"That's not it. When are you going to talk?"

"I said I will soon. There's no problem. Ralph, drive."

"Carol, you are so honest with everyone but yourself," Maxx said.

"What's that mean?"

"It means the biggest lie is the one you tell yourself."

As Ralph turned his car back up the road, she looked at the letter. A stamp of the coliseum covered much of one corner and was covered by multiple ink stamps. She didn't recognize the return address but recognized the handwriting right away.

Dear Lil' Sis,

I can't believe it's been weeks since you left. I never intended on staying away this long, and so I didn't think about writing, believing I'd be home tomorrow or the next day. I was going to email or call but somehow sitting down and writing just seemed right. Like we used to do when we were kids, away at summer camp or something. I thought I'd give you some time to get back to your roots and all. I hope things are going well with you and the fam on the farm. Say, if you get a chance can you stop by the hardware store and say hey for me? I'm sure they're wondering where I'm at. I hope they keep everything going until I get back. Tell Frank I left the key to the time clock in my top desk drawer, but he probably found it by now.

Anyway, Dr. Lazarus is good. He's back teaching and doing his thing. He's trying to keep tabs on the pagans. We call them "the family." It sounds better, especially when we're out in public. You know, like, "So have you heard anything from the family?" "Not really but I heard Mother got arrested for desecrating a cat." See it just sounds better, right? I think I saw Starlite at a record store, it's tough to tell. All those Goths look alike. Is that OK to say? Anyway, I went up to her and said, "Hi, any news?" And she just looked at me and said, "Go away old bird." Old bird? How rude! So, I said, "Whatever," and just left. I think that's what kids are saying these days.

I'm sure you're wondering about Antonio, right? He got a promotion at the museo, so he doesn't see Dr. L as much. He's an associate curator which is almost as good as an assistant curator, just not as much money, and he has to work weekends. He's as funny as ever. You know he's so cute. He took me to see his mother. I was more nervous than a pole cat on a porch full of rocking chairs in March. She didn't speak English, but I took care of her granddaughter while she got things ready in the kitchen. She wouldn't let me help with that.

So, with Antonio working weekends, it gave me time to travel around a bit, but I got bored and told him I was going to come home. That's when he got me a job. I show American students around the outside of the museum and give them a class on horticulture. You know, the outdoor products were my specialty at the hardware store, and growing up where we did, I know about plants and stuff. So now I tie it into Roman history and talk about how they had running water for their plants, and how they brought back plants from around the known world, and that if it wasn't for Rome, we might not have many of the plants and flowers we enjoy today. They knew how to graft, make hybrid plants, and all sorts of things.

Carol heard gravel crunch under the tires and looked up to see Ralph pulling into a gas station.

While he was filling up, Carol went in to use the restroom. The cashier had given her a key with an engine part attached to it, so no one would forget to return it. With one look around the room, Carol estimated the bathroom had last been cleaned sometime before the Exxon merger. She used most of the roll to paper the toilet seat.

As she made her way back to the car, she saw the *Harrisburg Times* for sale in a metal box dispenser. A picture on the front page drew her closer. The caption read:

HAROLD BAKER: 12 DEAD—12 DAYS TO DIE

She looked into Baker's vacant eyes in the mug shot, juxtaposed above a grimacing smile. She stood transfixed.

He looks so ordinary, like anyone's relative who talks too much about the good ole days. The one who doesn't know how to use a computer, drives fifteen miles under the speed limit, reads the Good Book, keeps his lawn mowed, and at night abducts little girls. Depraved derelict.

Carol's heart started to race. She took in a deep breath, pushed it out through her pursed lips, and returned to her safe place in the back seat of the squad car. After shutting her eyes for a few moments, her heart slowed, and she noticed she wasn't even sweating this time. *Progress.*

"Want one?"

She opened her eyes to see Maxx shoving a Cow Tale candy in her face. The long thin roll of caramel and cream looked tempting.

"Sure, thanks, it means a lot to me."

"It's just candy."

"No, Maxx, it means a lot to me that you are *here*. This isn't going to be easy for either of us."

"I know, Car. I'm glad I'm here too."

Carol liked it when he called her Car. No one else did.

Ralph returned to the car with his receipt in hand, and the three headed closer to Rockview, home to some of the nicest people in the county and some of the most dangerous people in the country. Carol went back to her letter.

Well, listen to me giving you a lecture on Rome, aren't I funny? I'm taking Italian and I work Fridays and weekends. Antonio and I have lunch together. I make him something with fresh bread and cheeses from the market and sometimes I make a fruit salad. And then we usually go out to eat late at one of the cafés. Guess what? I lost twelve pounds. Okay, I gained back four.

I can't believe I've gone on about Antonio and haven't said a thing about little Becca. I figured you haven't found her, otherwise you'd let me know, right? I want to support you, lil' sis, honest I do, but the longer I'm away, the more I realize how much I've been living in the past. I'm not saying you are, or what you are doing is wrong. I'm just saying for me, when Sid died, I died. Sure, I worked at the hardware store, went to church, looked after Mom, and the farm. But I wasn't going anywhere in life. I was dead.

Well, I'm alive now. I have a new life. It sounds selfish, so what? I don't know if you'll ever find Becca. Carol, understand, I'm trying to help. I've always been there for you but this thing of searching for her is only hurting you more. Maybe the best thing you can do to honor her is to move on with your life. Like I have. Go back to the beach, find a guy, find two (OK, I'm kidding). I did. (one, so far ... lol).

Antonio and I are getting married, lil' sis. Can you believe it? I can't. And we want you to be the maid of honor. When can you come back? We're planning for a fall wedding. You know I look better in earthy colors. You have to be here—you're the reason we got together. See, something good has come of this.

Carol put down the letter. "You little snip."
"What is it?" asked Ralph.
"My sister's getting married."
"You don't sound very happy."
"It's not that, it's just ... I don't know, it's how she says it. I'm not jealous, I'm happy for her, I guess, but she just says all this other crap. Maybe it's me."
Carol picked up the letter and read on.

Anyway, Antonio's brother is the best man and we're having it at the chapel at the museo, surrounded by all that culture.

Class, huh? His mother is making me a dress, and all his nieces and nephews are so excited.

I'm marrying a real Italian. Remember when those men in the airport were making fun of me and you told me they were complimenting me? I knew they weren't. Well, guess what, no one's laughing now, except me. I hope you don't mind telling Mom for me. I'm sure by now you two are just chummy. Tell Mee-Maw I miss her.

Love You More,
Sis
XXXOOOXXX

Oh brother. She sounds so different. I don't know if I like the new Sis. Guess we're all changing. Maybe she won't like the new me either.

"I can't believe she wants me to fly to Rome again. Why does she care if I keep searching?"

"So what's up," Maxx asked. "What does she want?"

"Oh, I'm not really sure. We'll talk about it later."

I can't give up. I can't stop. Not now. We are getting somewhere. We're close, I just know it.

"She's just so self-absorbed, like I was, I guess. I'm happy for her. She's coming out of her cocoon. Sometimes you just never know."

Carol hadn't realized they'd gone so far until the car came to a stop. She looked up at the immense chain-link fence towering at least fifteen feet overhead.

CHAPTER 18

Concertina razor wire looped around the top of the fence and signs posted in multiple locations warned people to stay back.

Even though the execution wasn't until next week, there was already a small group of protesters. Most of the signs protested the death penalty but one sign read, "HARROLD, I LOVE YOU," and another read, "MARRY ME." Burnt candles littered the ground and a makeshift pavilion housed more signs, a music box, and bottled water.

"You think she could have spelled his name correctly," Ralph joked but no one laughed. "The pro-death penalty group doesn't get here 'til dark. Maybe because they have jobs." Again, silence.

A buzz signaled the gate to open, and Ralph drove the car forward. The first building they could see looked more like an oversized concrete bunker than a prison but still conveyed a sense of impenetrability.

"Rockview was originally built to be a maximum-security prison," Ralph explained. "But the governor at the time—Governor Pinchot—was more interested in rehabilitation and changed it to a medium security prison with an elaborate farm and vocational center. The prison used to be self-sufficient. When inmates were released, they had an agriculture or a trades skill to get a job."

"Interesting," said Maxx. "I like history."

Carol shook her head.

"One thing that hasn't changed is the death house—it's what they call the execution chamber. They've always had one here. Early on, prisons like this one used death by hanging, but in the age of electricity, the chair was used until it was outlawed in the seventies. When PA brought the death penalty back, the death house moved to the old infirmary, and lethal injection was introduced. They haven't put anyone to death since 1999 in the state, so Harold Baker is drawing quite a crowd."

The trio went into the visitor's center and were instructed to pass through the metal detector. Then the guards searched their things and scrutinized their identification. A German shepherd laid at the feet of his handler near the door as the guard ushered them into a small waiting room. A list of regulations and an aerial picture of the grounds hung on one wall while the florescent light above them flickered. On the other three walls hung pictures from the twenties and thirties showing happy prisoners working the fields, building furniture, and washing laundry.

The world was a safer place before we knew about monsters like Baker who roam the back roads, select their prey, and blend back into the crowd.

An older woman with spiked black hair and a black leather folder walked in, followed by a young prison guard. The woman's eyes darted back and forth, and her hands continually repositioned the folder but never opened it.

"Hello, I am Mrs. Welch. I'm the social worker who made the arrangements for your meeting today."

After introductions, Mrs. Welch continued, "Remove anything that could come loose—scarves, pins, necklaces, large earrings—and place them in the bag to be retrieved later. Do not come within five feet of any prisoner or their cell. Do not talk to anyone who I have not introduced to you. And lastly, think now of three things you want to say to Harold Baker, because I guarantee you, when you get face to face, you won't remember. It is easy to forget."

Carol took a deep breath as the trio followed the young guard while the social worker trailed from behind at a distance. The guard's uniform hung on his small frame, and his hair was so short his hat slid up and down as they walked. The walls were made of cinderblock and were broken here and there with an occasional small window on their left. Carol could see an outdoor courtyard below where groups of prisoners milled about. On their right, bars separated them from more groups of inmates sitting around long metal tables. Some talked, others stared. Carol stayed close to the guard.

Carol heard prisoners shouting, "Mrs. Welch, Mrs. Welch," and heard the social worker telling prisoners, "Not now," or "We'll see," or "I told you already."

In front of them, two sets of bars opened to allow them access and then slammed behind them. Florescent lights were recessed into the ceiling and a duct coated with dust blew stale air from above. Another guard led them to a room devoid of any decoration except one large mirror.

"I'll be sitting behind the mirror, watching and listening to all interactions, you'll sit there and there." The new guard pointed to two metal chairs. "A guard will stand in the corner. Officer Peters, you can come with me behind the glass."

"I'll sit here at this end," the social worker chimed in. "Don't forget your three questions."

"I hear him coming," the guard said. "Officer Peters, come with me, please."

Carol heard metal doors slamming and soon could hear the echoes of people talking and yelling in the background.

"Baker, Baker!" someone yelled from a muffled distance.

"Mr. Baker gets a lot of attention from the others whenever he is moved," said the social worker.

Carol and Maxx sat on one side of a long table facing the metal door with a small square window. Neither looked at each other, but Maxx reached over to hold Carol's hand. They saw another guard look through the glass before unlocking the door and leading a short, thin, pale man with a few white hairs covering the top of his head into the room. His feet and hands were shackled causing him to shuffle in pronounced labor. The guard pulled out a chair, and the senior monster sat down. He stared expressionless at Carol with dull grey eyes as the guard locked the cuffs around his hands to a bar that ran the length of the table. Baker's transport then left the room, but the guard in the corner never moved.

Baker's grey shirt buttoned tightly to the top and around his wrists and had white numbers stenciled on one pocket. His pants, like the shirt, were neatly pressed and cuffed above his black shoes, which seemed old by any standard but were without blemish.

An overhead air handler kicked on, breaking the stillness with an unnatural rattle.

"Mr. Baker, I'm Carol." Her throat felt dry, and her voice weakened.

"And I'm Maxx. We're missing our daughter, Becca Davies." Maxx sounded as if he was presenting a project to his board of directors. "She disappeared October sixth, over one year ago, after you were arrested. After you told the authorities where you disposed of most of the victims' remains, they found a bracelet and some hair from our daughter on the edge of the pit. Here's her picture."

Baker took the 4x6 photo in one shackled hand and rubbed the edge of the picture methodically with his other. He slowly rocked back and forth as he stared at the photo.

Carol's throat tightened further, and her breathing shortened. She didn't like him holding Becca's picture. When he looked up, Carol sensed he didn't seem to be looking at her, or even through her. She felt as if she simply did not exist, and he stared into a void. She did not matter to his lifeless eyes and was no more a person than the chair she sat upon.

He began to speak.

"Davy, Davy Dumpling,
Boil him in a pot;
Sugar him, and butter him,
And eat him while he's hot!"

Baker licked his lips, sending a shiver up Carol's spine.

Maxx and Carol looked at each other, then at the social worker in the corner.

"I've been told he does this a lot. He speaks in nursery rhymes, sometimes for hours."

Maxx slapped a hand on the table and snatched back the photo. "Now, look here. Who do you think you are? We didn't come all this way for games."

"I am the baker man
I come from far away
And I can bake
What can you bake?
I can bake biscuits
Crunchy, crunchy, crunchy crunch
Crunchy, crunchy, crunchy crunch
Crunchy, crunchy, crunchy crunch
Crunchy, crunchy crunch."

Carol felt herself growing hotter and the room getting smaller.

"Mr. Baker. I am a mother ... Becca's mother. Will you help me? You led the police to think Becca was dead, but I want to hear it from you. Is my child still alive?"

Harold Baker continued looking in her direction. Then said,

"Monday's child is fair of face,
Tuesday's child is full of grace,
Wednesday's child is full of woe,
Thursday's child has far to go,
Friday's child is loving and giving,
Saturday's child works hard for a living,
And the child who is born on the Sabbath Day
Is fair and wise and good in every way.
Only Sabbath Day child goes away."

His voice, his intonation, and staccato froze Carol. Maxx stilled beside her, and even the social worker remained motionless.

After a few seconds passed, Maxx shifted in his chair and then laid down a large picture of the bracelet.

"Mr. Baker, this is Becca's bracelet. Do know anything about it? How did it get to your burn pit?"

Baker spoke once more.

> "Eeper Weeper, chimney sweeper,
> Had a wife but couldn't keep her.
> Had another, he did love her,
> Up the chimney, didn't shove her."

Tears sprung from Carol's eyes and her breathing slowed. Maxx scowled and she placed a hand on his arm. Harold remained stoic, alone in his own little world.

The social worker stood up next to the table. "Perhaps this would be a good time for a break. Let's step outside the room for a moment."

Carol trembled as they joined Ralph and the guard behind the mirror. When Maxx pulled her into a hug, she relaxed into the embrace and breathed in his familiar scent.

"I know what you're feeling," the social worker began. "Anger is depression turned inward. You're experiencing the anger stage of grief. This is healthy for closure. Ma'am, you have to get over this and have closure."

"I don't have to do anything." Carol's voice quivered as her hands continued to tremble. "What does that mean anyway? Closure? Closure is a crock. Have you ever lost a child? Did you ever cry over a plastic urn that looks nothing like your child, but they tell you it's all that's left from her lifeless body?" Carol's stare was resolute. "You don't have a clue what I'm feeling. What are you even talking about? I'm never gonna get over this. I don't *want* to get over this. I want my daughter."

"Carol." Maxx drew her in once more and both began to sob.

Ralph tried to embrace them both, but his short arms and gun belt made for an awkward moment. The social worker and guard stared through the mirror at Baker, now reciting nursery rhymes and rocking back and forth with his hands clasped together.

In the file Ralph had supplied Carol, an expert witness at Baker's trial had characterized him as an organized killer. His crimes had not been ones of spontaneous passion, the witness said. His anger lay buried deep inside, unnoticed by everyone, including himself, but he'd planned each killing as a methodic, meticulous surgery—everything in its place, no action wasted. His actions might have been the result of years of abuse, or he might be a genetic freak, but he was described at his trial as "the quintessential, stone-cold killer." They believed he'd relished each death and had a photographic memory of each one of the victims. Experts testified that while the world continued to remain distant and unapproachable to him, the deaths brought him relief.

"I can't go back," Carol said. "Let's go, Maxx."

"But you still have over a half hour." The social worker clutched her folder to her chest. "Ma'am, you didn't ask your third question."

"We're ready to leave." Ralph nodded to the guards and placed his hand at the small of Carol's back.

They retraced their steps to the outside air. The days were becoming shorter, and it had grown dark already. The central Pennsylvania evening cooled, making the air crisp. Overhead, bright lights cast long shadows.

The social worker talked to the group, "Any final questions? Thoughts? Feelings?"

Carol turned away, but then back. "Don't call me ma'am."

As Ralph drove down Route 322, Maxx was the first one to speak.

"Well, I'm not sure we got anywhere today. I guess that's police work, right, Ralph?"

"Not so fast, Maxx. I took notes while you were in there." He handed Carol a yellow legal pad from the driver's seat.

He'd written down the rhymes. Carol winced.

"What do we know about Baker?" Ralph started. "Remember, this guy is not out of his mind, not completely, otherwise they couldn't put him to death, right?" Ralph glanced at her in the rear-view mirror. "And remember, he's extremely organized. Everything has a reason for him, or he doesn't do it. But never forget, he doesn't care at all about other human beings—he just uses them."

Carol looked over the nursery rhymes. "Davy, Davy Dumpling," "I Am the Baker Man," "Monday's Child," and "Eeper Weeper."

"What did he say when you showed him Becca's picture?"

"Boil him in a pot," Maxx said with disgust.

Carol looked out the window.

"Right, he got excited," said Ralph. "He wanted her. But I didn't get the idea he ever saw her before. He was excited for the first time. I think he was telling you he knew something. In a way, he answered your first question."

"So, you think he was trying to help?" Maxx snorted. "Some help."

"What did he say when you accused him of playing games and asked him who do you think you are?"

"He said, 'I am the baker man.' Oh, Harold Baker, I get it."

"Right, everything he does has a point, Maxx. Carol, read what he said when you asked him your second question about Becca being dead."

Carol read through the verse silently until the end. "Only Sabbath Day child goes away."

"Mum recited that rhyme to me all the time," Ralph said. "I was born on a Sunday and that's not part of the rhyme. He added that. He was saying something."

"Becca was born on Monday," Carol added.

"In his file, it says that Baker killed Sunday's children— those born on Sundays." Ralph glanced at Carol.

"He was telling me she wasn't dead?"

"I think so."

Carol looked back out the window.

"Some thought he might have been religiously preoccupied because of his fixation with the Sabbath, but I don't think religion had anything to do with it."

"What about that crazy answer he gave me when I asked him how the bracelet got to his burn pit?"

Carol began to read,

> "Eeper Weeper, chimney sweeper,
> Had a wife but couldn't keep her.
> Had another, he did love her,
> Up the chimney, didn't shove her."

"The guard showed me Baker's prison file while you were talking with him. He had a wife, but she ran away with Baker's brother. After they arrested Baker, they went to the brother's house. They never found the brother, but guess where they found his wife?"

"No! You're kidding," Maxx said.

"The guard says it's his favorite rhyme."

"But the rhyme says, 'Had another, he did love her.' Was he married a second time?" Carol asked.

"No, but I asked to see his visitor log and he has a fiancé. Also, he twisted words by saying he *didn't* kill the second wife, and he *did* love her. That's not how the actual rhyme goes."

"So, he killed his first wife but loved his fiancé."

"Right."

"I asked him how Becca's DNA got to his burn pit and you're saying he told me it was his fiancé who put it there?"

"Pretty much."

"Who's the fiancé?" Carol asked.

"Carol, DNA cannot be transferred through ashes. Only through teeth or bone fragments. Ash alone contains no messengers. If the fire is hot enough, all DNA is wiped away. So, this burn pit was likely where they deposited the ashes after cremation. Now, the bracelet could have got some of her DNA on it, and certainly the hair if it still had roots attached, but they were guessing about the ash."

"You didn't answer the question."

"Ralph? Who is Baker's fiancé?" demanded Maxx.

Carol continued to stare at him as he drove along the highway that wound around the short Pennsylvania mountains.

Ralph glanced at Carol in the rear-view mirror before saying, "Rea Billingsley. She visited him regularly."

"Rea," Carol whispered.

Ralph turned his focus back to the street as they drove into Duncannon.

"Maybe you should have asked your third question," Maxx offered.

Carol turned to look out the window once more.

When they pulled into Ralph's driveway, she saw the light on upstairs, but it had gone out by the time Carol exited the car.

"Now what ... I mean, what next?" asked Maxx.

"Maybe we should just let this perk a bit," Ralph said. "Besides I gotta pull a twelve-hour shift."

"Well, I could use some time to catch up on some paperwork," Maxx added. "I'm heading back to my hotel. Call me tomorrow."

"I can't wait. I've got to find her," Carol said as she crossed the street.

Inside, Carol found a slice of pie with a note for Maxx. Mee-Maw had already retired for the night. Carol sat down and broke off the crust, always her favorite part, then poured a half glass of milk and finished off the slice. With her nighttime snack now filling her stomach, she walked upstairs, laid down on the bed, and turned off the light. Her mind reeled with the events of the day. Or maybe from the extra sugar from the pie.

I can't take much more of this. Psychopaths, death houses, capital murders. Life was better when it wasn't so real.

"God," she prayed, "I can't take it anymore. Why God? Why me? Why Becca? She's just a child—it's so unfair. Why are you doing this to me? And who is this Rea Billingsley?"

She began to cry and soon her sobs grew louder. She felt thankful her grandmother was such a sound sleeper.

"Why?" was an easy question to ask. "Why?" would have been her third question for Baker. But why didn't have an answer. Not tonight anyway. Why didn't bring Becca back.

As her sobs subsided, she prayed again, "Thank you, God. Thank you for Ralph, for Maxx, thank you for Mee-Maw. Thank you for Mother. I will talk to her. Just not tonight." She prayed like a little girl whose mother had just taught her how.

"How am I going to do this God? I'm just not strong enough. God, what are you doing to me? Take this from me. Bring me my Becca. I'll do anything, anything."

Carol looked out her window and saw Mrs. Peter's light had turned back on. Carol couldn't see anyone and pulled down the blind.

CHAPTER 19

"Well, darling, what's your plan for today? Aren't you the girl who always has a plan?"

"Mee-Maw, I don't know who that girl is anymore. All my plans are only as good as the paper they were written on. Yesterday proved that."

Carol poured herself a cup of coffee and grabbed her grandmother's marmalade in the fridge for the scones. She noticed her clothes were starting to fit more snugly again. And despite the emotional roller coaster, her complexion was clearing too.

"Honey, you're my fresh air kid."

Carol smiled as she remembered when they used to sponsor kids from Harrisburg to teach them how to milk a cow, stack hay in the barn, and ride horses.

"Yeah, I guess I am."

After Carol left for college, she'd bounced from Rome to DC, and finally to the Outer Banks. Incredible places that left her wanting. Now she knew—she wanted home.

"Well, we know Baker didn't kill Becca. That's good. You'll never believe what Ralph thinks. Rea Billingsley is or was engaged to him."

Mee-Maw *tsked* and then said, "That's crazy."

"She may have put Becca's DNA at the site. And maybe she has Becca or at least knows where she's at."

"That's incredible. That girl is evil. She needs to be caught and soon."

"I don't know what evil is anymore. Yesterday, I stared evil in the face and all I got were nursery rhymes from an old man. Is that evil? Evil is not having my girl, that's evil. Evil is people thinking they're God."

"That's the original evil, still just as true as ever. Here, this is what I just read this morning." Mee-Maw pulled her old Bible in front of her.

Carol recognized the large, black, worn front from when she was a child. She remembered the book, fat with church bulletins and filled with underlined passages.

Her grandmother read, "'The heart is deceitful above all things, and desperately wicked; Who can know it?' Jeremiah 17:9. Evil took your little girl—so evil, we can't understand it. But grace is going to bring her back."

"How do you know that, Mee-Maw?"

"Faith, honey. I believe it in my heart. I still believe that, in the end, God wins."

"I've been searching for almost three months and, right now, I believe I'm losing."

"Either way, you'll be right. I like my belief better than yours, Carol."

"Yeah, me too."

Carol thumbed through the local paper. She'd always looked forward to reading the *Duncannon Record* when she was younger. She didn't care much for who shot the biggest buck or who got arrested outside the Handimart, but she enjoyed the other local news. This morning, she recognized a kid in the sports section that she thought must belong to one of her old classmates. It was hard to imagine her friends were old enough to have teenagers and realized she hadn't seen them since they were teens.

Where has it all gone? I've been so busy, and for what? What does it all matter?

"I guess I'll go walk off some of this caffeine," she said as she grabbed her nylon jacket. The rain had started earlier this morning, and Carol thought umbrellas unnecessary.

As Carol walked through the neighborhood, she passed a bike laying in the wet grass and a tricycle abandoned on the pavement. Becca had been riding a bike for years. She'd been way ahead of all the kids her age with her bike riding skills. Carol had burst with pride when they'd ridden down the street with their pudgy little preschooler peddling a twelve-inch, violet Minnie Mouse bike. Becca had to peddle as fast as she could to stay upright, but the smile between her chubby cheeks let Carol know this girl would not be denied. She was always happy and on-the-go. Now she was gone.

Feeling warm from the sweat underneath her rain jacket after circling the block, she started across Ralph's empty driveway. As she walked by, she saw the window shade being pulled down. Mrs. Peters. She had only seen Ralph's mom through the window since she'd returned.

Mrs. Peters always liked me. I wonder if she's mad I used to ignore her son. Why does she watch from a distance? She's old, but so is Mee-Maw and she doesn't do that.

Carol walked up on the Peters' porch, much like her Mee-Maw's, and rang the bell. She could hear the melodic chimes.

I can't believe that old thing still works, I guess it doesn't get rung that often.

She waited a minute and rang the bell again. No answer.

I know she's in there.

Carol opened the storm door and knocked on the glass pane in the darkened oak door.

Maybe I should just walk in like I did when I was a kid, or maybe I should just go.

She heard the lock and then saw the knob turn. Too late to run now.

Mrs. Peters' hair had turned completely grey but remained in the same arrangement, tightly pulled back into a single barrette behind her head and curled around her neck. It likely hadn't changed since she got off the boat from Scotland. Her familiar broach clasped the top of her dress against her neck. Her stern expression no longer seemed fearful, but now, mixed with years, showed evidence of a lonely old woman.

"Mrs. Peters, I ... I never thanked you for identifying Rea in the picture."

That sounded stupid.

"Child, I did not hear you knocking. Please, come in."

Carol walked in, and her eyes went immediately to the pictures on the mantel. She recognized Mr. Peters in a picture with the State Attorney General. She remembered the wedding picture on the wall, and, of course, Ralphie's picture in his Boy Scout uniform getting his Eagle Scout badge.

"This one was always my favorite," Mrs. Peters said, pointing at Ralph and Carol's prom picture.

Her original date had stood her up just a few hours before the big event. Carol's grandmother arranged things with Mrs. Peters, and Ralphie showed up an hour early with a large corsage for Carol, flowers for her mother, and chocolate for Mee-Maw. He'd sat for an hour and a half before Carol came down the steps in a light pink chiffon dress. When she realized she could see over Ralph's slicked down cowlick, she ran back up the stairs to get a pair of flat ballet slippers in exchange for her high-heeled pumps.

"Your son was always a gentleman," Carol said. "My knight in shining armor."

"He has a rescuer spirit," Mrs. Peters remarked as she looked toward the ceiling. "Like his pap. He has been telling me about your investigation. It sounds like he is at it again. I hope he does not get hurt."

"I came over to thank you. You started us down this path when you identified Rea Billingsley."

"Would you like some tea, lass?"

"Certainly." *Why did I say that?*

Mrs. Peters walked toward the kitchen. "I will be right back."

A few minutes later, Carol heard the tea kettle whistling on the stove. She picked up a photo album off a pile next to the La-Z-Boy recliner. The pile had dust on it but looked out of place on the floor. A cardboard box filled with more albums sat behind the pile.

Carol recognized some of the faces and some of the names written in the margins of the albums. She recognized Ralphie and his dad fishing, riding in his dad's 1970's police car, and playing catch in the front yard.

She picked out another album from the box filled with pictures of Mr. Peters from the time he was a police recruit to the time he earned police chief. Newspaper clippings fell from the pages. One detailed how Patrolman Peters had broken up a moonshine ring, and one was about how Officer Peters had climbed a tree to rescue old Mrs. Klinepeter's cat.

Another described the time a family had been killed on Route 15 when a truck driver had taken the corner at the Clarks Ferry Bridge too fast and hit them head on. The paper's headline read "Truck Dead-On Clarks Ferry." The paper commented how Officer Peters had handled each person with respect even though he'd appeared visibly shaken when he commented, "This beautiful family met a tragic end."

"That man had a heart for everyone—every stray dog, anyone in need." Mrs. Peters startled Carol as she brought in a tray with tea and biscuits.

"Oh, I'm sorry. I didn't mean to pry."

"No, those were good times. When he was helping others, he was happy, and I thought we were too." Mrs. Peters set down her tea set and Scottish biscuits.

"I always respected you for your daring voyage from the UK, but my mother always said you were a loyal subject of the queen. I thought you and Mr. Peters were the perfect couple," Carol remarked. "You never fought like my parents. You both went to church and had one child who even had his own peddle police car."

"Scotland." Mrs. Peters' expression remained unchanged. She slowly stirred one sugar cube and took a brief sip of tea. "You remember that, do you?" Mrs. Peters smiled. "Well, lassie, things are not always what they seem. There are some things you do not know. There are some things Ralphie does not know either, and I would like to keep it that way."

Carol mirrored Mrs. Peters as she stirred her sugar cube with a tarnished silver teaspoon. Her cup rested on a saucer with a pink pattern of a castle, now chipped on the edge, and stained by the iron-laden water.

"Carol, listen to me, and never repeat this to Ralphie. He may be a state trooper, but he is still my little lad, and I worry about him every time he walks out of this house. He still believes his father's death was accidental. He refused to listen to the rumors, and there were plenty of them. Senior managed to keep his story sealed as part of a bargain to retire quietly. That way Ralph would have a chance to make his own way.

"When it got too much for Senior, I think it was too much to hold in, and he went out back in the shed with his service revolver. It was reported as an accident, that he was cleaning his weapon, but no one believed that. People respected him. Senior was special to a fault."

Carol shifted in her chair and focused on her tea, fearing she would spill it into her saucer. *Why is she telling me this? Maybe because I knew him before.* She looked at the old wallpaper.

"Ma'am, you told Ralph you knew Rea."

"I remembered Rea from the church camp when Ralphie showed me that picture of you last week. Too many memories came back to me when Ralphie came home from Miss Reba's the other day. That is when I remembered Senior would take her father home when he got drunk in town. He was the only police around here for years until they hired Thelma's boy."

Carol bit hard on her lip. The way Mrs. Peters referred to her husband as "Senior" sounded more like a rank than a nickname.

"Well, Senior always took care of domestic disputes. Back then there were no family services or child protection agency, not around here anyway. Senior knew some old spinsters who would take care of kids at risk until he could get the county to find a relative, or a foster home, or an agency in Harrisburg to take them. We took care of our own back then. Sometimes he brought them here for a meal and a place to feel safe."

The cat purred and rubbed against Carol's leg.

"Rea bounced from foster home to foster home. Sometimes she ran away. Sometimes they just could not handle her, especially after she came of age. Sometimes she made a play for the men. Sometimes they came after her. She never had a chance. She stayed with one family long enough for them to try to adopt her, but the father abused her, so she had to leave. She lived on the streets for a time, and Senior would give her a warm meal, pick her up in his car, and take her where he knew she could sleep. She would stop by the station and just sit in there to read because she felt safe."

Carol sat motionless—her spoon on her saucer, her tea growing cold in her cup.

"She was a pretty girl, and this is really hard to talk about, but some rumors about Senior and Rea started floating around town. You do not know this town like I do. You were born here, and I will always be an outsider. But I have lived here for over sixty years, and people talk in this town. They have always talked about me because I speak the Queen's English. I grew up in the garment district in Edinburgh. There is nothing special about that."

Carol smiled politely.

"Regardless, the rumors got to the town council, and they reviewed the police department. Thelma was the secretary, and her son was the only other policeman. Senior was never good with the books, not like he was with people, so money was missing. Time was not accounted for, and miles were missing from his police cruiser. He would help people out of his own pocket and never ask for reimbursement. On top of that, I never trusted Thelma. She always wanted to get her boy, Robby, a promotion."

Carol looked at the cat still at her feet. She was unprepared to have her memories of a quiet little town torn apart by a woman who was always so quiet and aloof. Somehow, Carol had pulled a small stone from the dam and couldn't stop the flood.

"Mrs. Peters, it seems like wherever I go, I get a strong reaction whenever I mention Rea."

"Well, I should say so. Thelma went to Rea who was easily swayed by money and men. She got her to sign a confession that she and Senior were in love. He would pay for motel rooms, and would give her money for food, and such things. But she always had name brands. No Ross's or K-Mart for her. How did she get the money for such things? They all figured it was the police chief, and even though she later swore the confession was coerced, the mayor believed Senior's accusers."

She shook her head and took a sip of her tea before continuing.

"That is when Ralph Senior made a deal to seal the records. He resigned and avoided a grand jury. He did it for us and for her. Ralphie still does not believe it was suicide but that is another matter. I do not know what Ralphie would do if he knew what I am telling you. It would drive him to distraction. He thinks the world of his father. I am only telling you to let you know what kind of evil you are up against with this girl."

Carol took a deep breath and held back tears.

"When Ralphie told me Rea was engaged to that monster Harold Baker, I knew she was up to her old tricks again, using other people for her own selfish gain." Mrs. Peters took a sip of tea and grimaced. "Cold. Anyway, Ralphie will be home soon for lunch, to check on his mum, and to provide me with some company."

Carol sat in her chair by the window while Mrs. Peters got up to pour out her tea. Carol no longer had a desire to look through the old black and white photo albums. She no longer desired the secrets of the past. This was a history she wanted no part of. A sordid tale about a nice old town cop and an abused teenage girl.

History is written by the winners. There were no winners in this history, only losers.

Carol noticed the service plaques of both father and son lining one wall. The smiles in Carol and Ralph's prom picture were the only smiles in the room.

So sad. These men want to help, to give of themselves. They want to be loved, but one was rejected by the very community he served, and the other never married. One died alone despite being married most of his life, the other comes home to a lonely house to live with his mother.

"Carol, you're here."

"Ralph, you're home."

"I'm making your favorite—leftovers," his mother called from the kitchen.

"She thinks she knows me," he said and smiled. "What have you girls been talking about?"

"I have to leave, Ralph. You know ... Mee-Maw."

"What a good girl you still are." Mrs. Peters poked her head out of the kitchen and winked at her son.

When his mother returned to the kitchen, Ralph walked Carol out the door. "I'm sorry for her meddling. She doesn't get out much anymore."

"We had a nice talk about the old days. Have you thought any more about yesterday?"

"Oh, I almost forgot. Maybe this is nothing, and maybe I'm stretchin' things, but you know how you told me about dimes always popping up?"

"Don't tell me Baker slipped you a dime."

"Maybe he slipped you one. When I looked up the nursery rhymes he recited, I realized they make an acrostic."

"Acr—what?"

"An acrostic. You must not play word puzzles." Ralph smiled but Carol simply stared. "Hey, don't be a hater, it gets boring in that squad car at three in the morning on a twelve-hour shift. There are only so many times you can clean the air vents with a Q-tip."

Carol crossed her arms.

"Okay, okay. An acrostic is a word puzzle in which certain letters in each line form a word. Look at the titles of each of the rhymes."

Ralph handed her a copy of the four rhymes: Davy, Davy Dumpling, I am the Baker Man, Monday's Child, and Eeper Weeper Chimney Sweeper.

"Okay, what am I looking at?"

"Look at the first letter of each title."

She looked at the rhymes and then swallowed hard before leaning forward and embracing Ralphie. She could feel his name plate digging into her chest and his holstered weapon pressing her hip. When she stepped back, Ralph took Carol's face in his hands and kissed her—not long or deep, but full of meaning.

They both stepped back. Carol felt puzzled. Ralphie looked dizzy.

"I think I should go now."

"You live here, Ralph."

"Right, I mean I think I should get some water."

Carol stepped down off the porch and crossed the street while her gentleman rescuer went to get a glass of water. She looked again at the first letter of the four titles.

Davy, Davy Dumpling

I am the Baker Man

Monday's Child

Eeper Weeper Chimney Sweeper.

"D-I-M-E."

Underneath the rhymes, Ralph had written "The unconscious never sleeps."

CHAPTER 20

"Carol, you almost ran over Ed."

"Who?" Carol looked back across the street.

Mee-Maw pointed to a man delivering mail a few houses down.

"You saw that?"

"That's not all I saw. I hope you know what you're doing."

"Mee-Maw, I haven't known what I'm doing for over a year now."

Carol walked inside and to the fridge looking for leftovers while Mee-Maw stayed on the porch working on a new needlepoint for senior club.

Her cell phone rang and Carol answered. Maxx.

"I have to go back to my office. Maybe for a week if you don't need me. I can stay if you do need me."

She said go, and he promised to stay in touch through a network of emails, texts, and calls. Carol felt guilty for being relieved at this news, but the tension among Maxx, Ralph, and her would have been intolerable.

Over the next week, she settled into a routine of internet searches. When that proved too monotonous, she took trips to the local libraries to search through the archives hoping to find a trace of Rea. She decided to visit Foster, the attorney in Lemoyne, since she'd never called Carol back.

The drive took her a little more than a half hour. Businesses crowded Route 15 on one side and the river the other as she drove past the stately mansions now converted into professional offices.

When Carol entered, the attorney's secretary smiled politely, informed Ms. Foster of Carol's arrival, and then went back to her computer. Carol had watched the faux bronze clock on the wall tick past fifteen minutes when the lawyer emerged carrying too many folders. She dropped her pile on the edge of the desk, exchanged glances with her secretary, and finally turned to Carol.

Bending down on one knee in front of Carol, she said, "Ma'am, I am truly sorry for your loss."

I know where this is going.

"But the law is pretty clear on the point that unless I have a court injunction, my hands are tied."

Carol sighed as she stared at the dirty linoleum floor.

"Can you tell me anything, anything at all? My daughter is missing, surely the mother would want to help."

"I can tell you I contacted the mother, and she is aware of the situation." She turned and looked at the wall clock. "I'm sorry, but I'm due in court."

Carol's eyes filled with tears and she clenched her jaw. "Can you at least tell me where she is? North Carolina? Pennsylvania ... Rome?"

"No."

"No, you can't tell me, or no, she's not there."

"No, I can't tell you."

Ms. Foster hurried back to her office, making sure to shut the door behind her. Carol sat stunned. A minute later, the door opened, and Foster stepped out with her coat on and brief case in hand.

"Ma'am, I feel for you—I do. You're good. You're close, you looked in Rome and Pennsylvania, but you haven't looked everywhere." Foster left before she could be stopped.

The lawyer's words kept coming back to Carol as she drove back to her grandmother's. She could chew on thoughts like a cow's cud and she couldn't let this go. *So, if I'm close and I looked in Rome, and I looked in Pennsylvania ... is she saying North Carolina, or am I reading too much into it?*

On the way back, she passed the Enola train yard moving diesel engines and freight cars. *All those cars, all going somewhere and not one of them lost.* She passed the Twin Kiss and thought about how Becca always wanted sprinkles on her soft ice cream. Carol would always laugh the way Becca would say the word *jimmies*.

Back at Mee-Maw's, she returned to her computer. She tugged on a thin thread at the edge of the internet. The right thread when tugged, might unravel a tapestry of lies, deception, and ugliness. She scanned obituaries, and combed police reports looking at low-level criminals who'd made a life out of stealing produce from hucksters, jack-lighting deer for venison, and falling down drunk on the railroad bridge.

Carol had led a life ignoring the poor, the disadvantaged, and the left-behinds. Sure, she donated at her church, made Christmas boxes for third world children, and helped with the annual missionary conference, but she would also stare straight ahead at the stoplight to avoid eye contact with the old lady panhandling on the corner.

Carol really didn't know a poor person, not any full names anyway. She surely didn't know anyone who'd spent time in jail. After settling into her placid beach life, she'd isolated herself from the misery and drudgery of the real world even further. Until the real world came looking for her. Now, she couldn't ignore the world any longer.

She also wanted to ignore Ralph. Since their trip to Rockview, he'd buried himself in familiarity by pulling extra shifts. Pop Warner football was in full swing so his job as line coach occupied his evenings and days off.

Days slipped past, and time eluded her. Needing to get out just as much as needing groceries, she drove out to Mutzabaugh's. Carol dodged Ralph in the produce section, but she couldn't avoid him in the bread aisle.

"Well, this is awkward," Ralph said. "I see you're out doing your stor'n."

Carol smiled.

It had been silly to make excuses for being busy when they lived a stone's throw away from each other. They had much to talk about, but little to say, separated by shopping carts.

"How's Maxx doing?"

"He's fine."

"You still owe me that canoe trip."

"What canoe trip?"

"You don't remember?"

"Isn't it getting too cold for a canoe?"

"It will be, but we can take advantage of Indian summer. How about Thursday? It should be warm. What'd ya say?"

Carol felt stuck. It was too much to think about as shoppers sidestepped their carts blocking the aisle.

I'm married, well for the most part. Maxx has been so supportive ... well, now anyway. Ralphie has always been nothing but nice. What about that kiss? What did I promise twenty years ago, and what is Indian summer?

"Look, Carol, the statute of limitations ran out a long time ago on that promise. It's fine if you don't want to go."

She shook her head. "Oh, no, I want to go."

"Great, come on over at seven." Ralph smiled.

Carol balanced sandwiches, brownies, and sun tea as she crossed the street. Ralph ran out to help when he saw her about to drop the old Coleman cooler and their hands touched.

"Such a gentleman," Carol said as they loaded up the old pickup. An aluminum canoe hung out the end of the bed. The Ford was his father's, and Ralph drove it only for certain trips—like to the Pub or to the hardware store to buy a bag of nails.

"I like driving Pap's truck to the diner on my days off—reminds me of better times."

Ralph followed Carol who drove her car to a parking lot in town across from the water's edge. Then she climbed into the Ford and sat next to Ralph's springer spaniel.

Carol had never been much of a dog lover, but Belle's big black eyes and long silky ears won her over as the pup licked her face and rested her head on her lap.

When they reached the edge of the Juniata, northwest of town, Belle sniffed through the weeds while Carol helped Ralph unlash the canoe and carry it down to the river's edge underneath the train overpass. Ralph steered with his oar at the stern, Carol paddled up front, and Belle sat in the middle, between fishing gear and the cooler. They floated down the river back toward Duncannon where they would take Carol's car back to the truck.

The warm sun shone directly overhead as Ralph directed the canoe toward the beach at his family's picnic lot. Carol remembered when their families would picnic together next to the river on the Fourth of July. The men would play horseshoes, the women would talk, and the kids would fish, throw rocks, and play tag. Everyone would eat, and everyone left happy.

Carol and Ralph used to sit in the middle of the canoe like Belle while Mr. Peters paddled. She hadn't remembered that tidbit until Mrs. Peters had showed her some pictures of her in a pair of shorts, a bikini top, an old orange life jacket, and a fishing pole. She wondered what else she'd forgotten and how much she'd lost of herself.

Today, the water rippled by the gunwales, and the paddles pushed through the current, bringing back a piece of her with each swirl from every stroke. The shallow Juniata flowed swift from the recent rains. Rocks dotted the waterscape and branches overhung the river's edge. They found a still spot and Ralph steadied the craft as Carol recalled how to cast. Belle propped her head on the center thwart.

"Okay, Ralphie, what promise?"

"When I took you home after the prom, I wanted to kiss you in the worst way, but I really didn't know how."

"What do you mean you didn't know how?"

"Carol, you were my first date. When I tried for a kiss, you acted like you didn't know what I was doing and stepped away. So, I said, 'How about going on a canoe ride,' and you said, 'Right now?' and I said, 'No, next Saturday,' and you said, 'Okay,' and I said, 'Promise?' and you promised."

"And you never forgot."

"Well, it was a promise. Later you said you were busy or something, but still a promise is a promise. Then you went to college."

"I'm so sorry. I'm different now. I'm glad you never forgot."

They drifted in the current for a spell and Ralph used his paddle as a rudder to miss the rocks.

"You know, Officer, I don't have my fishing license."

"I might have to issue you a citation." Ralph winked at her.

"It isn't really fishing, is it, if you don't catch anything? It's more like taking your fishing pole for a walk, right?"

"That sounds like something your dad would have told my dad."

Carol nodded. "Daddy had a 'live and let live' attitude when it came to fishing."

"Well, my pap had a 'by the book' attitude when it came to everything."

Just then, Carol's pole bent to the water and Belle's head perked up.

"I got a fish! I got a fish! What do I do, what do I do?" Her eyes never left the pole.

Ralph reached out to help. "Set the hook, set the hook."

Carol jerked the line.

"Careful, you don't want to launch him over the canoe. Just relax, relax. What is it you say ... breathe? Just breathe."

She pulled her pole back gently and reeled in her line. After a few turns of the reel, she stopped and lowered the pole to let the fish take up some line. The task seemed to take forever, but, in less than a minute, she saw a beautiful bass jump in the air in one last attempt to loosen her grip.

Ralphie scooped up the smallmouth bass with his worn net.

Carol admired how the fish shone in the sun. "He's so pretty."

"He'll taste even better."

"I want to let him go."

"Let him go? He weighs over four pounds, Carol."

"Ralphie, let him go."

Ralph sighed and then took out the hook that was caught in the fish's upper lip.

Then, he held the fish out to Carol. "I'm not letting him go until you kiss him."

Carol squirmed and shook her head, but Ralph persisted. "First fish always gets kissed—it's for luck."

Finally, she shut her eyes and leaned forward while Ralph held up the bass. Ralph and Carol looked at each other for an extra second when she opened her eyes.

The fish squirmed and fell into the canoe. Belle alerted and began barking and snapping at the fish, causing the boat to shake. Ralph bent forward on his knees and scooped the fish back into his watery home.

Belle jumped in after him.

When she did, the boat tipped to one side and Ralph, who had just stood up to take his seat again, went overboard too.

He came up with some type of vegetation covering his face. Carol was laughing so hard she didn't notice Ralph taking hold of the gunwale, causing her to fall in next to him. She came up coughing but ended up laughing and holding on to Ralph who pushed on her until she rolled back into the boat.

Carol sat to one side while Ralph pulled himself in. He may have been overweight, but he knew how to take care of himself on the water. They pulled Belle back in too, and then sat back, exhausted. Belle shook out the wet and then sat panting.

They were close now to the river lot and Ralph widened his stroke, then backpaddled to bring his craft to a stop among the weeds. He gathered their lunch while Carol and Belle walked through the soggy river edge and up the shallow bank.

The lot was overgrown, but the horseshoe pit and the brick barbeque pit remained. The crooked chimney, now cracked, supported the rusted through grill.

"Oh, look at the old outhouse." She pointed. "Hey, remember the time we locked you in it?"

"Carol, I don't forget anything."

Ralph propped up the old picnic table with a couple of river rocks and logs. Then, they both stripped to their bathing suits and Carol put their wet clothes across a sunbaked rock to dry. Then, she broke out a tablecloth.

"Well, that's like putting lipstick on a pig," Ralph said.

Carol gave him a look and unpacked the sandwiches and sun tea. She saw Ralph's eyes get big when she uncovered the brownies. She remembered that look from a long time ago.

After lunch, Ralph and Belle waded out into the water while Carol spread her towel on the narrow beach to catch some rays.

I forgot Perry County had a beach.

With the chocolate brownie in her stomach, the warm sun and cool breeze took Carol away to a blissful rest. After a while, she felt something wet on her face.

Belle.

She pushed the dog away and said, "How long was I out?"

Ralph was lying next to her. "Long enough to snore."

"No."

"Okay, if you say so, but we need to get going. We could come back here."

"I'd like that."

They edged the canoe back into the Juniata.

The day had grown dark by the time they pulled the canoe out of the river. Ralph chained it to a signpost that also supported a metal trash can. After slowly driving back to Ralph's house in Carol's car, Belle slept in the back seat as they rinsed off the gear.

"I'll get the truck tomorrow and I'll clean your car out," Ralph said.

"I had fun, Ralphie. This was ... special."

Ralph nodded and then looked down at his feet. "Well, I should check on Mum."

Before he could turn away, Carol reached out and pulled him into a hug. They held on to each other for a long moment—she didn't know how long.

Ralph headed back across the street and up the steps to his house. Carol sat down next to her grandmother on the porch swing and rested her head in her lap. Mee-Maw stroked her hair for a few moments before Carol stood up and turned toward the house.

"Maxx called."

Carol stopped and remained silent. *I didn't do anything, but why do I feel guilty?* "What did he have to say?"

"He wondered why you haven't called."

"I didn't have any news. I figured he knew that. I guess I should have told him about the lawyer. He's right, I should have called. Was he mad?"

Mee-Maw pushed the swing into motion once with her foot. "No, he wasn't mad."

"Then what?"

"I think he sounded worried. I never heard him like that before. He's always so confident, so upbeat. I got the sense he's feeling helpless."

"That's a switch." She tried to think of something else. "Did the paper come?"

"On the table."

Carol picked up the paper and noticed an amber alert listing a missing girl. They had printed only a silhouette of a girl's profile, but the description fit Becca—light blue eyes, light brown hair, and seven years old. The girl's name was listed as Shelby Myers. She'd disappeared from her foster parents the day before.

"It's been on the news all day," Mee-Maw said, stepping up beside her. "They think the girl's dad took her because he's mad at the mother for keeping him from her. They say he's been in and out of jail for drug-related charges and disobeying his restraining order."

"There's no picture."

"I know, but I still can't help but think about our Becca. I'm sure you do too."

"It's all I think about, Mee-Maw. Everything reminds me of Becca. Even the dandelions."

"Even the jasmine?"

"Especially the jasmine."

Ralph knocked on the porch screen and then entered. "I see you got the paper," he said. "I made a call into the Harrisburg station. There's a lot of coincidences. They don't have her picture but the description, her age ... it sorta sounds like Becca."

"It could be just a coincidence."

"I know but they didn't report everything on the news. The police report said she was carrying a stuffed turtle. Wasn't Becca holding a stuffed animal in the picture you got of her in Rome? And wasn't it a turtle?"

"She calls him Tutt because she couldn't pronounce turtle." Carol looked into his eyes. "What do we do?"

"We don't do anything. We wait. That's what police work is—one month of waiting, one minute of excitement."

"I've had one year of waiting. I'm not waiting anymore."

"I'll call again."

Carol and Mee-Maw waited while Ralph talked back and forth with another investigator.

When he finished the call, he turned to them and said, "All I know is two DSS investigators were driving out to the foster home to follow up on an earlier complaint. They told me I'd get an update the moment they had more news."

"We have to wait, honey. Cooking and life, it's all about the wait." Mee-Maw turned to start making dinner.

Tension meant food, and a lot of tension meant a lot of food. Mee-Maw pulled out a large heavy pot from a cabinet and started boiling water. Carol peeled potatoes and Ralph pulled the ham from the bone.

"Good thing I cooked the ham hocks yesterday." Mee-Maw broke out two jars of home-canned green beans and waited for the ham and potatoes to simmer together before adding the beans.

"It's the wait that's the hardest," Carol said.

"It's the wait that makes it the best."

"It's the wait that makes me hungry," Ralph said.

Mee-Maw and Carol smiled at each other.

After about thirty minutes, Mee-Maw pulled off the lid to the pot and took a sniff. "This will taste even better tomorrow, but I say it's ready now."

Ralph said grace, asking the Lord for a sign, for some reason to hope, and some peace for Carol. After they'd said "Amen," Ralph tried to scoop up some ham and beans with a piece of bread, but the bread fell apart, and he dripped green bean juice down his shirt.

"Peters, who taught you to eat green beans and ham?" Carol smirked as Ralph used his napkin to wipe up the mess.

"Nobody."

"Well, it shows. Look here, take a piece of bread."

"White or wheat?"

"It's all wheat, how 'bout it, Mee-Maw?"

"You *are* from Perry County." Mee-Maw laughed.

"Look, this is how Daddy taught me. Take your bread and butter it good."

"With margarine."

"Don't make me mad—margarine nothing. Now put in some ham and some green beans, and just a skosh of potato and real butter, and fold it over. Now you can dip it into your juice."

Ralph worked his bread and figured it out with his next try.

"That's it, Peters," Carol teased. "Aren't you from Perry County?"

"Carol, you're scaring the boy."

They ate until Ralph's phone broke the silence. He pushed back from the table and stood to answer.

"Send it ... uh-huh ... Okay ... Okay. Chief, can I go? Got it ... uh-huh, you won't, I promise. Out here."

After he'd hung up, Ralph sat back at the table, buttered his bread, and folded in more ham and green beans.

Mee-Maw pushed at his hand. "Ralphie, not now. What was that all about?"

He sighed and put down his bread. "Okay, here's the deal. They went out to the foster home, and they think they know where the father is. He called from a cell phone, and they pinged it to a motel along Route 22."

Carol pushed back her chair. "Let's go."

Ralph reached out for her arm. "Not so fast. It's out of my catchment, but the shift supervisor said I could go to be a secondary. In other words, I just watch and do anything they need."

"What do I do?"

"You wait."

Carol shook her head. "I'm going."

"Not this time. Sometimes these domestic things get touchy."

"Will you be in danger?"

"No way. I'll be in the background where no one ever gets hurt."

Carol and Mee-Maw walked Ralph to his car. Mee-Maw handed him a Tupperware. "I packed you some dessert."

Mrs. Peters joined them in the driveway as Ralph backed out the drive and down the road. Together, they waved goodbye.

Carol walked back into the house, went to the living room, and picked up a cross stitch her Mee-Maw had given her. She'd never had time for crafts before. There had always been something more immediate.

When Becca was taken, Carol did nothing for a long time. She didn't read, work out, eat, or sleep. She couldn't. Now, it surprised her to see her fingers working feverishly, and her mind focused on the needle and colored thread.

She had no words for the emotion her new craft evoked. *I guess its satisfaction, but it's just hard to think that about a little piece of material and thread. Maybe I'm still learning what's really important and not just immediate.*

When her eyes tired, she set the piece into her lap and dimmed the light.

"Carol, are you going to bed?" her grandmother called from the other room.

"In a little."

Carol kept watch out the window, the street illuminated by the light near Ralph's house. She saw the light in

Ralph's mother's room go off. Her own room had grown dark, illuminated only by the light of her cell phone. She checked and rechecked it to see if she'd received a text or somehow missed a voicemail message. Hours ticked by as the other houses along the street darkened. She waited for a phone call and tried not to think about it, but imagined hearing Ralph's voice, "Carol, it's Ralph, we have her, we have her."

Stop it, Carol. Don't get excited. It'll hurt too much. Just wait.

And that's what she did. She waited.

CHAPTER 21

His patrol cruiser moved along the narrow Duncannon streets with purpose. Speeding with his blue lights circulating overhead and his grill lights pulsating would have been easy, but driving controlled was fast and smooth. Quiet, with no siren needed, he hit the ramp for US Route 15 and drove down through Marysville and Perdix before crossing the river on the I-81 bridge into Harrisburg.

His thoughts remained on Carol and his hopes on bringing back her Becca.

By now, he had seen Becca's picture in hundreds of photos. He'd watched video clips, looked at drawings, and knew her likes and dislikes. He even knew she liked catsup on her hotdogs, loved all animals, and that her favorite color was hot pink—no other pink would do. She preferred water to soda, except for Sprite, French fries with lots of salt and more catsup, and preferred shows about animals to cartoons.

The road was well-lit until he took a series of exits onto US Route 22. His speedometer crept toward the top and around the other side of the dial as the urgency built within him. Ralph had never driven this fast, not in training or in pursuit. In his sedentary career, he'd mostly dealt with noncompliant motorists. Because he homesteaded in Duncannon, his career path had kept him away from the more dangerous aspects of police work. Special units of the state police dealt more with the hardened criminal element.

Still, Ralph had raised his hand and was willing to do whatever it took and go wherever to do the job he was sworn to do. After seventeen years, he still felt like an optimist who believed he was making a difference simply by putting on his uniform every day.

After radioing his position to the Harrisburg dispatch, he received further instruction on how to approach the Twilight Motel. Other Harrisburg units had the advantage of seeing a layout of the motel and surrounding grounds in their pre-ops brief, but Ralph was an outsider, a straphanger along for the ride.

He was there officially to observe but, unofficially, saw himself walking through the sticky storm door on Church Street with Becca in his arms and Carol rushing to greet him.

Okay, Ralph, don't get ahead of yourself.

He looked down at the speedometer and pumped the brakes too hard causing a short skid and a loud squeal.

Sheesh, I hope none of the boys heard me.

The dispatcher had told him to come in quiet. Domestic situations were always tense, and a show of force could make a tense situation worse. He drifted his car to the edge of the parking lot that bordered the highway. There was a ten-yard grass median that looked passable, but recent rains had made it soggy.

He could see the long dogleg-shaped motel with a lit office at the bend through his windshield. Most of the motel lighting was out but distant highway lights reflected off his trunk. Two unmarked cars were parked on either side of room 121. From the radio chatter, he knew two more cars sat at the rear of the motel. A command vehicle parked at the office.

Whenever he was anxious, he always cinched his vest too tight, and now the Kevlar pinched the rolls around his waist. He reached each side to loosen its grip on his torso and then sighed as he welcomed the space to breath once more. He eyed the sealed Tupperware on the seat next to him. After popping the lid, he grabbed the top two brownies.

The ops commander, a grizzled sergeant, made radio checks, but didn't mention Ralph's number. After everyone reported, Ralph hesitated, then pushed his call button. "Car 104—check."

"Who?" came the reply.

"Car 104, sir."

"That's Peters, Sarge, from Perry County."

"Right, 104, just stay out of the way. This'll be over before you know it. Sit back, watch, and learn how we do things in the big city."

Ralph was used to getting ribbed whenever he went for in-service training in Harrisburg. The troopers there acted superior because they dealt with the crime rolling into the city but mostly because they were closer to the flagpole. Somehow escorting the governor and dealing with state representatives boosted their ego. But Ralph and troopers at his station knew how to deal with people—to deescalate a confrontation with their disarming country ways. Ralph's charm was something you couldn't learn in training—it was bred into him and honed in the field.

"Unit 2, you're primary as discussed," the sergeant called over the radio. "Unit 12, you're back up. Be advised units three and six are in the rear, be mindful of your sight patterns."

Ralph swallowed when he realized each car, except his own, held two officers.

That's a lotta firepower for a domestic.

He sat out of the fire zone and, in all his years, had never been involved in an op that went hot. He checked his computer for the pre-op brief. Mug shot photos of the subject in question popped up on his screen. Justice Laredo had a rap sheet that spilled onto a second screen.

"Justice, that's ironic. Looks like Justice Laredo is in the drug business. Spent time in Camp Hill prison, even was in Super Max at SCI Greene after beating another prisoner into a coma." Talking to himself helped Ralph remember facts. "Held up a string of 7-Elevens and Turkey Hill convenience stores and shot a clerk who was handicapped. Nice guy. What's this? Former Army Spec

Ops. That could be a sharpshooter or a backhoe driver rebuilding Afghanistan. Psych discharge for antisocial personality … wonderful. Who knows what this guy will do if cornered?"

His conversation with himself was interrupted by more radio chatter.

"Lights on in room 121. Unit 2, send one man to see if you can see anything through the window—your partner plays back up."

Ralph watched as one trooper crept below the window while a second crouched behind their unmarked car. Ralph leaned to the middle to get a better view. The Tupperware lid started to slide to the floor and when Ralph lurched to grab it, he brushed his yellow hazard lights and turned them on for a hot second.

"What's that?" The commander screamed into the radio, "Turn that off. *Now.*"

The door of the hotel room opened revealing a silhouette in the darkened doorway looking in Ralph's direction. The officer below the window froze, while the other ducked behind his car. Ralph didn't move. He barely breathed. The silhouette turned and went back inside.

"Perry County, was that you?"

"Sir, yes, sir."

"Don't give me none of that sir crap. Just shut up and don't move."

"Yes—"

"I didn't see much, Sarge," the officer from Unit 2 responded. "Maybe a child lying on the second bed watching cartoons, and something lying on the bed closest to the door—possible multiple handguns, maybe a shotgun, a few boxes of ammo, I think, and a bag. Oh, and one suspect standing in the doorway breathing down my neck, stinking of liquor."

"Roger that."

Ralph sat back against his seat and sighed. *Who do you think you are anyway? Super Trooper? This is the big leagues, you idiot. Get it together.*

He could hear his academy trainer yelling in his ear.

He thought about Carol at home, swinging on the porch, waiting, and longed to be with her.

His radio crackled again.

"Sarge, there is no way we can storm the room without the hostage getting hurt."

"Right. Let's do this one by the book, like we discussed. Unit 2, negotiator, go in five. Acknowledge."

One by one—except for Ralph—the units checked in. He didn't move, and the commander didn't ask him to report. He wanted to be forgotten, but it hurt more because he was. He wanted to start up his car and turn around, but he knew he wouldn't even if he could. He sat there in the dark, on the end of the bench, and out of his league. He tried to tell himself he was lucky to be there, that he was one of the finest, but it felt like he was locked in the outhouse at the river lot. He wanted to punch the dashboard but was afraid he would set off the siren.

Five minutes ticked slowly by. On cue, Unit 2 moved to either side of the door while Unit 12 moved to the rear fender of each car, their doors remained open for cover. Ralph imagined the trooper from Unit 3 in the rear standing on a milk crate to look through a small window in the bathroom while his partner watched from the car. He could see the other unit who had stayed in their vehicle with the motor running.

The negotiator knocked three times on the door. Ralph could hear his next words through the officer's body cam, which directly fed to the units.

"Mr. Laredo, this is Truet Meinke. I'm from the State Social Worker division and I'd like to talk to you."

"I got nothing to say to you, you got the wrong room, go away."

"Now look, sir, can you open the door, just a crack, so we can talk? You can keep it chained."

"I can't do that, you'll break in."

"Sir, I'm a social worker, we don't do that. If we wanted to break in, we already would have done it."

"Who else is with you?"

The negotiator had already made a mistake by lying to him and by saying "we."

"My partner. We never travel alone at night, sir, you understand, I'm sure."

"Oh, I understand more than you know. This isn't my first rodeo. You sound like a cop."

"Look, I'm going to call your room, so I don't have to shout through this door. I'd like you to pick up the phone."

Ralph figured Meinke was trying to get some compliance from Laredo by getting him to answer the phone. Any movement would be seen as a step toward a peaceful outcome.

Ralph could hear over the patched-in radio channel as the negotiator called Laredo.

"Yeah?"

"This is Truet, Mr. Laredo. I'm really concerned about your little girl."

"I'd never hurt my girl."

"If you put her on, then I will know for sure."

Laredo agreed.

Smart, he never asks a question but gives him a choice. This negotiator is good. This is working like textbook. I'll be home for the eleven o'clock news. And the good news is, no one I know will be on it.

A little girl's voice sounded through the phone and sent a chill up Ralph's spine.

"Honey, listen to me, my name is Truet, you're going to be okay, we are going to get you home."

Laredo got back on the phone and the talking continued for the next hour. Ralph knew that as long as the suspect talked, the negotiation had a chance of working, and everyone would get to go home in one piece.

During a break, the ops commander came over the radio.

"I don't like this. Look, I gave it a chance, meet me at the motel office."

Ralph could see the negotiator and the commander in the window. He could see the commander's arms flailing as he walked about the room. The negotiator never moved.

This can't be good. He was certain they were in the midst of a heated argument. Eventually, the officers from Unit 2 went back to their car and the commander got on the radio.

"Look, Laredo is drinking—a lot." Ralph could see Laredo's shadow in the hotel room, waiving what looked like a firearm and a whiskey bottle. "This guy is getting more irrational," the commander added.

"Sarge, this guy is a chronic alcoholic, he can hold more liquor than a small brewery," the negotiator from Unit 2 responded.

"Not now, two! Meet me at the room," the commander retorted.

The commander creeped up to the edge of the door. Unit 2 didn't have time to assume a tactical position and ended up behind the commander.

"Look, Laredo if you don't send the girl out, we're coming in."

The negotiator shook his head.

"This can't be good," Ralph said under his breath.

"Okay, Okay," Laredo shouted through the door. "Just give me a minute and you can get her. She's sleeping. I didn't mean nothing by it, honest. I just wanted to see my little girl."

The commander lowered his weapon. As Laredo stepped into the doorframe, Ralph noticed he'd turned off his room lights. Suddenly, the commander was yanked inside the motel room and the door slammed shut. Pandemonium overtook the radio as the units started talking over each other.

With the door locked, the lights out, two hostages now inside, and no one in charge, it wasn't clear to Ralph what would happen next. On the radio, the negotiation team argued with the backup team. The chatter stopped as they saw the door reopening.

The commander shuffled outside with duct tape across his mouth and around his hands and feet. Ralph noticed a dark stain dripping down the front of his face. A sawed-off shotgun was duct-taped to his neck, with Laredo holding the other end. A little girl hugged Laredo's pant leg.

The other officers drew their weapons.

Laredo didn't give them another moment. He pulled the trigger on the shotgun, blowing through the sergeant's neck and paralyzing the team of seasoned veterans. Then, he opened fire at the four officers who stood at the back of their cars.

Laredo shoved the little girl into the unmarked police car and jumped in. He jammed it into reverse, running over one of the officers while the other three ducked and rolled. They shot at the car's tires. Laredo spun the car around in the narrow lot and careened toward US Route 22—right at Ralph.

Ralph pulled on his gear shift and mashed the gas pedal. He cut off the exit, causing Laredo to crash into the front of his cruiser, turning it across the grassy median. Laredo's tires sunk into the soggy grass spinning and spitting mud. The flattened tire spun off its rim. Units three and six from behind the motel came from both ends of the highway, blocking any chance of escape.

Laredo rolled out of his car which was now flanked by a squad car on the passenger side and Ralph's car on the driver's side.

Laredo sprayed them with three-blast intervals from a semi-automatic weapon then reached for a nine-millimeter pistol. Despite the normally deafening noise, Ralph only heard the tinkling of spent rounds hitting the curb, asphalt, and cars. Seconds were hours, minutes lasted forever.

"Cease fire, cease fire!" someone yelled, and silence finally forced its way onto the pandemonium. The escape car windows had been shattered. Bullet holes riddled the sheet metal. It seemed that nothing escaped destruction—the telephone pole, the cars, even the motel had taken damage, pocked with bullet holes.

"Where's the girl? Find the girl," the negotiator yelled.

The forensics unit worked until dawn picking up fragments of hair, skull, and teeth. Both the sergeant and Laredo were unrecognizable. The officer that Laredo backed over was transferred to the hospital with a compound fracture.

The little girl was found lying on the floor underneath the dashboard on the passenger side. Her forehead bruised, shards of glass in her hair, and she had a cut on her cheek, but she had remained untouched by the hail of gunfire. EMTs wheeled her into the emergency room with a stuffed frog by her side. No turtle named "Tutt" was ever recovered. Her arm was thought to be broken but x-rays ruled that out. Becca was also ruled out as her name, and she returned to her foster parents in Lemoyne.

Carol moved her watch to her grandma's porch on Church Street. She had long stopped swinging. She thumbed through the internet but had no interest in a koala bear stuck in a tree, the latest Oprah sighting, or the NBA season. She certainly didn't want to hear about a celebrity break up, and news from North Korea only made her feel worse.

She saw the light come on across the street and then saw Mrs. Peters walking toward her.

"Did you hear something?" Carol asked.

"No, I thought maybe he would call you first. I saw you out here and figured I would keep you company."

The two women sat together and soon Mee-Maw brought out a pot of coffee and a box of Ritz crackers.

"I couldn't sleep either."

Before long, a few lights came on in other houses as neighbors got ready to go to work.

The still morning made it easy to hear the patrol car turn the corner at the end of the street. The women even heard the police radio as they noticed the darkened lights on the car's roof.

"Oh, it's Ralph, it's Ralph." Carol jumped up from the swing.

Mrs. Peters looked at Mee-Maw. Neither moved.

As the car moved in front of the house, Carol ran out to stop it. The patrolman lowered his window.

Carol backed up as the stranger got out of his car.

"No, no, no." She sank to the lawn. Mrs. Peters and Mee-Maw went to her side.

"Ma'am, I regret to ..." he started. Then, "Ma'am, I am so sorry for your loss." The patrolman's flat brimmed hat and chin strap could not cover his tears. "I am so very sorry. Ralph was a good trooper."

Mrs. Peters had lost her husband, and now, she had lost her son. Some thought it odd they never saw her cry. Some said she was cold, but others who knew the hurt of a mother put an end to such gossip.

Maxx flew back for the funeral, which was too large for the Lutheran church in town, so it was held at the cathedral in Harrisburg. Carol thought Ralph would have liked the horse-drawn wagon, but she shrieked when they gave him a gun salute.

She held onto Maxx as they walked through the procession. He stood by her side and brought her a chair when he thought she needed to rest. He brought her a drink when he thought she should take in fluids and kept others from harping over her. And when Carol's mother showed up, he stepped between them, but Carol pushed him aside and held on to her mother like she was seven again.

One of the troopers had found Ralph slumped over his wheel. An errant round had entered his loosened Kevlar vest and nicked his aorta. Ballistics confirmed he'd been hit by a stray bullet from one of the troopers.

But Ralph's actions had stopped Laredo's escape.

After the funeral, the procession, the gun salute, the burial, after the flowers were taken away, and the cars driven home, after everything was put away ... three ladies stood alone holding on to each other.

"Mee-Maw," Carol said, pushing away from the tight hold, "I'm going home ... to the farm."

CHAPTER 22

Carol entered through the back door and made her way through the darkened house to the center hallway. She didn't stop to notice the odd spindle and didn't step over the squeaky stair tread.

Her mother met her at the top of the stairs in her robe. "I have your room ready for you. I didn't have time to dust, but there's a towel and a washcloth on the end of the bed. Just let me know if you need anything."

"I'm sure everything I need is here. Mother?"

"What is it, dear?"

"We need to talk."

"Of course, of course. Get some rest now, though."

Carol nodded and headed to her room. Nothing had changed since she first arrived except now there were three paint color cards taped to the pink walls. She didn't like seeing them, so she turned off the light and sank to the bottom of her overstuffed queen bed.

Carol hadn't realized how fond she'd grown of Ralph. He amused her, but she had taken him for granted. He had just been simply Ralphie, the kid who lived near Mee-Maw and who was always in the way. Twenty years later, he'd still been here for her. Now, he'd been in the way of a misplaced bullet.

Her stomach turned. *How could I have been so shallow? Why hadn't I seen how wonderful he was? Why hadn't I appreciated his commitment to life and to everyone around him?* She hated herself for not having that same commitment, that same love.

I'm the reason Joey rode his motorcycle that day, and I'm the reason Ralphie had been sitting alone at a dank motel along the highway.

She opened her bedroom closet door and shuffled though a stack of winter coats. She found all her bridesmaids' dresses and most of her prom dresses, but she took down the pink one, the one she wore when Ralph had picked her up the night of her prom. She remembered sitting on the edge of her bed for the longest time, not wanting to go downstairs until her mother threatened to get out her spaghetti strainer to smack her.

"That boy's been down there for an hour and a half waiting for you," she remembered her mother saying before Carol bounded down the stairs with a forced smile on her face.

Carol zipped open the dry cleaner's plastic bag and laid the dress on the bed. She felt the smooth pleats and ran her fingers across the ruffled embroidery, hand stitched by Mee-Maw. Carol laid down on the bed next to her dress and smelled the material. Tears flowed as she turned her head into her pillow—they wouldn't be denied.

A knock at her door startled her. She looked up to see Maxx leaning against the door jamb.

"Maxx, what are you doing here?"

"You called me, remember? You said you had some stuff for Goodwill when I told you I was making a run."

"Oh, right."

She pointed to several boxes in the corner that held clothes dating back to high school.

"I can't believe she kept this stuff." Carol handed him a box.

"Isn't it yours?"

She smiled. "Okay, you have a point."

They carried the boxes down and loaded them into the back of Maxx's SUV. Carol got in the front seat, and Maxx looked at her and started the car.

"I'm dead." She could feel Maxx's stare. She knew him well enough to know he didn't know what to say. *I guess he wants me to change the subject.*

"Whoa, what do mean dead?" His response startled her.

"Everyone around me dies, at least everyone I care about. I tried to stop caring ... about Dad, Joey, Ralph, even friends I had growing up."

"It's not your fault, Car."

"I know that. It's not that. There's this emptiness inside of me. I got nothing left."

As Maxx drove, Carol noticed the river receding due to the lack of rain and saw a dusty '76 Corvette sitting under someone's carport.

"Something's still there, otherwise I wouldn't be here, and you wouldn't be looking for Becca." Carol fidgeted with her phone but mostly stared out the window. "I don't know. There's this hole where all those people used to be, I can't get them out of my mind, and really I don't want to."

"You're ruminating again—like a cow chewing its cud."

"It's killing me. Just when I think I'm getting somewhere."

After they'd dropped off the clothes, Maxx began the trek back to the farm.

"On the trail, I learned this one thing—just walk."

"Just walk, that's it?"

"Pretty much, and one more thing. I realized in the rain no one was going to pick me up. At the shelter, no one was going to put me to bed. I had to just ... just walk."

Carol turned and saw tears forming in her husband's eyes. "Maxx, you said you learned one more thing."

"Yeah, yeah, I did. Every once and a while something inexplicable would happen. I'd get to a shelter and someone would give me a meal, sometimes the very thing I was thinking about for the last ten miles. One time, I lost a small piece of gear and someone handed me exactly what I needed at the next campsite. Thing is, when everything I needed was on my back and my only concern was the next trail marker, God's world opened up to me."

"That's beautiful. I want that for me."

"Keep walking, keep looking and asking, Car. Just like Becca, God knows where you are too."

They drove in silence along the highway that cut a path between the mountains and the river below. The sun shone bright, the sky was blue, and the clouds were exceptional.

"I think I've created a bit of competition between your grandmother and Mrs. Peters. I'm not sure which one is trying to fatten me up the most." He smiled at Carol, but she didn't reply. "The older generation here seem to have their own society, right in the middle of everything. They have their own values, hierarchy, you know, from who has their own teeth to who lives in a nursing home. They even have their own secret clubs. I think those senior clubs aren't as innocent as they appear. I think they're a front for the mob."

"Maxx, you're nuts."

"A little. I'm just glad to see you feel me."

"Oh, yeah, I *feel* you all right. Is that what you kids are saying these days?"

He smiled again. "It's getting late, what do you say we stop at the Ranch House?"

"No."

"Not hungry?"

She shrugged. "It's not that."

"I get it. How about the Red Rabbit, you always liked that."

Carol didn't say anything, so Maxx crossed the highway and pulled into the old-fashioned drive-in restaurant. Dusty spiderwebs connected metal posts to the tar paper roof. Stucco walls once white were bronzed with mud and car exhaust. Gone were the roller skates and bow ties but the carhops still served Bunny Burgers and French fries with extra Bunny Dust. Carol liked their vanilla shakes.

When their order came, Carol dug in, and Maxx laughed as she tried to talk with a mouth full of fries. She smiled and swallowed hard when Maxx reached over to wipe some catsup off her cheek.

He crumpled up the napkin but never took his eyes off hers. "So ... how you doing?"

Carol shook her head and watched a carhop serving another car. People had asked her that same question for the last two weeks, but she still didn't know the answer.

"I feel dead."

"What do you mean?"

"Dead. Empty. That's the best I can come up with. I'm empty."

"I know he was special to you."

"He *is* special." She pointed a fry at Maxx before shoving it in her mouth.

"I want to be there for you, Carol. I think you're special too."

"Maxx, I don't know what I want. I didn't know who Ralph was, not until he died. I only knew what he could do for me. I think that's how I've seen people for most of my life. Maybe since Joey died. I don't know if I married you for you, or if I married you for what you could do for me."

Carol crumbled up her napkin and took a deep breath.

"We built a life away from here, a beach life. Did you know Perry County has a beach? I don't even know if I want a beach anymore, and I don't know what love is. You're nice, and I'm married to you, but I've been so self-absorbed all this time. I don't know if I wanted a child for me or for her." Carol shook her head. "I hate myself for thinking this way."

"I guess we've both been pretty selfish," he admitted.

Maxx flashed his lights and the carhop came by and collected the tray that hung on the driver's side window. "Anything else?"

"How much for a dish of wisdom?" Maxx asked her.

The girl cocked her head, and he waved her off.

Maxx drove them back to Duncannon, through town, and back out to the farm. At the house, he turned off the car's lights but kept the motor running.

Carol shifted in the seat making the leather squeak. "Maxx, I need you. I just don't know if I want you."

"Man, that hurts, but I think you need more than just me."

"The only thing I know is I need my daughter back. Nothing else matters—nothing."

"That, I get. I feel you." He smiled at her and she smiled back.

"Come on out tomorrow. They're loading a truck with hay. I gotta go in before Mother comes out with her shotgun."

The next day, Mee-Maw roused Maxx early, made him eat a large breakfast, and gave him a jug filled with ice water. Before he left, she made him put on a pair of jeans and boots. She even made sure he had a good pair of socks and gave him a bandana to blow the chaff out of his nose. As he was pulling out of the drive, she hurried down to his car to give him a farmer's ball cap with a Dekalb Corn logo.

"There, now you look like a farmer, all but the tan, and you won't get hay stuck in your ankles or in your hair product."

The truck was already at the farm when Maxx pulled in, and the tractor trailer looked big enough to carry away half the barn. Maxx climbed up the haymow, and Carol followed behind him as the driver and his helper worked the step-down flatbed trailer. Maxx and Carol rolled forty-pound hay bales twenty feet below to the bed of the trailer, and the helper tossed them to the driver who stacked them. Maxx threw several bales that hit the side of the trailer and broke the strings, causing hay to fly everywhere.

"Look at each bale like it's a two-dollar bill. Every broken bale is money left on the floor that can't be picked up," Carol told him.

"Got it," he said, between gulps of cool water from his thermos jug. "What's a two-dollar bill look like?"

Carol knew how to step on the bales without falling through the cracks. Maxx learned. Carol knew not to get too close to the side or the haymow could collapse. Maxx learned that too, when he stepped on the wrong spot and hay bales tumbled to the floor, and he tumbled on top of them.

"Where did you get this one?" the driver yelled, pointing at Maxx.

Carol smiled.

Maxx climbed back up the haymow while the driver repositioned his truck and trailer. Carol hooked her foot on the strings of a hay bale and reached to help him with the final two rows. The helper smiled when he saw her saving Maxx from another fall while the driver tied each layer of hay together on his trailer.

Maxx's breakfast began to wear off as they worked through most of the morning, but no one else looked like they were ready to stop, so he kept dropping bales of hay on the trailer. He worried how he was going to throw forty-pound bales of hay ten feet into the air for the final four rows. But then they rolled the hay elevator into place, and Maxx felt a sense of relief. His relief only lasted a second as a black snake fell out of the top of elevator, almost hitting him.

They began dropping the hay next to the elevator, and the helper loaded the bale which was then conveyed up to the driver who walked it on top of his trailer to the other end. When they loaded the elevator too fast, the driver started cursing, and when they loaded too slow, he just stood on top and glared with his hands on his hips.

When they'd finished, the driver wrenched down the load with cable, chain, and come-along. Then the four sat against the trailer's wheels below the eight hundred bales of hay.

"How it's stacked determines if the load will stay together or get blown apart going sixty miles per hour down the interstate," Carol told Maxx.

"My wife and I used to load these ourselves before lunch," the driver said. "That was thirty years ago."

"Shame she couldn't do it today," Maxx replied.

Carol punched him in the shoulder.

"Well, son, she passed on last winter, but it ain't a shame. She was a good woman, we had a good life, and now she's got a better one. And that's all I know."

"I wish I knew that much," Maxx replied.

The driver rose and walked to the cab while his helper climbed in the other side. Carol laid her leather-gloved hand on Maxx's shoulder as the trucker backed up and drove his rig down the lane.

"Daddy used to say a farmer is the only one who works all summer long, not making a dime, only to see his efforts drive away, and still doesn't know if he made anything."

"I'm hungry."

"Yeah, me too."

The hay-dusty pair uncuffed their pants, took off their boots, and shook shards of hay from their shirts. Maxx stuck his head under the cold hose while Carol snuck inside in her dirty clothes to get cleaned up. Maxx got a pair of shorts from the car and went to put them on in the garage.

Carol, her mother, and Maxx sat around the kitchen table—satisfied with a day's work. Their lunch settled as Maxx reached for a last glass of lemonade. Sweat and hard work is a good elixir.

"Walk with me, Carol." The country couple walked back the farm lane and over the hill.

"You put your work gloves back on."

"I kind a like them. Maybe I'm a farmer after all."

"Maxx, you never like doing the same thing twice. Remember, when you drive your tractor to the end of the field, you have to turn around and do it all over again."

"I know, but I get to drive a tractor. Today, we did something together. Carol, did you hear me? We did something *together*."

"You're starting to scare me."

He took off his gloves and held out his hands to her. "Look, I got blisters. They're real too."

She shook her head. "Now, you're really scaring me."

"We could do this. You even said there was a beach in Perry County."

Carol looked away.

Maxx stepped closer and brushed a piece of chaff from her hair. "I'd like to see it. I'd like to see your beach."

Carol turned around and started back to the house. "Not today."

When they returned to the house, Maxx said he had to get going.

"I need to help Mrs. Peters sort stuff in her garage. She thinks it's time to do something with her husband's things. Put 'er there, pardner," he said, sticking out his gloved hand.

"Sure, partner," Carol said. "I'd kiss you if you didn't have that hay chaff between your teeth."

"Would you?"

She shook her head. "Like I said, not today. Do you want to say goodbye to Mother?"

"Oh, no," he said as he backed up to the car and opened the door. "You say it for me."

CHAPTER 23

Carol's forced routine of yoga in the morning followed by a long walk couldn't break her episodic crying jags and fitful sleep patterns. "Stop it, stop it now," she screamed in the middle of the night at the chaos in her head. Life crashed over her like waves on a rocky beach.

"Carol, wake up, darling. Wake up."

She awoke to find her mother sitting on the side of her queen-sized bed.

"Carol, you're dreaming, honey, it's just a dream."

"Mommy." Carol sat up and grabbed onto her mother's shoulder.

"You haven't called me that since you were a child."

"Sometimes I think I'm still a child." Carol flopped back down on the pillow. "What's wrong with me? Why does everyone that I love die?"

Her mother brushed some hair away from Carol's forehead. "It's only because you love them that it hurts."

"I'm cursed, Mother."

"That's nonsense. Don't say that."

"It's true. I'm the reason Ralphie is dead, and I'm the reason Becca is gone. If it wasn't for me, Joey would be alive. You even know that."

"I know nothing of the kind."

The small night light behind her mother cast a dark shadow that kept Carol from seeing the details of her face.

"It's all my fault. You never said it, Mother, but I know you blame me too. Just say it … say it now."

She shook her head. "I will not. It's not true. Look at me, both of you could have died that night. If it wasn't for Joey, you might be dead. But you didn't kill him."

Carol got out of bed and stood by her window that looked down on the dusk-till-dawn light lighting up the drive and barn. She used to get up at night as a child and stare down the lane. Carol imagined herself on her horse Blackie riding down that lane and never coming back.

Her mother walked over to the window and stood behind her.

"Remember Blackie out in the pasture?" she asked.

"You used to complain about Blackie, Mother."

"No, I complained about you not tacking and grooming Blackie."

"I loved Blackie," Carol replied. "But I hated cleaning her stall."

"Me too. I loved how she took you away from here."

Carol cocked her head toward her mother.

"You're not the only one who thought about leaving here, Carol."

"My life took me from here, but you love it here."

"I loved your daddy, so I learned to love it here."

"Where did you want to go?"

Her mother sighed. "Honey, that sounds like a question best answered over coffee. I might as well put on a pot. What is it your brother used to call it?"

"Level five."

"Right, I'll brew a pot of level five coffee."

Carol grabbed a robe while her mother turned on the hall lights and made her way downstairs to her coffeepot. Carol followed.

"Milk, no sugar, sugar?" Her mother put out a box of sugar and some milk.

"You used to say that all the time. You haven't forgotten."

"I don't forget much. I'll never forget what I felt when your daddy took my boyfriend's pie. I knew then he was my guy. Mee-Maw asked me if I knew what I was doing, and I really didn't. I was going to be a Harrisburg lawyer.

I had been accepted to Messiah College and had my plans made, but your daddy changed all that. He visited me my first semester, and my roommate snuck him into Sollenberger Dorm. We thought we knew what we were doing until baby Joey came along."

"I had no idea."

Her mother shrugged. "We never talked about it. It's something that wasn't supposed to happen to good girls. I loved your daddy, so it was never a question. I came home at the end of the semester and never went back. We married in the Lutheran church, had a small reception at the Legion, and a honeymoon in Niagara Falls. I had morning sickness that week, though, and couldn't even look at the falls or your father." She sat down at the table next to Carol. "The years went by, and I thought I'd forget about being a lawyer, but I never did."

"Is that why you always read those legal mysteries?"

"I guess so." Her mother laughed—a brief, innocent, and familiar laugh, but one lost to time. "I was so happy to see you graduate from college and from graduate school." She looked at Carol. "It was what I wanted."

Carol could hear the grandfather clock, its ticking now especially loud. Everyone had their picture taken in front of that old clock. Graduations, birthdays, and prom nights had been recorded with a Kodak camera using the clock as a backdrop. Carol's mother always said the clock pictures marked time.

"I always thought you didn't want me to move away."

"Nonsense." Her mother rose to grab the coffeepot and some mugs. "I wanted you to take me with you. And when your daddy died, we had so much to talk about. I wanted to know about Rome, your archeology, and your life. But when Joey died, everything changed."

Carol got up to get more milk but knocked over the box of sugar. She cursed.

"Don't swear, college girl, it doesn't make you sound very smart."

Her mother cleaned up the sugar while Carol retrieved the milk.

"I know you don't want to talk about it, but you need to know this—it was not your fault."

Carol poured some milk into her mug. "I thought you always blamed me."

"No, I was lost in my grief, honey. I am so sorry I couldn't be there for you, but I had lost my son. I wasn't there for anyone. I just laid in bed for days. I didn't have anything to give you. I feel so ashamed."

Carol took the towel from her mother to wipe up the last of the sugar. Her mother had never been a cleaner. A good cook, a creative decorator, but her real joy was the garden and anything that kept her outside. Carol moved the papers and mail cluttering the middle of the table to get the last remnants when she noticed the Roman postmark.

"Hey, is this a letter from Sis?"

"She knows how I am with a computer, so she writes real letters. That came today. You didn't tell me your sister is married."

"I wanted to tell you."

"It's too late now. She says she wants to bring her man home to meet everyone. Of course, she's already planning a big party, she wants to have it out in the barn." Her mother laughed. "Your sister is still crazy."

"She is, but she was a big help to me. It's good seeing her get out of her cocoon." Carol shuffled the rest of the papers and picked up a manila envelope. "What's this one?"

"Oh, that came last week. I completely forgot about it when Ralphie ... you know."

She took the envelope from Carol, opened it up, and read the note aloud.

Dear Mrs. Beck,

I am sending this report to you because I think you should be the one to get it first and show it to Carol. I don't know if you know about this, and I'm pretty sure Carol doesn't, but it's the state police results of the investigation after your son, Joseph, was killed on the square in New Bloomfield. I found it while working on Becca's investigation.

I hope I am not making things worse by stirring up old memories. But Mum always says, "Dinner is spoiled if the pot isn't stirred."

Respectfully,

Officer Ralph Peters

P.S. I still think your daughter is special and would not do anything to hurt her—ever.

Ralphie

Carol wiped her eyes with the edge of the dishcloth. Her mother tried to excuse herself to the bathroom, but Carol stopped her, and they stood in front of the big picture window holding on to each other. The dusk-till-dawn light cast shadows across the driveway that stretched to the horse barn as the gelding and mare whinnied in the paddocks.

They pulled out the three-page report.

Carol pointed to the accident scene diagram. "Mother, have you seen this before?"

"Oh, no, I couldn't. Maybe your father did. To me the only thing that mattered was Joey, and he was dead."

"Look here, this is the motorcycle ... this is the monument ... here it shows Joey making the first turn, but then he ended up cutting across the pavement, and into the middle of the square. That doesn't make sense. Why would he just drive across the sidewalk like that?"

"What's this symbol back here mean, Carol?"

"I don't know. You're the lawyer."

Her mother frowned. "Very funny."

"It's a P, the legend says MV is a motor vehicle, MC is motorcycle, and P is pedestrian, here by the tavern."

Carol picked up the last page of the report—a series of eyewitness reports.

"Look what it says here." Her mother took the paper from Carol. "'Mr. Walter Jones (P) reported seeing a car coming from the NW corner, slowing down then picking up excessive speed. MC swerved to miss MV, crossed the corner of the sidewalk and ended up hitting the monument. The MV then backed up, paused at the monument, but drove away. Driver was identified as female, driving a small sports car with one headlight. Mr. Jones admitted drinking at least six beers, needing glasses. Eyewitness may have been in the street and caused the accident.'"

Her mother stood, stunned.

"Mother?"

"Rea."

"What?"

"Rea Billingsley. She had a little foreign convertible."

"Rea Billingsley? Mother, that's who we think has Becca."

Her mother collapsed into a chair and then looked up at Carol.

"You never told me you were looking for Rea."

"I guess I just thought you knew. I figured Mee-Maw would have told you. Mother, what's going on? What's happening?"

Carol's mother held her coffee cup in one hand, but the liquid spilt over the rim and onto the saucer in her other hand. She raised it to her lips and tried to take a sip before resting both on the table.

"Rea Billingsley must have run your brother off the road."

"Why would she do that? How do you know? That makes no sense." Carol shook her head.

"That girl was bad, Carol. She grew up wrong and ended up worse. I'm going to tell you some things I never said before, things I didn't think you needed to know about your brother. You adored him so, and I don't want that to change. Promise me that won't change, honey."

"I promise. What is it?"

Her mother turned to face her. The dated colonial light over the table revealed every line in her face and the crow's feet around her eyes added to her weathered sadness.

"Families ... some families have their own secrets. They don't start off as secrets, they're just memories too painful to voice. They turn into background noise out of respect for the person, and out of a feeble way to protect the family. In the end, they get woven into the fabric of family life and just are. No one intentionally hides the secret—it simply becomes something that just never happened. But it did. And everybody knows something, they are just not sure what."

Carol's mother's eyes filled with tears, but they didn't stop her from looking at her daughter.

"'Now is not the time to bring up the past,' they think. 'Let's not upset her,' they say. 'Everyone is so happy, why ruin the day?' they ask. Families rarely handle confrontation well. So, the secrets are buried in the layers, lurking between the sheets, and smothering life.'"

"Mother, what are you talking about?"

Her mother held up a hand and kept talking. "Joey and Lydia were having their third child. Money was tight. His insurance business had taken several losses, so I worked part time as his secretary and helped keep the books. Rea Billingsley had her car insurance with Joey but was behind on her premiums. I called her about it, and she told me not to worry—she'd worked it out with Joey." Carol's mother wiped her hand across the table. "Well, Joey acted funny and told me he would take care of it and, next thing I know, it's paid in full. Your brother often helped people by giving them extensions and even small loans when they needed it. For an insurance man, he wasn't good with records."

Her mother began collecting small crumbs left on the table.

"Anyway, he and Rea dated back when he was in high school, but we forbade the relationship. You were too young to know anything about it. Your father was mad and told Joey he wouldn't help him with college if he kept seeing her. But they kept on anyway in secret until he went away to college and met Lydia. I guess Rea never forgot about him."

Carol grabbed her mother's hand.

"Through the years, he and Lydia grew distant. He and Rea must have started up again. The news would have crushed Lydia, who was pregnant and on bedrest at the time. Money was missing from the business. It's probably how she got that little car."

"Mrs. Peters told me the township thought Chief Peters was giving her money."

A look of pained guilt came across her mother's face. She looked down at the crumbs now in a neat formation. "No, honey, it was your brother. I heard the rumors about the police chief and her, but I knew where her money was coming from. It killed me to keep that secret from old friends, but what could I do? I guess I should have come forward, but I didn't. Maybe if I had, Ralphie's dad would have kept his job. Maybe he would be alive today. I live with that." She shook her head. "It's terrible. A little secret you keep for your kids turns into the lie that hurts them in the end." Tears started rolling down the lines in her face.

Her mother wiped her nose with a tissue and said, "Anyway, Rea came into the office one day, demanding to see Joey. She smelled of alcohol and told me she needed money. I told her if she needed a bank, go down to the square. Sounds like me, right?" She smiled. "That's when she tells me she's pregnant and needs money for an abortion. I told her if she was pregnant, she shouldn't be drinking, but she sped off in her MG."

"Mother, I had no idea."

"Remember, you were in Rome. It wasn't something I could put in a letter or even say over the phone. Anyway, I figured she was just bluffing and forgot all about her when your daddy died."

"That's when I came home," Carol said. "I asked Joey to take me for ice cream on his motorcycle after the funeral. I wonder if she saw him with me on the back of his bike and went after him and me."

Her mother stood and gripped the back of her dark walnut chair. "That makes sense. I guess they never caught up to her. They probably never believed Walter. Everyone knew he was a drunk and used to stand in the middle of the road hollering at that statue at all hours of the night. I bet she got rid of that car out at her parents' place in one of those hollows. Even the Game Commission doesn't go out there. Chief Peters was the only one who could go there without getting shot at, and I doubt if he would have followed up with all his pending allegations. It would have looked like he was using Joey's death to get rid of her and save himself."

Carol looked up. "You would have made a good lawyer. I've been searching for her all this time. You were right, we did need to talk."

Her mother nodded, her lips firmly pressed together. "You didn't kill Joey. That was put into play long before you were even on the scene. And you didn't kill Ralphie. If anything, you gave him something to live for. To him, you were special. That's what he always said to me whenever I saw him at the supermarket or at church with his mom. 'Mrs. Beck, that girl of yours is special,' he'd say. Then he'd wave and smile and be on his way."

Carol looked down at the table. "I've wasted a lot of time. I need to find my little girl. I still don't know where Rea is—I don't even know what she looks like—but I got to find her. I just have to."

The grandfather clock in the corner rung six chimes.

"Carol, that old clock reminds me of something. I never throw out anything and you know it. Let's dig through some old photos."

The two went back up the stairs.

"Watch the squeaky step," her mother said, "We don't want to wake up the parents."

"Mother!"

They walked down the hall to the attic door and stumbled up the dark stairs. At the top, her mother reached overhead and found the string to the bare lightbulb. Toys, dolls, Christmas ornaments, mounted deer heads, and stuffed birds cluttered the room. Three steamer trunks filled with military uniforms, memorabilia, and papers lined one wall. The underside of the roof peaked in the middle and the early morning wind whistled through the cracks in the windows on each wall. Carol could see the edges of daylight creeping through the distant trees.

"I think Joey's school stuff is in this one," her mother said as she opened one trunk.

Carol noticed his high school varsity letter for track, and even his Boy Scout merit badges and little league glove.

"I can't believe you kept all of this. Why?"

"It means something. Don't you have Becca's baby things?"

"Good point."

Toward the bottom of the chest, they pulled out several albums. Birth announcements and baby pictures fell out of the pages. Each school year was arranged in order and complete with a class picture.

"Mother, this won't help. Rea didn't go to school. She did home study."

"Maybe not, but she did go to a prom." Her mother pulled out a picture from Joey's senior year. "Your father was furious when he heard Joey was taking her. I convinced him not to fuss, the tickets and tux were already paid for. He was so mad he went out to the barn when Joey showed up with her. I didn't know what to do so I made small talk. Joey asked me if I was going to take a clock picture like I always do."

Carol stared down at the back of the picture where her mother had written down their names and the date.

"Your daddy never saw this one—I kept it from him. Go on, Carol, aren't you going to turn it over?"

Carol had wondered what she must look like and had conjured up all sorts of possibilities.

"Oh, just give it here." Her mother turned the picture over.

Carol gasped as the picture fell to the floor.

"What? What is it?" her mother reached out to touch her arm, and Carol fell into her mother's embrace.

Next to her foot lay a picture of her brother, a clock, and an eighteen-year-old Daphne, her North Carolina neighbor.

CHAPTER 24

Maxx's drive out to the farm took only a matter of minutes. His car kicked up rocks as he sped down the lane, only slowing for the diversion ditch.

One time, Maxx had told Carol's father he should level that ditch so he wouldn't have to slow down.

Mr. Beck had replied, "Boy, what the heck are you thinking? That ditch is there to divert the water and keep the topsoil on the field."

Now, Maxx nearly bottomed out his SUV in the gully. The car slid when he braked behind Old Brownie in the driveway. He left the keys in the ignition and made his way through the garage and into the kitchen. He didn't knock.

Before sitting down, he put his hand on Mrs. Beck's shoulder, then bent down to hug his wife. They sat together as Carol's mother reached for the coffeepot and donuts left over from the day they'd loaded the hay trailer. Carol still looked shaken, her eyes red, her voice soft, but her movements seemed smooth and her thoughts clear.

Maxx looked at the picture and confirmed what Carol already knew. "That's our neighbor. Unbelievable." In the photo, Daphne even wore her silver dime, partially obscured behind a yellow feather boa, above her low-cut gown. "Would you look at that dress. How did this happen?"

"I haven't figured it all out yet, but I will. What I know ..." Carol took a deep breath. "What I *think* I know is that Rea Billingsley might have gotten pregnant from my brother, Joey. You never knew him. Joey was married, but not to her. Rea ... Daphne had an abortion that he might have paid for, and she probably hated him for it. Anyway, Rea saw him one night with me on the back of his motorcycle. Maybe she thought he was with another woman, got mad, and drove him off the road."

"Mad is the right word, but how does she become Daphne, our neighbor?"

"That I don't know ... yet. But I think she has Becca."

Maxx frowned. "Whoa ... that's a stretch."

"I know. I was wrong before. I was wrong in Rome when I relied on my deductive reasoning, and I was wrong in Harrisburg when I was going on gut instinct. But somehow this is different. It's here." Carol placed her hand across her heart.

"The same heart that's been giving you panic attacks?"

Her mother stopped pouring milk into a server. Too late, he realized he'd just stepped on a landmine. Her mother didn't know about the attacks. He stared at his cup and stirred the sugar at the bottom.

Carol glared at him. "Yes, the same heart. Well, not exactly."

Maxx sighed and laid a hand on hers. "Carol, I'm sorry. I'm just upset, but I'm here for you."

"What panic attacks?" her mother asked.

"It's something I've been dealing with for a while, but they're getting better. I can't explain it all right now. I know if we went to the police they'd want more, but for me, it's enough. I still don't know where Becca is, but I know who has her."

"So ... Daphne is Rea." Maxx took a sip of his coffee.

"I'm thinking, after the accident, she had to get out of town. She was probably thinking the police would be after her and knew someone saw her, so she ditched her car and left. Remember her saying she had a husband on the West Coast? She must have thought she would be safe in California, changed her name, and got married. She probably got a whole new identity, blond hair and all."

"All that makes sense, but why did she come east, and how did she find you? Was it all one big coincidence? That's some coincidence."

Carol shrugged. "No, not a coincidence. I don't know everything, not yet. Maybe when we find Daphne, I mean Rea, it'll all make sense."

Maxx sipped his coffee and then said, "I remember her telling me one day that she moved east because of family, but we never saw any, did we? Maybe she kept in touch with people in Perry County and found out about you living at the beach in North Carolina."

Carol's mother had been putting dishes away and throwing out junk mail. Now, she went into the bathroom and came back out carrying a copy of the *Duncannon Record*.

"What about the *Record*, Carol?"

"Mother, not now."

"No, remember the article they did on you after you came back from Rome? An archaeologist from Perry County—that was big news around here. It mentioned where you were living, and that you'd adopted a little girl. She could have read that online."

"The *Record* is online?" Carol raised her eyebrows.

Her mother nodded.

"So maybe she's still mad at Joey for making her get an abortion, and when she hears about our daughter, she figures Becca should be hers."

"That's crazy," said Maxx.

"That's right—it is crazy. Maybe not crazy like Harold Baker, but she's still messed up."

Maxx stared at the ceiling and began to pace. "Maybe when she talked to Baker, she found out about his burn site and seized the opportunity to plant some evidence. That way people would think Becca was dead."

"She was attracted to his power in the same way she was attracted to Joey and Chief Peters." Carol scooted back her chair. "Come on."

"Carol, listen to Maxx."

"Daphne always scared me," admitted Maxx. "She was overly flirtatious, so I always made sure someone else was around if I talked to her. You know I saw her when I went back home."

"No, you didn't tell me that."

"Well, I didn't think anything of it. When I went back for business, I went down to check on the beach house. I know where the spare key is, and I did a walk through. The place looked lived in. It wasn't messy or anything like that, but it looked like someone had been spending a lot of time over there. Cushions were out of place, there was some food left on the counter, and some towels in the bathroom."

"Maxx, you should have told me." Carol pressed her hands against the chair back.

"Like I said, I didn't think much about it. I knew you had Daphne, I mean Rea, watching our place so I guess she thought that meant she could use the place. Anyway, when I walked outside, she was out in her yard. I could have sworn she was looking at me when I came out, but when I called over to her, she turned away and headed into her place. I thought it was weird, but I figured she must not have heard me."

"So, she's still there." Carol pulled out her phone. "We should call the police."

"Hello, Emerald Isle Police Department," the receptionist said. "If this is an emergency please hang up and dial 911."

"This is an emergency, but I need to talk to Detective Krinshaw."

"Hold, ma'am."

"She called me, ma'am." Carol rolled her eyes.

"Krinshaw here."

"Detective Krinshaw, this is Carol Davies. You told me to call if I had anything." Carol tried to tell her story as briefly as possible. "I'm certain Becca is still alive and with my neighbor. Or my neighbor knows where she is."

"And what makes you think that, ma'am?"

Carol told him Rea's story, about being involved with her brother years ago and how she'd probably caused his death, changed her name, and had now mysteriously ended up living next door to her. She also explained about Rea's relationship with Harold Baker, and how she'd been able to convince the police that Becca was dead by putting her bracelet and some hair near his burn pit. Then she'd alerted the police to the location.

Carol could hear the detective's skepticism in his silence.

"Ms. Davies, you make your neighbor sound like a psychopath."

"Sir, can you just go and find out if she has our little girl? If you don't do this, and later find out you were wrong, you're going to have a hard time explaining yourself."

"Okay, okay. I'll go by and knock on the door."

"Thank you, sir. And please don't call me ma'am."

After Carol hung up, her mother asked, "What happens next?"

"We wait," Maxx replied.

Carol remembered the night she'd waited for Ralphie while sitting on the porch. "I'm not waiting. I'm going." She got up from the table and headed out the back door.

"Carol, wait," yelled Maxx, "Wait!"

"I'm not waiting."

"At least take your coat!" her mother shouted.

Carol turned back to grab her coat off the clothes tree in the corner.

"Just a second," her mother said. "How long will it take the police to check on your neighbor?"

Carol stopped and turned. "Ten, fifteen minutes."

"How long will it take you to pack up your things?"

She sighed. "Fifteen minutes."

"Well, why not pack for fifteen minutes, get the phone call from the detective, and then you'll know better what to do. You'll need your things if you go home anyway."

Carol looked at her mother and then at Maxx, who diverted his attention to the floor. She put her coat back on the rack and started for the stairs.

"I'll go to Mee-Maw's to grab my stuff," Maxx said. "Pick me up on your way out of town."

Carol nodded.

"Thanks, Mom." Maxx gave her mother a quick kiss on the cheek and then turned to leave.

Her mother followed her up the stairs and watched silently from the bedroom doorway as she threw toiletries and various other items into her bag. Carol's mind ran wild with what might happen next, and she swiped at tears pooling in her eyes as she closed her duffle bag.

"I'll go with you," her mother said from the doorway.

"Someone has to wait, Mother."

"Someone always has to wait. Carol, do you have a plan?"

"Ha! Mother, I don't have even have a clue."

"Well, if she's as evil as we think, you're going to need a plan and a good one."

"I know. I'll come up with one before I get there."

Carol carried her duffle bag out of the bedroom and down the stairs as her mother followed behind. Carol managed to grab her coat while balancing her bag on her hip but her heavy duffle kept pushing the door closed when she reached for it.

"Just set it down," her mother said softly, and Carol surrendered.

"It's been twenty-five minutes and no call. I'm leaving." She pulled open the door and dragged her bags out onto the porch.

"How about calling them back?"

"I'll call on the way," Carol said as she shoved her bags into the car and got behind the wheel.

Carol sped down the lane, passed through town, and pulled onto US Route 15. As she rounded Peter's Mountain, she pulled over at the Cove and made an apologetic, albeit hurried, phone call to Maxx.

"I forgot to stop. I'm so sorry. I just can't wait any longer."

"Okay, I'll call the police department and get on the road. I'll catch up to you on the way down," Maxx replied.

Maxx called the Emerald Isle Police Department and found out Krinshaw's shift had ended.

"Sir, we haven't heard anything from Detective Krinshaw. I'm certain he went home for the weekend."

Maxx called Carol to relay the information as he said goodbye to Mee-Maw and got into his car. Mrs. Peters scurried across the street with some no-bake oatmeal cookies. "My favorite," he said.

After thanking her, he pulled out of the neighborhood. He looked in his rear-view mirror to see the two gray-haired matriarchs, each barely five-feet-tall, arm in arm in the middle of the street. Waiting. Again.

CHAPTER 25

Carol had always liked the riverfront town of Perdix but driving thirty-five miles an hour through the idyllic hamlet now unnerved her but not as much as the blue lights flashing in her rear-view mirror. As she pulled over, the state trooper sped past to flag down a tractor trailer. Carol thought of Ralph and the last night she'd seen him.

Maxx's number lit up on her cell phone. "Carol, pull into the Summerdale Diner, and we can go together."

Carol turned into the diner, parked her car, grabbed her duffle, and jumped in with Maxx. When they entered the highway, Maxx's grip on the wheel tightened.

"All I can think about is the time we first went to get Becca. It felt like I could hardly keep the car on the road," he said. This time Maxx held his speed, stayed close to the passing lane, and weaved around slower cars and trucks. The DC beltway traffic choked the highway and brought them to a crawl.

"Where is all this traffic coming from on a Wednesday morning?"

Carol looked around. "I don't know. From all over the world, I guess."

The traffic didn't let up even when they passed the sign "Virginia is for Lovers."

"Now watch your speed down here, Virginia might be for lovers, but its fines are pretty steep, Speedy."

"Very funny."

"Maxx, I thought I saw Ralph in Perdix when the trooper sped by me."

"Ralph was special, Carol."

He is special. "How are you doing for gas?"

"We're good. I'm starting to think about what we should do when we get down there, but I'm not coming up with much. I'm going to need to stop before Richmond."

"For gas?"

"Yeah, that too," Maxx replied.

"What did the Emerald Isle police say?"

"The woman who answered the phone said she thinks he went home for the weekend. I'm guessing he didn't call you back."

"No, and that worries me."

"He probably didn't find anything and went home."

"Maybe. I hope so. Do you have any ideas about what to do when we get there?"

"I've been thinking about a plan since we got up from the kitchen table at the farm," Maxx stated. "It's in my DNA to plan."

"I know. It's why you're always late."

"Hey, before I get out of bed in the morning, I wrap my head around a P.O.D.

"P.O.D.?"

"Plan of the day. It's what gets me going. I check things off my list in my notebook at night."

"Is that why you sleep so good? Must be your navy training."

Carol watched two small cars with loud mufflers pass them at a dizzying speed.

"Everything on my ship had a backup system, from the engines to the life rafts. Failure was anticipated, disaster was trained for, and crisis was drilled as opportunity. My surface warfare world of algorithms served me well in business."

Carol had heard his story before.

Maxx continued, "This is what I got so far, but this is so far outside my wheelhouse. What I was thinking is that Daphne—Rea, or whatever her name is—knows my car. I could pull into our house and just do some things out in the yard that would get her attention. You sneak over on the other side of her place and find a place to slip in, like a window or something."

"A window. You want me to climb in through a window? That's your plan?" Carol adjusted the visor overhead and redirected her air vent.

"You got something better?"

"What's Plan B, Maxx?"

"I go through a window?"

"Why does anyone have to go through a window? Why don't I just walk up on her porch? That wouldn't arouse too much suspicion."

"Yeah, that could work too. I was just thinking the police already did that, and it didn't work."

"They probably didn't get past the porch," she said. "I will."

Maxx nodded. "Hmm. Good point. Then what?"

"That's as far as I got. Maybe while I'm talking to her in the living room, you could slip in and sneak around."

"Through a window?"

Carol let out a breath. "If that's what you need to do, then fine, climb through a window."

The highway narrowed to two lanes each way and somewhere below Fredericksburg they stopped for gas. Carol left the car to go inside for an over-sized cup of coffee. Maxx hustled to the men's room, then bought an Arnie Palmer and a pack of Krimpets before returning to his car.

"Did you know, the wheel, the automatic gas pump shut-off, and the Tastykake Krimpet revolutionized modern travel?" Maxx shouted across the gas pumps.

"What about the no-bake cookies?"

"Finished them."

When they were back in the car and speeding down the highway, Carol said, "I've been thinking, too." Her voice cracked and she cleared her throat before continuing. "What if Rea was bluffing Mother that day in the insurance office? What if she really was pregnant but never got that abortion? I've been doing the math. What if Becca is Joey and Rea's baby?"

Maxx took his eyes off the road. "I don't know if I can go there." A brief look at his wife was long enough.

"It's a lot, I know, but just listen. Remember, the only stipulation was that we had to keep her name? Well, Reba and Rea are nicknames for Rebecca. In Rome, I learned the mother's name is Rebecca. And remember how Daphne would always call Becca Rebecca even when we corrected her? But I think that's why she wants Becca, and that's why she moved here. Not because of revenge ... because she's Becca's mother."

"Carol, *you* are Becca's mother."

"Rea doesn't think like that. She's delusional, you said it yourself. Now, we're not just getting Becca back. We're getting back Joey's baby."

"It does make sense. She was always taking pictures," Maxx added. "And she always bought her things and asked us if she could babysit. Remember how mad she got one time when she found out we had someone else babysitting?"

Maxx sipped his tea from the tall can and then explained about the time Rea tried to get alone with him and Becca. "It creeped me out. I never said anything, but it seemed like Rea was playing family. One time she said to me, 'I could be a good mother.'" He took another sip of his tea. "Please don't be mad, but do you remember when you asked me to take her home from the beach when she had too much to drink? When we got to her house, she threw her arms around me and said, 'We could be a family.' I smelled her breath and figured it was the wine talking. But maybe it wasn't just the wine."

Carol shook her head. "She's delusional. We have to get our daughter back."

Hours later, Carol's heart fluttered when she saw the sign, "Welcome to North Carolina." After months of searching and over a year of waiting, she was now only three hours from realizing her real dream. She could see Becca playing in the sand with her shovel and bucket. She could feel Becca in her lap as she read to her in the rocking chair, and Becca drifted to sleep. She envisioned Becca pedaling her Minnie Mouse bike with the twelve-inch tires.

Her memories brought on a certain angst, a gnawing feeling in her gut. A little piece of Carol had died in Rome when they hadn't gotten her back at the pagan ritual. Another piece had died when Ralphie hadn't come back with her. And a big piece died the day Becca had disappeared.

For over a year, she'd refused to think of that day, but when Maxx exited I-95 she saw a sign for fresh crab cakes, and the memory came blowing back—the windy day at the Seafood Festival, and the wrapping on Carol's crab cake sandwich that flew between her fingers.

Please, God, no! Take this memory from me.

The memory was replaced as the next billboard come into view—a Harley ad with a guy and a girl cruising down the highway. The girl's hair streamed out from beneath her helmet as she hung on.

Oh, Joey, we were so young. You were so good. You were better than me. You were always better.

Carol's thoughts flashed back and forth between Becca and Joey. Happy thoughts of tricycles and ice cream mixed with a cold hotdog and a crushed motorcycle. Tears no longer rolled down her face as her eyes fixed on the highway and mile post signs that broke up the flattened tobacco fields.

She could hear Becca say, "Lookey," and her reply, "Whatever." She could hear her brother's laugh, and she could see the stiff way he'd danced at his wedding.

"I love you both," she said softly.

Maxx reached out a hand and squeezed her knee, bringing her back to the present. Rain had now turned the road to a dark sheen, and their windshield wipers kept a steady rhythm. Headlights flashed by as pine trees moved gently in the breeze.

"The radio keeps talking about a tropical storm—it may get upgraded to a hurricane. Here's the sign for Maysville." Maxx pointed. "The last half-hour is the longest." Maxx drove down the narrow highway with certainty. He drove fast, passing two cars crossing a wet double yellow line.

Carol reached out to brace herself on the dashboard. "Hey, don't forget the roads are wet."

Maxx lowered the speed, but just a little.

The bridge over the sound and Intercoastal Waterway usually brought solace to Carol at sundown, but not this time. In the fall, the sun set at the extreme west of the island and she loved seeing the purples, pinks, and blues laced through the sky. But now there was only grey as the rain came down in sheets. A couple of sailboats with a single white light in the middle of their masts labored down the waterway to winter in the Caribbean. The hurricane season was almost over, and the boats were looking for warmer sun and bigger water.

A trio of shrimp boats chugged to the ocean inlet looking for their home. Carol often watched the trawlers from the beach with Becca. Dolphins sometimes surrounded the boats in a playful dance. They'd race head-on at the bow and change their path at the last second as if playing chicken with the large trawlers. The dolphins risked getting caught up in the nets, but their reward would be a belly full of chum or shrimp.

The last of the baby sea turtles are hatched, no doubt.

Carol recalled taking Becca to see the mother sea turtles, measuring up to six feet and struggling up the beach in the middle of the night to lay over one hundred eggs. At the end of the summer, the eggs would hatch, and baby turtles would make their way to the surf's edge. Volunteers kept watch on nature's miracles to increase survival rates but only one baby turtle in one thousand would make it to adulthood. Some hatch when it's low tide, and they don't make it to the water. Some hatch at high tide and drown.

The thought of all those helpless baby turtles, separated from their mother and fending for themselves, saddened her.

Who decides who makes it? It's not fair that some get eaten by birds. Life isn't fair.

"Life just is," she lamented. "God give me faith."

Cars had backed up on the bridge and Maxx eased once more off the gas. Carol could see yellow jacketed policemen, orange cones, and red flares. The delay unnerved her more.

As the town limits came into view, Maxx said, "Focus, my love, focus. Breathe, just breathe."

Her eyes widened, and she could feel blood rush to her extremities. Her hearing excluded any unnecessary sound. She wasn't just entering her town—she was entering her flight or fight mode. She sat up straight in her seat.

Both lanes were now being used to allow people to exit the island and the police had stopped the traffic to allow occasional vehicles to return for official business.

Maxx reached a cop wearing a neon green vest on top of his yellow jacket and carrying a long red directional light.

"Evacuation, sir, I can't let you on."

"We're residents, here's our entry pass." Maxx held up a four-by-six cardboard sign.

The officer shook his head. "Doesn't matter."

"Officer, I'm part of the auxiliary ambulance crew."

"We have an auxiliary ambulance crew?" the cop asked.

"Only for emergencies. You're an auxiliary cop, right?"

"Yeah."

"Well, I'm an auxiliary ambulance worker."

"Oh, I see. In that case, show me some identification."

Maxx pulled out his old military ID and flashed it at the cop. Cars continued to line up in both directions creating a greater commotion, and the officer received a loud message on his walkie talkie chastising him to keep the lines moving. Looking flustered, he glanced at Maxx and then waved him through.

"What was that?" Carol asked.

"I saw his badge and thought I'd go with it." Maxx flashed her a smile. "Guess it worked."

After the bridge, Maxx took to the shoulder to get around the traffic that was using both lanes to leave the island. No one honked. It seemed that in this emergency state, the only rule that applied was every man for himself. A few discarded trailers and boats had been left at the side of road along with cars that had broken down due to the heavy rain now pounding the island. Windshield wipers could not keep up, and headlights could not illuminate the road, but Maxx kept on going. He drove through long puddles that reached the bottom of the SUV. Water poured over the bumper, but they couldn't turn around now.

After making the first right onto Coast Guard Road, Carol saw the sign for her development. Her heart pounded through her chest, as much as any panic attack but she only thought about the life of her child.

Maxx turned into their neighborhood and stopped before he got to Daphne's house.

"I'm getting out. You park the car and sneak around back."

"I can't let you go in there alone," Maxx protested.

"I'll be fine. If she sees me, I'll just distract her while you look for Becca or climb through a window or something."

"No, Carol."

It was the last thing she heard as she shut the car door.

CHAPTER 26

As Carol scurried past Daphne's car, she noticed bags of groceries in the passenger seat. She turned off her cell phone and slipped it into her pocket. She knew Daphne's house, like hers, had a reverse floor plan—bedrooms on the second floor with the kitchen and open living space on top. The home was a typical Carolina beach house built on ten-foot-tall pressure-treated stilts that had been driven into the sandy barrier reef and bolted together to form a foundation that gives but doesn't break in the high winds and hurricanes. The ground floor had been enclosed fully—without windows or doors—to serve as storage. Daphne had once bragged about the builder doubling the thickness of the walls and the insulation for the storage room—to better protect it from storms, she'd said.

A patrol car passed by the house, the loudspeaker barking out an evacuation order. Everyone needed to be out by sundown. Carol felt a gust of wind and wondered how much time they had to get in and out. If a hurricane was bearing down on them, a direct hit might cause a tidal surge. Emergency services would shut down and they might be stuck. She shook off the thought. She didn't have time to think about the weather right now.

Carol fixated on the front door instead as she moved up the steps. The porch stretched across the front of the house and rocking chairs moved back and forth with the wind. Carol softly placed the ball of her foot on the porch before putting her full weight on each board. She stopped with each step, reminiscent of deer hunting with her daddy when she was twelve years old. She walked across palm leaves littering the wooden floor and stayed to the side of the glass pane door, not wanting to alert anyone inside should they be looking in her direction.

She crept up to the door and peered through the glass. Then she looked through the window next to the door but saw nothing. She tried the door. Locked. Carol couldn't remember a time when Daphne locked her doors.

Carol lifted the door mat and found a key. It stuck in its slot—perhaps not used much before. She massaged the rusted tumblers inside the lock by moving the key up and down, back and forth. It was slow, tedious work, not unlike cleaning the dirt and rock from centuries-old Roman fossilized bone.

Then, the knob turned with a click. She felt certain Daphne would have heard the click releasing the knob if she were inside. Daphne could probably also hear Carol's heart now pounding in own her ears.

Careful not to cause a squeak, Carol held onto the door, pushing it just wide enough for her to slip into the hallway. She took as much time shutting the door as when she opened it. She didn't close it entirely to avoid the noise from the catch finding its pocket in the door frame.

Carol stood inside the hallway, wishing the tremor in her thigh would subside. She scanned the stairs leading up to the kitchen and living space before making her way down the hallway. The umbrella stand made her think she should have a weapon but knew she wouldn't know what to do with one if she had it. She stepped into the first bedroom.

Where could she be?

As she looked around the sparse bedroom, a noise stopped her. She moved closer to the walk-in closet that connected to a bathroom and realized the noise had come from the kitchen upstairs. She heard footsteps on the ceramic tile.

Thank goodness for carpeted bedrooms.

Carol backed out of the room and into the next.

Only one more after this.

Her adrenaline soared and heightened her senses—she could hear the hum of the digital clock on the nightstand. The muscles in her legs ached.

This isn't as easy as all those cop shows make it look.

She entered the last bedroom, the smallest of the three, just as she heard footsteps coming down the oak steps. Carol ducked into the closet that extended across half the length of the room.

She heard Daphne say, "Let me see, I know I left that somewhere." Although her footsteps were now muffled on the carpet, her voice seemed close.

Breathe, Carol, breathe. Slow, deep, breaths.

Daphne slid open the closet door to Carol's right and then pulled a chair closer, stood on it, and reached to the shelf above a row of dresses. Carol sank back against the corner.

"Here's my pasta maker." Daphne closed the closet door and Carol exhaled.

Who keeps a pasta maker in their bedroom? Who makes pasta in a hurricane?

Carol stayed in the closet to think about her next move. There was no sign of Becca on this floor—no toys, no clothes, not even laundry.

Maybe she's not here. It would be silly to think she would keep her right next door to me this whole time anyway.

She hated waiting but remembered Mee-Maw telling her: "When you don't know what to do, sometimes it's best to do nothing." As the minutes ticked by in the dark closet, she began to hear the wind pick up outside, whistling through the aluminum shutters that kept the rooms dark and dry.

Then, from upstairs, came the sound of a ringing phone and muffled speaking.

Daphne's footfalls came back down the stairs and Carol heard the door click shut.

She heard Daphne's car pull out of the drive and the sound fade as she drove down the street. Carol remained quiet as she pushed open the closet door and then made her way upstairs. Cookbooks, the pasta machine box, and flour were spread across the open counter that divided the kitchen from the living space. The series of sliding doors and overhead windows had been covered with plywood.

Daphne had left the lights on making it easy for Carol to survey the room. She looked through a desk and read a whiteboard that hung next to the phone. The board held a list of numbers, including hers and Sis's.

She sat down at the top of the open stairs. The noise of the increasing winds now echoed inside the house—so loud, Carol didn't hear Daphne return until the door flung open, and she hustled up the stairs carrying three paper bags filled with groceries. Thankfully, the bags blocked Daphne's vision as Carol scrambled away from the stairs and behind the sectional sofa in the middle of the room.

"Stupid roads, flooded again, I still need olive oil," Daphne said out loud.

Carol felt exposed and vulnerable. When Daphne put down her packages on the counter with her back toward the steps, Carol made her way quietly back downstairs with her shoes in one hand.

At the bottom, she put her shoes back on, turned, and headed back down the hallway. As she contemplated a good place to hide, she noticed a bolted door at the end of the hall. She slid the two bolts and opened the door. Another set of steps made of unfinished plywood led down to the ground floor storage space.

Of course.

She pulled the door shut behind her and reached for her cell phone.

Her flashlight app lit the steps in front of her as she made her way down to the concrete floor. She could see the white drywall seams on the unfinished walls but little else. Beach stuff, boxes, and clothes sat on moveable metal racks and took up half the room.

"Mommy."

Carol froze.

"Mommy?"

A new jolt of adrenaline shot through her veins, her senses once again at full alert. She turned to her right and walked around a stack of wardrobe boxes.

Becca sat in what looked like a large dog kennel with fencing that stretched across the room, from floor to ceiling.

"Becca, oh my Becca ... Mommy's here, baby. Mommy's here."

Inside the fence, Becca had a small light, a child's bed, a chair, and a plastic vase that held jasmine, withered but alive. One end of the kennel led to a small bathroom and Carol could smell the musty odor. Her stuffed turtle, a few picture books, and crayons littered the floor. Becca's hair now fell past her shoulders in long strings.

"I want to go home," her child whimpered.

"Mommy's going to get you out of here. Mommy's going to take you home, baby."

"See, Tutt," Becca said to her stuffed turtle, "I told you Mommy would come back."

Carol jiggled the combination lock—there would be no key under the mat this time.

She turned to the small work bench and found a rusty hack saw. She tried to cut through the lock, but the steel seemed stronger than the blade. Returning to the workbench, she found an old toolbox with a crescent wrench and a socket set sitting at the bottom.

Sis would be proud of me.

She began unbolting the fence where it joined a pole at the end of the room.

Her fingers soon tired as she had to hold the wrench inside the kennel while she worked from the outside. Becca stood on her little chair and held the wrench for her mother, making the work go faster. They loosened the edges of the fence but there was still not enough space for Becca to escape, so they worked together on the third bolt.

Maxx pulled next door to their house and called the police. Everyone was busy, however, with the evacuation or gone home to secure their house. As he got out of his car, a shingle flew past his face and scraped across the roof rack on his SUV. Despite spending time at sea in a typhoon and being an experienced sailor, wind still made Maxx nervous. He had seen what its fury could do in other places of the world. He couldn't see it and couldn't control it.

Maxx dove onto the front seat when he saw Daphne leave the house and stayed slouched in his seat when he saw her red sports car return a few minutes later.

She didn't get far, maybe the flooded road.

Suddenly the streetlights and surrounding lights in the other houses went out.

Maxx texted Carol hoping her phone was on. When he received no reply, he knew he needed to act.

He made his way toward Daphne's house and considered going through a window, but then noticed the front door had been blown open by a gust of wind.

CHAPTER 26

Carol worked on the remaining bolts.

"Mommy?"

"Almost done, baby."

"MOMMY!"

"What, baby?"

As Carol turned to look, a metal flashlight came crashing down on Carol's head at the same spot she had hit months before beneath her shower. Her chin hit the floor and her teeth caught her tongue. She looked down at the blood pooling on the concrete as if it wasn't hers. When she looked up, Becca had begun to cry. Carol pulled herself to her knees.

Daphne ... or Rea ... stood over her, snarling.

"Stay down. Stay *down*." The crazed woman bounced on her toes like a prize fighter in the neutral corner.

But Carol didn't stay down. She rose to her feet only to get the handle end of the long flashlight across her jaw.

Carol staggered to her feet a second time, her knees now wobbling. Rea lunged at her and jabbed the end of the light into her gut. The filament in the bulb broke and the room went dark once more except for the faint glow from Carol's cell phone.

Like a feline, Rea pounced onto her prey. Carol groped along the floor. She slipped in her own blood and coughed up phlegm. She clutched a cardboard box to steady herself, but it collapsed, and she fell sideways. Her fall delayed Rea's assault for a moment. Carol's hand landed on a short wooden flagpole inside a box in time to thrust the metal end into Rea's oncoming abdomen. Her neighbor's eyes went wide, and Carol broke the wooden pole across the crazed women's shoulders.

Instinct activated an ancient part of Carol's hind brain and flooded every cell in her body starting with her spinal cord and terminating at the tips of her fingers and toes.

She leapt on her assailant who was down on one knee and breathing heavily. Boxes and shelves crashed down around them and on them. Her senses came alive as she made out grey shapes against a black backdrop. She could feel Rea's hair brush against her face. She smelled jasmine. They rolled on the floor. Carol threw a knee into Rea's ribs, and Rea punched at Carol's eye but hit a metal pole supporting a floor joist instead. They tore at each other's flesh—Carol biting Rea's finger so hard she could have choked on it.

Carol reached for the socket wrench, but Rea grabbed her leg and pulled her back. They separated in the darkness but found each other when they stood up and traded punches once again. Rea reeled back from another blow. When Carol's next punch missed, her crazed neighbor wrapped a strand of garland around Carol's neck and stuck her knee into the small of her back.

Bloody bubbles formed below Carol's nostrils. There was no room in her trachea for any air to escape except through the pores in her skin. Her strength evaporated as Rea's grip tightened, and a sense of calm took over Carol's body.

She collapsed to her knees and landed on the socket wrench. Grabbing her only hope, she stabbed it into Rea's right foot causing the mad woman to loosen her grip. Carol seized the moment, turned, and smashed the wrench across Rea's shin.

Rea let out an unnatural howl. The garland fell from Carol's throat as she lunged for Rea. She wrapped her hands around Rea's neck and pressed her thumbs against her larynx.

Rea's grey eyes rolled up into her head.

Carol pushed harder.

Rea's hands dropped.

Still, Carol pushed.

Rea stumbled backward, gasped, and slid to the floor. Carol looked at Rea lying on her side, a knife stuck in her back. Dust floated through the thickened air as silence settled on the room.

"Mommy, look."

Carol's chin was on her chest.

"Mommy, look."

Her hands fell limp by her sides.

"Mommy!"

She looked back at Becca who pointed to the bottom of the steps.

Sis.

Maxx came down the steps with a light in one hand but stopped short when he saw two women standing motionless and a third lying dead in a pool of blood.

Maxx pried back the kennel fencing and lifted his daughter to freedom. He held her like the day they'd first brought her home, shutting his eyes and swaying her back and forth. His one hand on the back of her head felt her long hair. His other hand wrapped around her back and felt her ribs.

"Daddy?"

"What, baby?"

"I want to go home."

Maxx lifted her into his arms and smiled. "Me too, baby, me too."

They walked upstairs with Carol and her sister. "I wanted to surprise you guys." Sis's speech sounded pressured, and her sentences flowed into each other. "I flew into Philly and called the farm. And then rented a car and headed right down here when I heard about Daphne.

I figured you needed my help. I parked on the road, then I saw Daphne's door was open. I went upstairs, but when I heard the commotion in the basement, I grabbed the first thing I saw and ran to help."

"How did you get past the bridge patrol?"

"Who, Billy? He's from Pennsylvania. His family has a farm in Carlisle."

Carol shook her head and took Becca from Maxx's arms.

"I grabbed a knife when I heard all the commotion and ran down the steps, not knowing how dark it'd be. When I got to the bottom, I stood against the wall, and barely saw something coming at me. When Daphne fell, I didn't even know what happened. Then I saw the knife and knew she'd backed into me. I must have killed her."

"Sis, you didn't kill her, it was self-defense. You're no murderer, you're a hero." Maxx squeezed his arms around his sister-in-law.

Carol held on to Becca. "I am never ever going to let you go."

"Me too, Mommy."

"Let's get out of here," Maxx said.

As the four left the house, Maxx noticed the rain and wind had lessened. They walked across the grass and through clumps of wet shrubs and broken tree branches to their own house.

"*Dopo la pioggia, arriva il sole.*"

"What, Carol?"

"Something someone told me before I left Rome—*after the rain, the sun comes.*"

Despite the cessation of emergency services, two police cars and an ambulance responded to Maxx's call. Neighbors who hadn't evacuated came out of their houses to gawk at the yellow caution tape wrapped around trees.

One officer started to set up lights in Rea's basement until the electricity could be restored.

Next door, an officer talked to Carol, while another talked to Sis. Maxx led Becca to her room and away from the action.

"Peggy!" Becca said as she hugged her stuffed Pegasus. Maxx sat in the rocking chair and lifted her into his lap. Something shiny caught his eye as he looked at the chifforobe.

"Daddy, why are you crying." Becca patted his wet cheek.

"I'm happy, baby."

"Then, why are you crying?"

"Someday, I'll tell you."

Upstairs, Sis repeated her story to the detective who had been joined by his superior.

"I told you, I don't remember stabbing anyone. I had a knife in my hand because ... well, because it was on the counter. I just grabbed it, ran downstairs, and now she's dead. It was dark, that's all I know."

"Thank you, ma'am. We're going to need to follow up, but that's it for now." The detective closed his notebook and turned to Carol.

Carol rocked back and forth on the couch as a paramedic wrapped an Ace bandage around her rib cage, checked her pupils, and gave her a mini-mental status exam to rule out a concussion. Carol held a bottle of water against her forehead and held her ribs with her other hand.

"Can you shut those blinds?" she asked. She could see two neighbors standing on the other side of the street, but the streetlight bothered her more.

"Ma'am?"

"Mrs. Davies," Carol replied.

"Mrs. Davies, I have everything we need for now, but I just have one more question. Why didn't you call us sooner?"

"I did. Someone came out here. Detective Krinshaw."

"What happened?"

"You tell me. We never heard from him."

The police officer made a quick phone call to the station.

"We'll get to the bottom of this. I'll send a patrolman out to his house. This never should have happened."

"I have my little girl. That's all that matters." Carol looked at her torn clothes, smeared with dirt, blood, and basement mold. Her hair hung at her shoulders—her braids unraveled.

"Yes, Mrs. Davies, that's what matters."

"I'd like to get cleaned up. I want my daughter."

Carol refused to go to the hospital and had to sign several forms before the paramedic left her alone. She put plastic wrap around her bandages before stepping into a warm shower. The water made her wince but when she lowered her head into the waterfall, her eyes shut, and her muscles started to relax. It hurt to move and to breathe. She stood motionless with the shower water pouring warmth and safety and thought of nothing until reality forced her back.

She dried herself off and put on a T-shirt and yoga pants. Sis brought Becca out from her bathroom, her hair still wet but combed, and the three walked upstairs to the open kitchen and living area.

At the breakfast bar, Maxx made Becca a chocolate milk and PB&J. He had found a snack pack of potato chips and had put some between the bread, the way Becca liked it.

Carol stroked Becca's hair as she and Maxx blew bubbles in their chocolate milk. She turned to her sister. "Where's Antonio?"

"Up at the farm, planning the party with Mother."

They looked at each other and laughed as they imagined the conversation going on between her Italian husband and their mother.

Maxx checked his phone for weather updates and heard the hurricane had turned north and was downgraded to a tropical storm, taking its full force to the middle of the

Atlantic. Roads were already surfacing while drainage ditches filled with water.

Sis sipped on wine as she explained their notes to Maxx, which were still taped and written on the mirrored wall. He looked at the books piled in the corner, and the legal pads and sticky notes scattered around the great room.

Sis nudged Maxx when he remarked, "You two did a lot of work—you should call Dr. Lazarus."

Carol shrugged. "This was our brain work. It wasn't until I did some soul searching that it all came together. And now we have our daughter." Her words brought tears to her eyes.

"So anyway," Sis broke in, "about the party—it'll be great. We're gonna clean out the barn, string lights, get a country band, and have ourselves a pig pickin'. Like when you and Maxx got married on the farm. Just, you know … better."

"What does Antonio think about all this?"

"I dunno. We'll see, I guess. I kind of took over after getting the green light from his mother."

"I see."

"Antonio has been single for so long he welcomes my whims." Sis took another sip of her wine.

"Maybe Sis and Antonio's party will be just the distraction we need to get away from all this," Maxx stated.

Carol stood and took Becca downstairs to get ready for bed. She tried to tickle her, but Becca began to whimper, so Carol pulled her close instead.

Becca slept in her mother's arms while Carol watched her daughter's little chest raise and lower the bedsheet. At Becca's insistence, she'd left one light on. As she stroked her hair, Carol could not help but be amazed at how long it had grown—a gauge of how long they had been apart.

We're going to do something about that.

Carol fell asleep propped against the headboard, still watching her little girl breathe.

The next day, Maxx packed their car and called the police station for any updates and to tell them where they were headed. He didn't get an argument but was told they were still searching for Krinshaw. The group decided to travel together—no one wanted to be alone. They called the rental agency to pick up Sis's car. Carol didn't ask about the cost, it no longer mattered.

Their first stop was a diner filled with truckers and construction workers. The building resembled a rail car, clad in aluminum and about as wide as a single wide trailer.

"I love a good diner, I do," Maxx remarked.

"I do too," repeated Becca. It was the first thing she'd said all morning. She'd cried when Maxx carried her into the diner and just stared at her Minnie Mouse pancake.

It took them at least an hour longer to return home, but it seemed a lot shorter to Carol. As they turned into the farm lane, they saw a banner draped across the porch: "WELCOME BACK, BECCA."

"Hey, why does she get top billing? I came all the way from Rome," said Sis.

Everyone but Sis laughed.

Mother, Mee-Maw, Mrs. Peters, and Antonio stood under the banner and shared hugs all around. They hugged so much, Carol felt she was being hugged even when she wasn't. Becca allowed herself to be hugged but her arms stayed rigid at her sides.

Carol was the first to step through the door into the kitchen.

"Surprise!"

"Dr. Lazarus!"

"You didn't think I'd miss this party, do you? For years, I never even knew where you lived, and now I'm here."

Her mother slipped an arm through hers. "Your professor's pretty good at shoveling pig poop too."

"Is that what we call it in front of Dr. Lazarus, Mother? Pig poop?"

"Wait 'til he loads a hay trailer. I still have blisters," Maxx added.

CHAPTER 27

In the morning, the entire family worked together in the barn and grounds preparing for Sis's party.

"No, Maxx, loop the lights across the beams, just don't string them," Sis insisted. "Antonio, even Mother carries two straw bales. Oh, and arrange them like benches in a park, for conversation, you know."

Sis's mother tied corn stalks and pumpkins around posts and fixed fall flowers in Ball canning jars.

"Yes, perfect, Mother, perfect. Oh, but some of the leaves are looking a little dead." Sis headed for the door. "Keep going everyone, chop-chop. I have a few calls to make."

She hustled up to the house to call a local cover band that played country and western and 80's rock. Inside, she noticed Mee-Maw in the kitchen. She'd enlisted Dr. L to roll pastry.

"Don't over-knead the dough, Dr. L, it happens sooner than you think," Sis chided as she came through the door. Dr. Lazarus worked the pastry while Mee-Maw called a cadre of seniors to make their finest potluck. "Mee-Maw, I need the phone. I have to get back to the barn—it's crazy down there."

After making her calls, Sis walked back to the barn and nearly tripped over Becca. "Becca, honey, help your mother tie these napkins around this plasticware."

Becca picked up a fork and spoon but froze when she felt the knife in her hand. Carol picked her up and walked into the sunlight.

So much for that task getting done.

Sis waved as the local pastor drove up with a truck full of tables, chairs, and a punch bowl. She directed Maxx and Antonio to unload the truck and then turned and announced to the group, "I called Sammy—he still has his barbecue trailer. He's showing up the morning of the party. I told him 'And I want an apple in the pig's mouth. I mean it.'" She laughed with those around her.

Three days later, people started showing up while the band ran power cords to the garage. Sis, with her hair piled high on her head and dressed in a floral-pleated dress, stood at a small door cut into one of the large barn doors with Antonio to greet their guests. Antonio smiled, and laughed whenever he didn't understand a guest. Antonio laughed a lot.

Sis walked over to where Mee-Maw and Mrs. Peters stood behind the long tables that held everything from casseroles to whoopie pies to a pig with an apple in its mouth.

"Maxx, honey can you keep an eye on the beer keg? Oh, and on the bartender, too? I absolutely love you using the old panel door for the bar. Great idea."

"It was your idea, Sis."

"Well, whatever, it works."

"Where's Carol and Becca?" her mother asked.

"You know Carol, she'll be here."

Cymbals crashed, the base drum thumped, a fiddle wailed, and guitars sang while a thin, bleached blonde in long black tights tested the mics.

"Maxx, it's getting hot. Help me open these barn doors."

Sis and Maxx lifted the plank and pushed open the twelve-foot high wooden doors. As the doors swung open, the Christmas lights strung overhead cast their brilliance onto two ladies walking up the grassy knoll leading to the barn.

Everyone stopped to look at Carol and Becca—even Sammy, the barbeque man who stood poised to ring the dinner bell.

Becca's little black dress matched Carol's LBD from Rome. Carol had bought them both believing they would be needed someday. She'd been right. Both ladies wore a simple silver sphere around their necks. Carol had cut Becca's hair a day earlier, and her curls barely touched her shoulders.

Sammy rang the old cast iron dinner bell that hung from a post.

The bell made Becca cry.

"Honey, don't cry," Maxx said, "That's the bell you ring when you want someone to look."

Carol had taken down her trademark braids, and now, her thick hair bounced just below her shoulder blades.

"Where did you get those beautiful eyes?" Sis heard her mother ask.

"They're yours, Mother."

"I didn't know you had so much hair," her mother replied. "Carol, you're beautiful."

Maxx walked up to his wife and daughter and hugged them both. "My family," was all he could say.

After dinner, Sis stopped talking to one of her old classmates in the band and wrapped her arms around her sister.

"Welcome to *my* party," Sis whispered in her ear as the band struck up the first song of the night.

Sheets of plywood covered the planked barn floor in front of the band. Carol watched as little boys and girls formed a circle and created their own dance, but Becca didn't join the group. Maxx lifted their daughter up and turned in circles to the music instead. Older couples found each other for one song, and younger couples stayed for more.

She'd noticed Dr. Lazarus talking to her grandmother all day and noticed he'd finally convinced Mee-Maw to leave the dessert table for one dance.

"Stop it, Carol," Mee-Maw said when the song ended.

"What? I didn't say a thing." She smiled and nudged her grandmother with her elbow.

Dr. L and Mee-Maw, both full of smiles, walked back to the dessert table.

Sis sat down on a straw bale next to Carol with a piece of shoofly pie.

"I love Pennsylvania Dutch cooking, don't you? Are you having fun?"

"I am." Carol watched Becca observe a little girl running with another and carrying orange streamers around the bales of hay.

"As much fun as your wedding?"

"I guess. How are you, Sis?"

Her sister shrugged as she shoved a piece of pie in her mouth. "Any word from North Carolina? Did they find your detective yet?" Sis asked.

"Yes, Detective Krinshaw called. He was locked in the trunk of his car, down by the pier. Someone named Tomlinson found him."

"Odd. Did they say who put him there?"

"No, but it must have been Daphne."

"Oh, right. I guess that's where she got her flashlight."

"Yeah," Carol said, touching her head where she'd been struck. "He asked when we're coming back to the beach. He needs to complete his investigation. I said I didn't know. But I don't feel settled here. I feel like I'm back in school and I'm sneaking around Mother again."

"Skipping over the stair step."

"Right. I want to be back at the beach, but I don't want to hurt anyone's feelings."

"I can't go back," Sis said. "I can't ever go back. Daphne ... Rea, whoever she was ... got what she deserved. I never liked her fake hair extensions or her green contacts. And all her matching outfits."

"She had green contacts? How do you know?"

"I don't know, they just looked fake, like her boobs. Didn't they?"

"They were fake?"

"And all that make-up. Even on the beach. Really?" Sis rolled her eyes.

"Did you know her before?"

"I never met her." She speared her last piece of pie. "This shoofly pie is incredible. Want some? I'm getting more." When Carol shook her head, Sis stood. "I'm going to find Antonio."

Carol watched as her sister led her new husband out on the plywood floor for their slow dance. Her mother came and stood next to Carol.

"I have to take their picture in front of the clock. Sis never went to her prom, you know. She always told me she wanted a picture like Joey's and yours."

"She knew about their picture?"

"Sure, she did. She was there."

"Are you certain?"

"You know your sister. She was always getting in the way. I even took a picture of her with Joey and Rea. I just saw it this morning when I put away the lock of hair I snagged when you were cutting Becca's hair yesterday. Why?"

Carol stared at her sister. "She told me she'd never met Rea."

"I don't know why she would say that, honey. She must have forgotten."

The dance ended and Sis bounded back to Carol and her mother.

"This is the happiest day of my life! Thank you both. I love you to the moon and back."

Their mother put an arm around Sis's shoulder. "I love seeing you sisters together. My fondest memories are of you two riding your horses when you were girls."

"We should do that again," Sis said, bouncing on her toes.

"Yeah, right." Carol waved her away with a flick of her wrist.

"No. That's a great idea," their mother said. "You could ride the mare and the paint. It's been a while since they've been ridden. All the tack is there."

"Whatev—"

"We're doing it. Tomorrow. Me and you, lil' sis." Sis's smile was too wide for Carol to object.

Maxx walked over with Antonio. "You definitely should do it, Carol. Antonio and I are going to be working in the barn all day."

"Let's go down and see the horses now," Carol said. "Maybe that will cheer Becca up."

Maxx and Carol walked with Becca down to the corral where the horses chewed on the last of the hay. Their tails were matted with briars, their manes had grown over their eyes, and their winter coats were beginning which made it look like they had patches of hair. But their ribs didn't show, if anything they were a little on the fat side. Their backs looked straight, withers strong, and their hoofs solid.

Maxx held Becca's hand as she reached out to stroke the paint's nose.

"It'll be fine, Carol, you used to love to ride. What's the problem?"

"Maxx, maybe I'm making too much of this, but Sis told me she never met Rea before when Joey was dating her. Yet Mother told me Sis was with Rea and Joey before their prom."

"That was a long time ago. I'm sure she just forgot. And Rea changed her looks when she changed her name, so she looks different."

"I guess you're right. I'm thinking too much again. Sis has always been there for me, and we have Becca. That's all I need to know."

"If there's one thing I learned, it's everything has a purpose, " Maxx stated.

"What are you two love birds doing down here in the dark?" Sis, walking with Antonio, startled them. "Looks like you had the same idea as us—checking out our trusty steeds. I bet you're wondering what you got yourself into."

"It's been a long time since we rode horses, Sis."

"I feel like there isn't anything I can't do." Sis lifted her chin. "Bring it."

Antonio let go of Sis's hand to pick up some hay and entice the horses who jerked it out of his hand. Their worn halters hung loosely around their heads.

Becca climbed up on the middle rail to reach over and pet their foreheads. As she did, the painted mare jerked its nose. Becca's hand, caught between the halter and the paint's face, forced her to lose her balance and fall into the muddy stall.

Before Carol could scream, Maxx had leaped over the rails and picked his daughter out of the manure. The paint stood back and whinnied as Becca cried.

"It's okay, baby girl, she's a good horse. She was just scared of being trapped."

"Like me, Daddy?"

Maxx kissed her cheek. "I guess so, yes, like you."

"I was scared, too, Peggy, but we'll be okay, we have Mommy and Daddy." Becca's words quieted the paint.

"Is that her name, Becca?"

"Yup, Peggy, like my Pegasus. The other one is Tutt, like my turtle. She's a good horse, Mommy. We were scared. You'll be all right too."

The group walked back to the barn where the party was breaking up. Sis and Antonio stood at the doors to thank everyone and say goodbye.

The barbecue man packed up his trailer. "I'll come by tomorrow when the coals die down to get it."

"I can't wait to open these gifts," Sis said, looking over the vast array of pretty packages.

"I'm ready for bed," said Mee-Maw. "I think I'll head home. Thank you for our dance, Dr. Lazarus."

"Ezekiel," he answered, and kissed her outstretched hand.

"Have you ever been to Hershey, Ezekiel?"

"No, I haven't, but I'd love to see it someday."

"Yes, I'd love to show it to you."

"Come on, Mee-Maw," said Sis. "I'll drive you home. We can open our gifts tomorrow."

Antonio got in the back seat and Mee-Maw got in the passenger side of Sis's car. She sat quietly in the seat, holding her kissed hand in her lap and looking out the windshield at her family as they backed out of the driveway.

Carol turned to Becca. "You 'tink, little lady. I think it's time for a bath and then bed."

Dried leaves blew across the shingles and filled the gutters while twigs fell from tall trees. In the woods, bucks lost their velvet, marking their territory by rubbing their antlers against thick saplings. In town, children thought about what they wanted to be for Halloween, and parents thought about what they wanted to be in life. But for now, it was time to make sure they had dry wood for the stove, a turkey for Thanksgiving, and money for Christmas.

"Could be a cold one this year," Carol's mother said to her granddaughter.

Since her husband had died, she'd taken on the farm work, stiffened her back, and tightened her grip. When she shook hands with a man, he knew it. She had a way of getting someone's attention. Her assertiveness had toughened as she'd secluded herself with acres of soybeans and woods.

Yet, every night since her two men died, she'd prayed that God would take her soon so she could be with them. And every day she worked to that end.

She prayed that same prayer every night but this night. On this night, she caught a glimpse of her maker's plan, and she let it be as the October breeze blew through her soul. She knew winter was coming, but she gathered in the fall. She kissed her wet grandchild as Becca got out of the tub and headed for bed wearing a cotton night gown with printed jasmine flowers.

"Dry your wet head, Joey ... I mean Becca."

"Who's Joey?" Becca asked.

"Grandma gets names mixed up. Joey was my son."

"Silly Grammy."

"We'll talk about Joey some other day."

CHAPTER 28

Carol pulled on a pair of stretch jeans and hiking boots and then found a flannel shirt in her closet and headed downstairs. Becca slid down the banister while Carol held her hand.

"My mother would have swatted my butt with the spaghetti strainer if she saw me do that."

"I still might," yelled her mother from the first floor.

Carol poured herself some coffee into a personal thermos and added cream. Sis's car pulled in as she was walking down the porch steps.

"We won't be riding until we clean up the horses," said Sis. "Well, hello, Becca."

"I'm Joey."

Carol's mother walked out of the kitchen and said, "She's been saying that all morning."

The four girls walked across the dirt lane and through the wet grass to the corral.

Carol gasped as she saw the horses. Gone were their unruly manes and the briar-filled tails. In their place stood a well-groomed gelding and sleek, painted mare. Their coats had been curried, their hooves filed and picked.

"Mother, the horses are beautiful."

"I got up early and got them ready for my girls."

Sis had made lunches and packed them in a sack that she now tied to the saddle horn.

"Here're some snacks. Tie them on your saddle, Carol." Her mother lifted another cloth sack to her.

Sis moved Tutt closer to the fence and then stood on the second rail to mount. When she put her foot into the stirrup, the bay gelding shied away, causing her to do a split between her horse and the fence. She grabbed at the horn and her mother pushed on her free leg to swing it over Tutt's hindquarters.

"It ain't pretty, but I'm up."

The bay and painted horse headed out of the corral. Becca and her grandmother watched the sisters' ponytails bounce above their flannel shirts until they disappeared over the last hill.

★★★

The jolt in the horse's trot jarred Carol's bones and her saddle slid from side to side. Nothing but a strip of leather and a piece of metal in the horse's mouth guided it down the path. She preferred to walk, but Sis liked to canter, to feel the smooth gait when one hoof touched the ground and the other three were air born. But Carol feared the gallop when all the hooves were airborne at once and a rider could be thrown from a horse fresh from the barn.

Now, Carol and Sis ducked under the low hanging branches on the edge of the field that led down into a hollow. The grade was steep on the only trail made by deer and small game. Thorns jutted out and caught the two at their calves and pulled at their pants. A rabbit jumped in front of Peggy. The mare's ears stood up and her nostrils flared.

"It's just a bunny, girl." Carol patted her skittish horse.

"Look there, Carol."

At the edge of the field stood an eight-point buck—its thick rack wider than his ears. He pawed at the ground and shook the branches around him with his antlers to let a younger buck know this was his territory.

The older buck could wait no longer and loped into the field, meeting the young buck at the top of the ridge. After one clash of antlers, the younger ran off. The old buck followed a doe to the other side of the field and disappeared.

"Miraculous. Everyone has a role in God's world, everyone," Carol commented.

Carol and Sis smiled at each other and rode on. Sis took a side trail that led through a stretch of wide flat wetlands. The horses hesitated but trusted their riders and stepped across a shallow stream. The slippery rocks at the bottom caused a hurried stride up and out the other side. The river shimmered in the distance. Carol didn't recognize the lot until they were on the steep road that led down to the picnic site where she and Ralph had paddled their canoe.

They tied the horses and left them munching on the lush grass. "I hope you two don't get sick," Carol said.

Sis retrieved the lunch sacks and carried them and the water bottles to the picnic table. The sandwiches and the salty broken potato chips tasted good. Laying on the wooden bench soothed Carol's ribs as the warm wood and gentle sun enveloped her.

While Sis took a pair of apples to the horses, Carol grabbed the second sack to look for some home-baked snacks from the night before. A picture fell to the bench when she reached for a no-bake chocolate oatmeal cookie. She turned it over to see her mother had included the picture of Joey, Rea, and Sis in front of the clock. "I told you" was written on the back.

"Oh my."

"What, Carol?"

"Mother. She put this picture in with the snacks." She handed it to Sis and her sister's face flushed. "You *do* remember her, don't you?"

Sis swallowed hard, placed the picture on the picnic table, and then took a sip of water.

"What do you want me to say? Yes, I knew her. So, what?"

"So, what? You lied, so what. Sis, what else did you lie about?"

"Nothing. I knew her." She shrugged. "She used to be fun."

"You were friends?"

"Sort of."

They sat looking at the river. The current flowed, carrying stray branches and fallen leaves. "What's that supposed to mean?" Carol asked.

"We talked. She called me when Daddy died."

"When Daddy died? What did you tell her?"

"I just said I couldn't believe you and Joey were out riding on his motorcycle."

"You did what?"

"I didn't think she'd find you. It wasn't 'til later I found out Rea was pregnant with Joey's baby, and I knew you wanted a baby, so ... it's all good."

"You knew Becca was Joey's?"

Sis took another sip of water but said nothing.

"Sis, you knew Daphne was Rea ... and Becca." Carol put her head in her hands. "Oh, my!"

"I just wanted you to have a baby and be happy."

Carol looked at her sister and said, "Wait a minute. You really didn't want me to go to Rome, and then you wanted me to give up looking. You didn't even want me to come here. You kept trying to talk me out of it this whole time, didn't you?"

"I just wanted you to be happy, Carol."

"*You* just wanted to be happy. And you wanted me off the scent just like that old buck. You wanted to be in control. You wanted to be the rider on the horse, and you wanted me to be your horse."

"Carol, that's not fair."

"Was Rea your horse too? Is that how she found me? Did you tell her? Did you?"

"Carol, a lot has happened. You're tired. You don't know what you're saying. I did it all for you, lil' sis."

"Did you tell her where we were living?"

Sis shrugged again. "I just thought she should know where her daughter was. I didn't know she was a pagan, and Lord knows I didn't think she was crazy. I didn't think she'd move next to you. By the time I found out, it was too late. She was your neighbor and your friend. She was your babysitter. You liked her."

"It was all a big lie. You knew the whole time. You knew she took Becca. Did you help her to do it? How could you?" Carol stood now, full of rage. "You weren't trying to help me at all!"

"Becca was Joey and Rea's baby, Carol. Becca is not your baby."

Her words cut into Carol like the knife cut into Rea. She stood stunned, dazed. "You are sick," she finally said.

"Carol, you got everything, your fabulous job, your wealthy husband, and your beach house. If I'm sick, I'm sick of you always getting everything you ever wanted and never being happy about it."

"You're so jealous—you wanted me to suffer."

"You had everything, all while I looked after our grieving mother. What about me? I lost my father, my brother, and my husband too. But it was always about you. You put me through so much pain."

"Sis, do you have any idea how much pain you put me through?"

Sis looked out across the water again and said nothing.

"You could have put that knife through me."

"I wanted to."

Both sisters sat motionless as the river moved toward the Chesapeake. Some words can be taken back, excused, or ignored. Some words last a lifetime.

"You wanted to? Were you upstairs with Rea?"

"You're thinking too much about this, Carol."

"You knew about the detective, too, didn't you?" Carol paused and considered her sister, a woman she no longer knew. "That knife was meant for me, wasn't it?" Carol started to walk back toward her horse.

"Carol, wait."

Carol untied Peggy's reins, put her left foot in the stirrup, and mounted as the horse started up the hill. She dug in her heels when she saw Sis gathering Tutt. By the time Sis had led Tutt to the picnic table to mount, Carol had fled over the first hill.

Peggy and Carol cantered down the country lane. The horse kicked up an occasional stone and avoided the holes worn by the rain. When Carol urged Peggy to jump a fallen tree, she was back in 4-H form, but still let out a yelp and clutched her aching ribs. Peggy slowed down when she got to the hollow and the branches closed in on her. Fallen branches broke under the horse's hooves. Peggy's lack of conditioning caught up to her as she staggered to the top of the hollow.

"Carol, stop. I just want to talk!" Siss yelled but Carol kept going. Sis closed in and swung a birch branch at Carol but missed when Peggy stepped into a groundhog hole and stumbled to her front knees. Carol's feet brushed the tops of the soybeans, yet she somehow hung on by hugging Peggy's neck and grabbing onto her mane. The branch fell out of Sis's hand.

Now both Carol and Sis reached the top of the hill and saw the barn below. Smelling the safety of home, both horses broke into a reckless gallop. A fear overtook them that neither rider could subside.

Carol saw Becca outside peddling Joey's toy tractor. Her little girl looked up and her eyes widened when she saw the horses racing toward her. She jumped off her tractor and reached for the rope hanging from the large cast iron dinner bell. Hearing the loud gong, Maxx and Antonio hustled out of the barn, and Mother stood up in the middle of her garden.

Becca pointed to the horses.

Carol jumped off her horse at the corral, with Sis following close behind. Before Carol could reach the safety of her family, her sister tackled her from behind and the two fell into the muck. Antonio and Maxx hurried across the fence and separated them, but Sis kept kicking and clawing at Carol, at Antonio, and at the air.

Maxx held onto Carol who whispered, "Maxx, she's crazy. She was behind it all."

"It should have been you!" Sis screamed. "I'll kill you, Carol. It should have been you."

Carol's mother walked to Sis with deliberate steps. Holding her leather gardening gloves in one hand, she smacked her across the mouth.

Everyone froze.

Sis stopped screaming, went to her knees, and began muttering. Her murmuring streamed into sentences before she broke down and cried. Then, a moment later, she broke into a maniacal laugh before crying some more.

"Come on, let's get inside." Maxx ushered Carol and Becca inside while Antonio took Sis to the family room and sat between her and the woodstove. As Carol began walking up the stairs, she spied Sis rocking back and forth and still mumbling. Dr. Lazarus held one of her hands while Antonio sat on the other side of her. Their mother stood with the phone at her ear, looking from Sis to Carol.

After Maxx cleaned Carol's wounds and rewrapped her ribs, he brought her some food she wouldn't eat. She lay on top of her bed and looked out the window to the top of the fields. Maxx sat in one corner of the oversized room with Becca, who played with some of her mother's old Care Bears. Carol shut her eyes and saw herself and Sis galloping down the lane. It hurt her ribs to remember.

"Here, you're the daddy, and this one is the mommy." Becca handed Maxx two stuffed bears. "I'm the girl bear."

"What's the girl's name?"

"Joey, call me Joey."

Maxx and Becca played with the bears as the sun went down, and Carol fell asleep on her bed. When Becca's eyes started to droop too, Maxx lay her beside her mother and saw two vehicles driving away from the house. He went downstairs and found Dr. Lazarus sitting beside Carol's mother.

"Sis had a breakdown," he told Maxx. "We called the clinic and they sent out an ambulance. The police always ride along. The officer took the whole story and said he'll get back with Carol when she's rested. Her mother wouldn't let him interrupt her rest. Antonio went with Sis. We think she'll be committed and will be on a psych unit for a while."

Maxx looked out the window and ran a hand through his hair. "This is incredible."

"Yes, it is.

Becca walked into the room and climbed into her grandmother's lap.

"Oh, Sis ... Carol ... I mean, Becca."

"I'm Joey, remember?"

"Okay, Joey, I'll try to remember that. Are you okay, sweetie?"

"Yes, I'm happy."

"Happy? Why?"

"Because I have Mommy, and I have Daddy, and I have you right here."

At the bottom of the steps, Carol sniffled, and her mother looked up at her.

"How long have you been there, Carol?"

"Long enough. I'm fine, Mom. How's Sis?"

Her mother looked down at Becca and then back at her daughter. "I don't know."

Carol walked over to her mother and reached for Becca. "You should go to her. I'm fine."

"You could have punctured a lung."

"But I didn't. I have my family. And Sis needs to know she still has you."

Her mother sighed and then stood. "Okay. I'm going. I like when you call me Mom. Right, Joey?"

"Right, Grammy."

CHAPTER 29

It had been months since Carol and Sis raced to the barn. Now Carol lay on her beach house bed as her phone rang.

"Carol, it's Maxx. I just pulled a breech-born calf from its mother and breathed air into its nostrils! You should have seen her wobbly knees and stretched-out neck as it suckled."

"You sound ... happy."

"I am happy."

"That's good," Carol replied.

"No, you don't understand, Carol. We could be happy. I want to live here for real. I could farm."

Carol looked out her window at the crashing surf. "Maxx, you're not a farmer."

"That's only because I don't farm."

"Whatever," Carol said and started to say goodbye. "Wait ... If you want to farm, go for it."

"Whatever" would never be her last word again.

After Dr. Lazarus left the farm, he took a partial appointment at the Smithsonian in DC. Maxx, Carol, and Joey visited him there during the fall break from school, saw the Roman artifacts, and walked the halls lined with sculptures, frescoes, and paintings. For Carol, it felt like another world she recognized but no longer knew.

"Who's this, Mommy?"

"That's Libertas, Joey."

"She's pretty. Is this her cat?"

"Yes, I suppose so. She's special," Carol said rubbing her necklace between her fingers.

"I want to be her," Joey said.

"You are, in your way, a lot like her … in a good way."

"How's Sis?" Dr. Lazarus asked, "And my old assistant, Antonio?"

"Pretty good, I suppose. I don't hear from them much." Carol didn't want to talk about her sister's commitment. "The DA reduced her charges when I refused to testify against her, so she did community service and was placed on probation."

Dr. Lazarus looked at Carol. She could see his concern and felt his caring eyes, but like her daughter, she was at a loss of words and began to twirl her hair.

"She went back to her old house in town," Maxx said now, breaking Carol out of her reverie. "I guess she felt like an outcast, but she took her medication and kept to herself. Antonio has stuck by her side."

"No," said Carol. "She's not there anymore. Mother saw a realtor putting up a for-sale sign. The realtor said she'd moved out and had gone to Italy."

"Without saying goodbye?" Dr. L asked.

"Her probation was up. She stopped to say goodbye to Mee-Maw on her way to the airport."

"She loved Rome, Carol. You studied it, but she lived it. After you left, Sis learned Italian, her mother-in-law taught her how to cook Italian, and she took classes at the museo. She blossomed into a different person."

"What do you mean?"

Dr. Lazarus sighed. "Well, she became authentic. Being on her own, without family or people who'd known her for years, she reinvented herself and grew into the person she wanted to be. I think being home forced her into her old self and she hated it."

"I always thought she was angry at something, but she always had a smile and laughed at everything, even if it wasn't funny."

"Me too," Maxx added. "She would say these little things that burned, but it was always too small or too late to ask her about it."

They said their goodbyes to Dr. Lazarus and then walked back to their hotel. Tourists scurried by with pamphlets mapping out the museums on the mall.

"Hurry up, kids, we can still make the Air and Space Museum by lunch," one dad yelled.

Maxx smiled and turned to Carol. "What about us?"

"I don't want to go to the Air and Space Museum."

"No, I mean, what about us?"

Carol knew what he meant. His tone and look told his intent. She waited for the question to go away. It didn't.

"I don't know, Maxx. Our current situation seems to be working. You like working on the farm and I need to be at the beach with Becca ... Joey."

"For now, it works, but you know I need a plan."

"I know you think you need a plan."

Maxx stopped her with a hand on her elbow. "This is important."

"I know it's important, Maxx. You don't think I know that? You don't think I hear Joey saying her prayers every night asking for her daddy? It hurts knowing I'm the one keeping her from you, but it's not my fault—not totally anyway."

"Look, I don't what to fight. That's not why I asked. I just want to know what you're thinking."

"Well, I want you to know that I *am* thinking, but I don't have a plan. Just not now anyway."

"When? When will you have a plan, Carol? I can only wait so long."

Joey tugged on Carol's hand. "Mommy, let's go!"

Carol nodded and then turned to Maxx. "I don't want to keep you from being happy if you want out."

"I don't want out," Maxx said, putting his arm around her waist and pulling her closer. "I want you."

CHAPTER 30

Lazy waves lapped at the edges of the beach towel. A plastic pail, rake, and shovel floated in the oncoming tide. The breeze felt cool now that the sun was on the way down.

"Joey, come pick up your toys before they float away."

Her daughter seemed not to hear as she frolicked with Ralph's dog Belle in the waves. Carol had agreed to take the black and white springer spaniel from Ralph's mother. Belle was good medicine for both. Together, child and dog rose over the smaller waves and under the big ones.

Carol turned back to her novel—*Rebecca* by Daphne du Maurier. Her floppy jute sun hat shaded the pages, and her dollar sunglasses colored the glare. The sun-bleached pages stuck together, and the cover was ripped. It had taken her the whole summer to read, but she was determined to see it through to the end.

As she read about the unnamed heroine and her new husband Maxim, and his first wife Rebecca, she recalled the adoption agent's words when she'd heard their three names. *I wonder if this book is what she meant?*

She put down her paperback to see her little girl and dog bouncing over the crest of a shallow wave. The salty sea air, the scent of coconut sun block, the sun on her back, and the sand between her toes told her she was home. The question she'd asked so many months ago sitting on this same beach, came floating back to her at this same spot.

I got a second chance when I got her back. Not everyone gets another chance. Thank you, God. I don't know if I said this before, thank you for my life—all of it. Like Maxx told me, your world is opening up to me. Thank you.

Carol watched the waves washing in and out and knew it would be going out in about eight hours. She looked to the right and observed the setting sun.

I wish I had another chance with my brother. I just want to hug him, just one more time.

Carol put down her book and walked to the water's edge.

"Joey, come on in," she yelled. "It's time to go, honey."

Joey took off her goggles and waved her mother in. Carol ducked under the next wave, and her body warmed to the water.

"Well, I guess we can stay a little longer." She lifted her little girl over a wave and held her close. The spaniel pawed at her back.

"Belle wants up too, Mommy."

"Joey, that dog thinks she's human."

"She's my sister."

The three made their way to the beach and shook out the sand from the chair and blanket. Carol loaded her chair with as much as she could carry and used its straps to wear it all on her back. Joey rolled up the mat and held on to one end of the dog leash. Then they walked up over the dunes and onto the boardwalk to home.

Carol's mother met them at the door.

"Grammy's here!" Joey squealed as she ran up the boards to her grandmother.

"I told you I would come see you, Joey. I missed you so much."

Maxx stepped out from behind her. "I drove. Don't I get a hug?"

Carol kissed Maxx on the cheek. "Thank you for bringing Mother through the awful weekend traffic."

"She complained until she fell asleep."

"She must be happy."

Carol led her guests inside and showed her mother her room.

"It has its own bathroom," her mother said, looking around at the spacious accommodations.

"All the rooms have their own bathroom, Mom."

"Now I know why you like it here so much, but I wouldn't want to clean them all."

Pictures of Joey, her grandmother, and great grandmother filled the nightstand. Carol's mother looked at every one while Carol put her things in the narrow closet. Conch shells and an old fishing net decorated the room that had a door leading to its own deck.

"My own deck too. I'll take my coffee right here tomorrow morning."

"She's happy," Maxx said.

"It's been a long time since I've seen her this happy. As a kid, I remember Mom after the Christmas meal. The presents had all been opened, the turkey picked over, and the pie served. She'd stand in the living room and stare at the tree. Then she'd move an ornament or two and take a step back. She seemed content, like she is now."

"Who seemed content?" her mother said returning with her granddaughter.

"Nothing, Mom. Still want to see the beach?""

"Well, I didn't drive nine hours for nothing."

They headed for the beach with Joey and Belle.

"Joey, don't get too far, it's getting dark." The girl and her four-footed sister ran back and forth, wetting her lighted sneakers in the surf.

"Lookey, Mommy, Grammy brought me bubbles." She began to blow bubbles and waved them at the creeping waters.

Becca in a bubble.

Carol remembered her game of imagining Becca trapped in a bubble. She looked at her mother whose tight-lipped smile matched hers.

"You're fortunate, Carol."

"I know, Mom. I got the second chance you didn't get."

"Why would you say that?"

"I just mean Daddy died, then Joey died, and you didn't get a second chance with them. You don't get to hug them. You don't get to love them like I love my Joey."

"But you're wrong, Carol. I talk to Daddy every day and Joey too. Butterflies come to me, a feather lands in front of me—they all tell me God is taking care of my men. Look what I found in your outside shower today." Carol's mother pulled a shiny new dime out of her pocket. "Don't worry, I'm not crazy. I'm just a mother too."

Carol grabbed her mother's hand and hugged her. Water seeped around their feet as they sunk into the wet sand.

"I can't explain these dimes. No one can. But they helped point the way when you were lost, and they picked you up when you were down. Honey, that surf keeps coming, and that tide will be back tomorrow. Today, I got to see the sunset when we drove over your bridge, and Lord willing, I'll see it tomorrow. Doesn't that tell you something?"

"God gives us another day?"

"Another chance. Joey's not dead, he's with his Father in heaven. And Carol, look." Her mother pointed at her granddaughter. "Don't you see him too? You get to hug him every day."

Carol looked up with tears in her eyes as she watched her Joey blowing another bubble that popped as it touched a wave.

"God's world is right in front of us. You got up, Carol, you went searching, and you found yourself back home. And when you did, you gave me a chance."

Carol pointed at Joey and Belle. "I love y'all, but my world is here."

"I love *you'uns*." Carol's mother laughed.

"Right, Mom, I love *you'uns*."

"Your sister got another chance, too, but she didn't see it, not here anyway. Maybe she'll see it someday. You found what I found when Daddy and Joey died—life matters. If you don't know that, you are just wasting your time on this beach."

"That's what I used to do," Carol said. "Waste my time."

"You were healing."

Carol looked at her mom and nodded. *"Nient'altro questioni dettit."*

"What's that?

"Something a cab driver told me, 'Nothing else matters.' The sand, the sea, even that plastic rake floating away in the tide. They only matter because of one thing." Carol watched Joey standing in front of the last bit of sunshine.

As the three girls held hands, walked over the final dune, and onto the boardwalk, they met Maxx.

"Life, it's all that matters." Carol embraced her family.

Therefore choose life, that both you and your descendants may live. (Deuteronomy 30:19b)

ABOUT THE AUTHOR

In the fourth grade Andy's teacher laughed so hard that she sent him and his story next door to read his story to another teacher. His "dark humor" letter to Mom from Valley Forge in which the soldier gradually succumbed to frost bite and died showed early signs of seeing the world differently (my humor really hasn't matured much). In the eighth grade his English teacher asked him to rewrite a story to submit it to a national writing contest (so I wrote a neater version proving my need for a good editor at an early age).

After graduating from The Christian Academy in Brookhaven, PA, Andy went on to play soccer and major in Behavioral Sciences at Messiah College where he met his wife, Lori. They raised their three children, Aaron, Ali, and Robby in Duncannon alongside their sheep, goats, and horses until moved to Indiana. Andy earned a doctorate in Clinical Psychology at Indiana State University. He accepted a commission in the US Navy to complete his internship at the National Naval Medical Center.

After retiring from the Navy, Andy and Lori settled on the coast in North Carolina. Everything changed when their son Aaron was killed while riding a motorcycle in 2014. Andy escaped to the 2,198.2-mile Appalachian Trail to deal with his grief when God gave him a story, *When Sunday Smiled,* which has been an Amazon Best Seller (ok, one day) and won second place in the Memoir category at the Selah Awards.

You'll want to read Andy's award-winning book, *When Sunday Smiles.* The first chapter follows.

CHAPTER 1

No Regrets

Lori held my hand. In the early hours of March 30, I took my place in a line of travelers waiting for the Greyhound bus at a nondescript gas station/ convenience store. Some hoped for a new job, others looked for a new life. I looked for a change. We stood together in the darkened parking lot in New Bern, North Carolina. I was the little kid trying out for the big kid's team. And the big kid's team was at Springer Mountain in Georgia, the start of the Appalachian Trail.

"No regrets," my wife whispered in my ear as she handed me a small pack of trail mix and some Jolly Ranchers. Her words sounded like something Adrian would have whispered to Rocky, but not something my wife would say. I expected her to say, "Have fun, good luck, or hurry home." But, no regrets? Lori's message sounded strong, sounded powerful—sounded like something that I needed. I made those words my vow.

No regrets, I repeated, *no regrets*, as I made my way to the middle of the bus. *No regrets.*

The problem is I regret everything. When I raised my hand at my Navy commissioning over twenty years ago, I stated, "And I do this with no mental reservations." I lied. I don't even walk to the bathroom without mental reservations. Regret defined me. So, as I sat alone on the bus watching Lori drive away in the darkness, I had a lot to think about.

I scanned the bus looking at my new companions, who were also looking for a new chance somewhere along the line. They looked too big, too old, and too casual in out of style and faddish attire. I easily judged people, put them in boxes, and often looked down on them. We were headed different places, but we were together, bound by more than an aluminum bus. The next nine hours on the Greyhound were my first lessons in grace as we traveled down the same road.

By the time we pulled into Durham, I was comfortable in my seat with no one next to me. I ate most of my snacks before we picked up more travelers. As they made their way down the aisle, I avoided eye contact to protect my space.

The woman across the aisle cursed into her cell phone while holding a baby with the other hand.

"We're not doing this here!" she yelled.

Actually, we are. In fact, we are all doing this here.

After a stop in Charlotte, I got back to my familiar seat in my temporary home as we headed to Georgia. *What are you trying to prove?* The question came back as the highway miles rolled under the wheels of the ungainly bus. The question, asked several months before, rang in my ears as if my friend Dave was right next to me.

I needed to prove I could do it, whatever "it" was. Not everyone can walk 2,189.2 miles in one year. The Appalachian Trail Conservancy or A.T.C, estimates that only one-in-four will complete the hike from one end to the other—a thru-hike. An accurate count is difficult. Many people skip sections but still consider themselves thru-hikers. I believe the count is less than ten percent. I wanted to be a ten-percenter.

I wanted to walk off my grief like Earl Shaffer in 1948—the first thru-hiker. After returning from World War II, he walked from Georgia to Maine to walk off the war. No one thought a thru-hike was possible until Shaffer. Since his feat, over ten thousand people have hiked the trail in a calendar year.

My grief was born on a warm Sunday afternoon in North Carolina. I had just finished painting a small wooden boat when a local police sergeant with a flat-top military haircut walked up our overgrown stone path. He opened the wooden gate, looked around, and hesitated.

"Excuse me, Mr. Davidson?"

Did I do something wrong? Puzzled, I wiped the grey paint from between my fingers.

"I ... regret to inform you ... son ... motorcycle ... sometime this morning ..." His voice faded as he handed me a scrap of paper. "Here's a number to call. I am sorry for your loss."

My question was "why." Why has no answer. Why did God let Aaron die? *Why? You could have stopped the tragedy. Why didn't you stop that minivan?* Why? As a Navy officer, I knew when a ship runs aground the captain is responsible regardless of who is at the helm. *God why aren't you accountable for Aaron's death?*

"Why" drove me to depression for almost a year after Aaron's death. Depression is anger turned inward, and I was furious. I am a psychologist and a Christian, but psychology came up short, and religion followed close behind. I needed more. I needed real. I turned to the trail.

My goal was to finish the trail. "If you don't finish you are nothing," said a fellow hiker. At the time, I thought he was right, but finishing isn't everything. Nine hours on a bus increased my resolve to walk the trail as I promised to never get back on a Greyhound before Maine.

It was dark by the time the innkeeper met me at the bus station. I loaded my pack in the back of her aging Suburban and got in with a thirty-year-old lawyer-turned-barkeeper from New Orleans, also determined to become a thru-hiker.

"I hike a lot," she said, "but nothing this big. I hope my pack isn't too heavy ... I don't think I forgot anything, did you?"

"I hope n—"

"Do you have AWOL's book?"

"I'm gonna carry parts of it," I said.

"Oh. I have the app."

We had nothing in common but the trail, which proved plenty until we arrived at the Hiker Hostel. "Breakfast at 7:00," was the last thing I remembered before falling asleep.

THWACK! A canvas bag for linens landed on my shoulder and slid off the side of the bed. I woke to the sting of canvas.

"Huh? Wha ...?"

"You're snoring so loud."

"Wha ...? What?" I asked, dazed.

"You're snoring so loud," he repeated in an Irish brogue.

"Oh, I'm so sorry," I stated in my 'tired brogue.' "It's a real problem. Good thing you're not my wife, right?"

My new roommate didn't laugh. I heard him roll over. I checked my phone in the early hours of March 31. The hostel system along the trail is an inexpensive way to get a hot shower and a real bed, and a hostel was a good way to begin my hike. It's a case of "you get what you pay for" and in this case, he got to pay to sleep next to someone who snores too loud. I got to sleep next to someone who hit me in the middle of the night with a canvas bag.

I lay on my stomach, hoping anyone else who was still awake would fall asleep, and maybe I could get some sleep. I was in a large room in the basement of a log cabin. My roommate and I were the only ones in the room but there was another group of hikers in the next room. I just wanted morning to come; I wanted to be a thru-hiker.

Beginning at Springer Mountain in Georgia, the Appalachian Trail traverses through the Appalachian Mountain chain until the terminus at Katahdin Mountain in Maine. That last two-tenths of a mile of the trail is special, but I focused on the first of over 165,000 three by six-inch white blazes—painted rectangles that mark the trail. I wanted to see my first white blaze at the summit of 3,780-foot Springer Mountain in north central Georgia.

I stayed away from the Irishman at breakfast the next day. I wanted no bad will coloring my walk. I ate as much as I could, weighed my pack, and climbed into a cramped van to the approach trail. I wanted to be in the woods to rid myself of the grief toxins that pulsated through this fifty-seven-year-old body. I wanted to be a NOBO, a North Bounder, to walk in one direction for the entire trail route. "Blue Blazers" take alternate routes that bypass mountains marked by "blue blazes" on the trail. I didn't start this venture to hike the Alternate Appalachian Trail, the A.A.T. I was there to hike the A.T. "Yellow Blazers" skip large sections of the trail by getting rides. They pass the yellow lines on the road to keep their hike alive.

"Flip Floppers" often start in the middle of the trail in West Virginia, go north to Maine, then drive back to the middle and walk south to Georgia. Flip Floppers get the benefit of better weather but lose the continuity of the trail and the camaraderie of the other hikers. That was too complicated. I hiked north. I carried everything I needed on my back. I walked looking for one thing— the next white blaze. That's what I did. I walked.

I stepped out on the eve of the busiest day of the trail and the birthdate of my youngest son. March 31, and I was in the middle of the "the bubble," when most hikers go north. My adrenaline rushed as I hurried past disillusioned hikers ill-prepared for the challenge. The trail contained all shapes, sizes, and configurations of backpacks. Backpackers resembled crazy cars from a Richard Scary children's book with cups, shoes, tents, and sleeping pads dangling from over-stuffed shells strapped on hunched-over backs. I breathed heavily through the early miles and passed hikers whose dazed stares of bewilderment mixed with a hint of helplessness.

"Fine," was always their weak reply when I asked

how they were, but their eyes betrayed them. Their eyes conveyed, "What did I do?"

Stopping for lunch at the first shelter, eight miles along the trail, I met a large hiker. He was bent over, holding his back with one hand while the other hand gripped the edge of the picnic table.

"My Special Ops instructor in the Army always asked me why I carried so much weight. I used to carry a hundred pounds," he said.

I doubted if he was in Special Operations, but I didn't question him in his pain. His contrite partner clutched his hamstring and lamented how he thought he was in better shape. In the background, his wife, on her cell phone, tried calling for a shuttle ride back to town. I didn't know there was a shuttle or a town. I didn't want to know and pressed further.

I was hurting too. From the beginning my knees hurt, more so when going downhill. On the first day, I cursed aloud, then prayed as I staggered down a large hill. Six months didn't give me enough recovery time after my orthoscopic surgery. Because of my brief recovery, I only did ten training hikes of various distances along the North Carolina coast. The only hill I faced was a bridge. I trained on flat and short courses compared to what I would face in the upcoming days.

My lunch of salami, cheese, and flat bread seemed adequate when walking beach miles, but the Appalachian Trail is no beach. Worry crept in as I walked away from the impromptu infirmary at the shelter. I pressed on.

Before he died, Aaron and I talked about hiking the two thousand-mile, five million steps of the Appalachian Trail. July 27, 2014, changed everything. In the fall, after I spent my workdays staring at my computer, my company asked for my resignation. By January, I didn't recognize the desperate and bearded old man in the mirror. Lori said I'd feel better if I cleaned up. She filled her time with pictures, friends, and flowers. At night, I listened to her sobbing. Nights were forever.

I read how the Appalachian Trail is life-changing. I watched videos of people persevering in the wilderness, alone in their thoughts, surrounded by the night. They walked a simple life. I wanted that. No, I needed that. I was dying inside, if not dead already. I wanted to die. I didn't want to kill myself, but I wanted to be with Aaron. I was running away from something, but I was running to something. What, I didn't know. In the mountains and miles, I would find out. After losing Aaron, I would find me. I had to do something. I had to get up—I had to walk.

Along with researching the trail, reading books, and talking to anyone who would listen, I started a blog before I left. My blog became a source of motivation as my growing group of readers developed into a support group. I needed them, and I prayed for them thinking what I would write as I traversed the next six miles. An early blog entry I entitled "Sleepwalking":

> For the last seven months, I've been walking in a haze, "sleepwalking," a therapist friend called it. I like that. Grief will do that to you. Robbed of happiness, devoid of joy, missing a reason to go on. Not sure if I want to live or die, just knowing I need to put one foot in front of the other. I'm afraid. I didn't want to sleepwalk the trail. The number one rule, every thru-hiker knows it, is HYOH, Hike Your Own Hike.

After fourteen miles, I settled into a site alongside Justus Creek. I set up my tent, ate the first of five months of Knorr noodles and tuna, and climbed into my sleeping quilt.

As I slept, a soft rain woke me from my sleep and I realized, "THAT DUDE HIT ME WITH A CANVAS BAG."

After eighteen hours and fourteen miles, the Irishman who woke me because of my snoring at last touched my anger. Too tired and too far away to do anything.

Let it go. I fell asleep to the harmless patter of rain on my nylon tent. *Let it go.*

My first morning on the Appalachian Trail meant the start of a routine that repeated itself for the next five months: let the air out of my sleeping pad while lying on it, pack up my clothes and sleeping bag, make breakfast, then break down my tent.

Breakfast consisted of Mueslix which must mean "mush" in German. I read online that Mueslix is high in fiber, but I didn't read German mush tastes like hay seeds and wallpaper paste. Fiber is good, but I couldn't eat mush for the next week. I ditched the rest and broke camp after eight as I headed towards Neel's Gap to buy more supplies.

At the end of the day, I found a stealth site halfway down a water trail. Stealth camping is pitching your gear at a site not established by the A.T.C. I later found out that it's frowned upon because of the mark stealth camping leaves on the wilderness. The official sites where backpackers corral after a long day of hiking miles through the wilderness are good for safety and good for the environment by decreasing the impact on the trail. I found a site barren of vegetation and other humans. As the sun went down, my fear went up. There are a few fatal incidents that are now part of the

Appalachian Trail lore. When I shut my eyes, visions of Jeffrey Dahmer danced in my head.

In the morning, I hiked back to the trail. Rock music blared from a tent at the intersection.

"Hey, I'm Sparrow," the bearded thirty-year-old said when he stuck his head out of his tent. Sparrow looked like a young Elton John and seemed too happy for so early in the morning. Still shaking out the cobwebs, I pretended a greeting and kept moving.

Blood Mountain loomed ahead. The climb was as intimidating as its name. While I climbed at a strong pace, the younger, stronger, and more experienced Sparrow blew by me. On the first day, Mountain Squid told me, "It's not a race, the last one to Katahdin [the end] wins." Mountain Squid is a retired Navy Chief who volunteered to count thru-hikers. Thru-hikers had trail names. I was still looking for mine. Squid is a negative label for a sailor, but Mountain Squid turned squid into a good thing. Well, I was winning as Sparrow's pack disappeared into the green canopy.

Alone in my thoughts, my mind drifted home. Lori told me she needed her time alone. Although she had backpacking experience and felt comfortable in the woods, she had no desire to hike two thousand miles. Her first child's death left her vulnerable. She needed familiar, she needed home on the North Carolina coast. The ocean's ebb and flow brought certainty, and the warm beach under her feet grounded her. Watching the sun set off our deck gave her hope. Her garden, her friends, and intentional butterflies gave her security.

The trail was well-suited for reflection and meditation. The footsteps of so many hikers wore a gully lined with rocks, roots, and mud. Even without the white blazes painted on trees every hundred yards, the wear made the trail discernable until you came to an intersection. When other trails intersected, I often went wrong. The repetition of my footsteps put me into a hypnotic trance that allowed for reflection and for getting lost with regularity. The physical exertion, matched to my rhythmic breathing, freed my soul to transcend the trail. I drifted to God, to family, back to me, to my fellow hikers on the trail of life, and always to my son.

Still early, I stayed dry, fed, and healthy, but as I hiked uphill, a fog surrounded the crest of Blood Mountain. A solid stone shelter stood at the top as a testament to the Civilian Conservation Corps. The CCC was part of the New Deal that Franklin Delano Roosevelt instituted to help lift the country out of the Great Depression. Across America, evidence of the CCC remains in National Parks and monuments as beautiful stonework and significant infrastructure from highways to dams.

It was easy to imagine the workers lifting huge stones and carrying the massive amounts of concrete, wood, and hardware for food and a few dollars in their pockets. Content to have a job, they worked to get themselves and this country back on its feet. Today, the shelter was an impressive structure with a huge chimney. The foreboding stone building's door was locked, leaving me to look in a windowless opening from the cold and damp.

Made in the USA
Columbia, SC
14 May 2021